Learn more about this series here:
www.SuperAlphaSeries.com
Copyright © 2017 by JA Huss
ISBN: 978-1-944475-24-6

Edited by RJ Locksley
Cover and Interior Drawings by Ambro Jordi
Cover Design by JA Huss

ANARCHY

A SUPERVILLAIN ROMANCE

CHAINED

ALPHA THOMAS

JA HUSS

CHAPTER ONE

Someone died early this morning.

I know this because I have his memories, and let me tell you, there are some fucked-up people in this world—people you should never know anything about—and he was one of them.

I sigh as I gaze out the tall window. The view is looking down at Cathedral City. From where I am, I can see three of the towers I built on the edge of the city boundaries. They are all pushed up against mountains, just waiting for their instructions. The whole city is surrounded by mountains.

I can't see the northern tower because it's behind me somewhere, but I don't need to see it to know what it's doing.

Even though it's spring, there's still snow on every peak higher than the foothills. There will be snow on them well into summer. That's just the way of things up here. Cathedral City is a microcosm of industry, people, and society the world over. But it's a secluded microcosm and that's what makes it the perfect place for Lincoln, Case, and me to enact our plan. It's almost like fate has put us here for this purpose.

"Are we going to talk?" Yasmine asks from behind me. "Or are you just going to stand there in front of the window all morning?"

I can see the inner-city towers too. Just the peaks of them because they mark the compass points of City Park in the middle of downtown and are mostly hidden by buildings. But again, I don't need to see them to know what they're doing.

"Someone died this morning?" I say. It's a question, just to keep Yasmine occupied while I enjoy the view.

"I'm not sure, but it doesn't matter," she replies.

Must be nice to think like that.

Unfortunately, I can't afford to be so... *laissez-faire* about things. Capturing the memories of dead people is a side effect of my superpower. I had it one hundred percent under control until Case fucking shot me with that drug a few months ago. Since then... well, things have gone a little wacky in my head. That's another way of saying... *crazy*. I had all this shit figured out until he did that. I had a drug that would last months and didn't need to be taken daily to keep my mind in working order, but that won't fix things anymore. Even the old version is useless. I've made several dozen batches of new drugs trying to get things under control again, but with no success.

At least it was still working when we killed the Blue Boar. I can't even imagine what was rolling around in that asshole's head when he died.

Your father's head, my inner voice amends.

Right. My father.

The point is, I say to myself—chastising the inner voice—I'm lucky it was working. I have no idea what it would be like to capture his memories, and I don't *ever* want to know.

This guy who died this morning is bad enough and he's just your run-of-the-mill crazy. But there will be more. So many more.

I feel sick just thinking about it.

"Thomas," Yasmine says, losing patience with me. "Can you please turn around and look at me?"

Nope. Not gonna do it.

My hand goes to my throat to loosen my tie a little. The shirt is new and scratchy. I hate it, but appreciate it at the same time.

Kind of like my inhibitor.

Growing up in Prodigy School wasn't fun either, but I knew how to appreciate the little things back then too.

"Eventually," Yasmine says, raising her voice, "you *will* have to talk to me."

Nope. I really don't think so.

"We can't just pretend none of this is happening."

She underestimates me.

"I need answers, Thomas. We can work through this."

There's nothing to work through. I was fine, then Case went crazy and shot me with some weird drug. And ever since then dead memories have been flooding into my head.

It's been so long since I had to deal with the effects of what they did to me, I'd forgotten how awful it was. But you don't shoot yourself up with the kind of drugs I've been taking for thirty years and not understand why.

Drugs that make me numb to everything and everyone.

I needed those drugs.

I still need those drugs.

"Have you talked to Case?" Yasmine says. She's really fishing for a way in now. "Or Lincoln?"

She's trying to get me to react. I know this. But I'm angry anyway. She has no right to invoke the names of my friends.

Still, I hold my words and feelings in.

I can still do this, I decide. I can still shut her out and keep her away. I can still control the feelings. I can still control my reactions.

But I cannot control the dead memories.

This guy who died today was a mess. So many things flooded into me. It took me down instantly. It made me weak, and pathetic, and powerless.

But I've got them corralled now. It only took a few minutes.

Still, in the heat of an important moment, those minutes count. Hell, *seconds* count.

"Well, that's it, I guess," Yasmine says. "It's over. I can't play nice with you anymore."

Yup. It's over all right.

"Take off your clothes," she commands.

This is when I finally turn to face Yasmine. She is tall and, if I'm being honest, very fucking beautiful. Thick, long, medium-brown hair that falls over her shoulders like a soft waterfall. Large dark eyes. Full lips. High cheekbones. And she has one of those shapes that drive men wild. Not too thin, not too thick. Not too straight, not too round. Large breasts, wide hips, big ass, and tiny waist. She's a cartoon character, I decide. Not real.

"I'm tired of talking to myself, Brooks. If you won't cooperate, I'll make you cooperate."

I loosen the tie some more, then bring it over my head and drop it on the floor. The suit coat comes off next. I let that fall to the floor as well. Then I start unbuttoning my shirt. Slowly. Looking her in the eyes.

She's breathing heavy. She likes this part. She likes *me*, I decide. She wants more than I'm offering.

I'm just using her. But I don't feel bad about it. She's using me too.

She tries to hold my gaze as I undress, but she falters when I take the shirt off and toss it aside. She stares at my chest and then her eyes wander down to my fingertips. I don't have a belt on, so she watches as I unbutton and unzip my pants.

I kick off the shoes and let my pants fall to the floor until I'm standing there in my black boxer briefs. She unabashedly—and unapologetically—studies the muscles of my legs, then moves up. Her eyes stop, perhaps checking to see if I'm hard.

I'm not.

Then she continues to the flat plane of my abdomen, my chest again, and then—finally—my face.

"I had high hopes for us, Thomas. We could've made a great team, you and I. But our time is up. I'm sorry you decided to waste it."

I'm not sorry.

I pick up the worn-thin scrub pants and pull them on. Then slip my arms into the matching shirt and bring it over my head.

Yasmine kicks the standard-issue shoes at me, disgusted that I wasted her time. She presses a button on her desk phone. "We're done here."

But I don't care if she's mad. I don't care about anything anymore. I can't afford to care. I can't afford to feel. I can't afford to be weak.

I slide my feet into the slip-on sneakers and hold my wrists out for the handcuffs when the orderly comes in to take me back to my room.

"Maybe tomorrow then?" Yasmine says as I walk past her.

No. Nothing about tomorrow will be different than today.

"Thomas," Dr. Yasmine Bates calls, once I'm in the hallway. "I won't let you wear the suit again until you talk to me."

I don't even bother shrugging. It was good while it lasted. It made me feel normal for a few minutes. It made me feel sane.

But I'm not sane.

If I was sane, I wouldn't be locked up inside Cathedral City Asylum.

If I was sane I wouldn't have to worry about the next person to die on this floor.

Or the memories of madness that will come afterward.

Or the way my psyche will deteriorate from the capture.

Or the way I might have to scream my way back to reality.

Or the real me, hidden away for all these years, dying to break free.

No. I'm not sane. I will never be sane again.

Like it or not, I am chained to the anarchy in my head.

CHAPTER TWO

"Do you understand what to do?"

I do. One hundred percent. I have no idea who I'm talking to. I don't know if the voice asking the question is male or female. I don't recognize it at all. But I absolutely know what to do.

"Yes," I say.

"Tell me," it says.

"Leave here. Travel through the tunnels to uptown. Exit through the D Street station. Travel one mile northeast to the laundry facility. Secure the truck. Proceed to Cathedral City Asylum. Secure target. Bring him back here."

"Yes," it says. "Do you foresee any problems with the plan?"

I think really hard about that question. So hard I can feel my eyebrows knitting together on my forehead. "Why would there be problems?"

"Good girl," it says.

Male, I decide. This voice is male. Then I stop that thought. I don't need to know.

"When was the last time you were"—it hesitates—"on assignment?"

I have no idea.

"A month ago?" it prods.

I'm still thinking.

"A few months?" it continues.

"It's been two years," another voice says. "She's been… in training." This one is definitely female. She forgot to activate her scrambler before she spoke.

The other voice rebukes her with a hiss and says, "Then why did we choose this one?"

"She's special."

I reluctantly smile. Because I *am* special.

"She's the only one who can manipulate her way through the asylum security. Don't worry, she's never been a troublemaker. She's as well-trained as they come."

The second voice has still not disguised herself. Her failure to follow protocol unsettles me.

"You're not convinced?" the female asks.

"Not even a little bit. Why are *you* here? Where's—" But it stops short of saying a name. I'm not to associate my handlers with anything. Not a name, not a gender, not a face. My eyes are blinded by the mask, my hands and feet secured to the table with tight straps. I have no idea where I am or how long I've been here.

But that doesn't matter. I have the plan programmed into my head. It's all I need.

"Trust me," the female says as a needle pricks my arm. "This injection should alleviate your concerns. Set her free and watch."

I can almost feel an eyebrow rise in response.

"Don't worry, we'll be tracking her. We can switch her off any time we want. Right, Sadie?"

"Yes," I answer immediately. "I am yours to command."

"See?" the female says. "You don't need to worry about this one. She is the best of the best."

Best of the best. I smile.

"Fine," voice one says. "Let her loose."

A motor whirrs to life and the table begins to slowly right itself. Blood rushes to my head as I become vertical. My body slides down the table with the force of gravity until the soles of my boots touch the floor and I am standing.

It takes a moment for my legs to remember what to do. But only a moment. The program in my head tells my muscles everything I need to know.

A door opens with a creak. "After you," the female says. Footsteps as they leave. A second creaking of the door as it closes behind them.

Then the straps holding me tightly to the table retract.

"Sadie," a scrambled voice says through a crackling intercom. "Take off your blinder."

I reach up, pull the mask down my face, and open my eyes.

The room is nearly dark so my eyes can take a few seconds to adjust to light. I feel them focusing, my lenses opening and closing as they find the right aperture.

"Exit when you're ready," the scrambled voice commands.

I step away from the table, testing my legs. Giving them a few moments to remember what to do. They are a little achy, like they feel the need to stretch. Or run. Something more than stillness.

I take in the room and the word *Exit* overlays on my vision screen when I look at a door. There are several other doors in this room but the only one I'll be able to pass through is the one marked Exit on my overlay.

I bend over and stretch since I'm unable to run. Touch my fingers to my toes, my forehead to my knees. I wrap my arms around my legs and force myself to stay there for a moment of relief. Perhaps even pleasure.

"Sadie," the voice interrupts. "We're on a deadline, sweetie. Please become ready now."

I slowly uncurl from my stretch, take a deep breath, then crack my knuckles.

"Yes," I say. "I'm ready."

I proceed to the door, open it up, and step out into the tunnel. A map overlays my vision now. A path lit up in red, for my eyes only, telling me where to go.

I follow it down the dark, wet tunnel for a long time. Miles, at least. I want to run so bad, but there's a command on my vision screen telling me to *be cautious*. Which means I shouldn't. So I don't.

After thirty-three minutes of wishing for something to change, the lighted path points to a metal ladder leading up to the surface. I climb up one level, but the path continues upward, so I ignore the people on that level as I pass through. The next level has no people, but I'm not supposed to stop, so I don't. When I get to the tenth level the path leads me to a door.

The trains are loud here. Down below they were just a faint rumble. Now they shake the floor, the walls, me.

I'm in a small room with a single door with an actual lighted exit sign. There's a keypad mounted on the wall. I don't need to touch it or punch in a code. Everything is controlled by my handlers.

I pull on the handle and it opens. I step through into the D Street station. People see me, but I'm wearing a uniform that makes them think I work for the Cathedral City Transportation Department, so they look away, quickly losing interest.

I'm almost sorry I don't attract more attention. My superpower has been dormant for so long, I'd like to let it loose. Take it out and see what it can do.

But the vision screen is still blinking *be cautious* at me.

So I don't.

I walk past everyone, hit the stairs, and take them two at a time. The adrenaline is pumping through my body now, my muscles primed from the long climb back to the surface.

The world assaults me. The noise, the traffic, the people. But that assault doesn't bother me. Nothing *bothers* me.

The compass on my vision screen points the way to the laundry facility so I walk that direction. I take in the smell of coffee shops, restaurants, exhaust fumes. I don't know how people can live up here. I prefer the dark, wet underworld.

I keep going, leaving the tight city blocks behind until I'm in a more industrial area. I'm still wearing my quasi-uniform, which not-so-coincidentally looks a little bit like the uniforms the people at the laundry facility are wearing.

There is no guard at the front gate. Just a chain-linked fence—open to allow workers to enter—and dozens of people who look a little bit like me. A man looks at me, his eyes squinting as he tries to figure out who I am and what I'm doing there. But the caution sign on my vision screen is no longer blinking so I take the superpower out and give it a whirl.

"Jennifer?" he asks, walking towards me. The timer on my vision screen is counting up, letting me know how long I have for this interaction. I glance across the parking lot, find a woman's face, and change the illusion. "Oh." He laughs. "Sorry, Lisa."

I turn away as he deals with his confusion, letting my face become someone else. It changes every five to seven seconds. If people look at me and see the change, they stop what they're doing. Wondering how they could see something so... impossible. But then they just shake their head and shrug it off as… what? What do they think when they see my illusions? They are crazy? Not at this level of trickery. They need more coffee? Probably that. It's Monday morning, after all. People chalk a lot of things up to Mondays.

My truck is number 219187 and it's parked just to the left of the main loading dock. The driver assigned to this truck is not here. She's sick today. I'm not sure why she's sick—or if she's even still alive—but Prodigy doesn't need me to know those details. All I need to know is what she looks like so I can steal the truck and not have anyone know.

People nod to me as I become who I need to be. Each time I trip the illusion the timer on screen resets. All my interactions need to be precise or the trip wears off.

But it's Monday. People are tired and busy. There are dozens of trucks and hundreds of people. So I slip inside, start the engine, and back out before anyone has a chance to realize what I'm doing.

I wave to a few people on my way out, tripping into the woman who should be behind this wheel instead of me.

And then I'm free to do my job.

I head north, up towards Cathedral City Asylum where they are keeping a man called Thomas Brooks. He's a crazy motherfucker. Really. My vision screen actually says "crazy motherfucker" in the notes section.

I will have him soon. I will take him back to Prodigy and he will be one of us again. He thinks he got away, but no one actually gets away from Prodigy.

And once I have him, I'll get his friends too. I won't fail. I never fail. That's why they only take me out for special occasions.

When you use me, the job gets done.

Thomas Brooks, Lincoln Wade, and Case Reider will all be mine by end of day.

CHAPTER THREE

My room is ten by ten. Bare concrete floor with a drain in the center—I don't even want to know why. One concrete bed. One stainless-steel sink. One stainless-steel toilet. And one stainless-steel desk.

This is the new building. It might as well be a prison. I'm not sure if everyone on this floor has a "room" like this, or just the dangerous patients, but this is what I have. There is no window in the door. Just a slot where they fasten the tray of food three times a day. They don't let me out except to talk with Yasmine, so standing in front of her window this morning was my only chance at seeing the real world.

I've been in here seven days, but I was in a nicer room before that. I spent almost three weeks there. That was before I became... difficult. Now I'm here. Apparently, this is where all the high-maintenance patients go.

It's been a little over a month since the Alpha plan went awry. One month of questions, and temptations, and a constant struggle for self-control.

The suit was a nice touch. I made that deal yesterday. Yasmine was about at the end of her patience with me and I just needed to buy a little time. Plus, the suit felt good—cheap as it was. It felt normal for the few minutes I had it on. That, in combination with the window... well, I could almost pretend things were OK.

Thing are decidedly not OK.

The little slot in my door clanks as someone on the other side opens it. I'm expecting a tray of food for lunch, but instead a piece of paper is shoved through and the slot is closed.

I know they have cameras on me, so I know I'm being watched as I walk over and pick the folded piece of paper up. But I don't care.

It reads:

Be ready.

I take it over to the sink, waiting for the sound of footsteps on the other side of the door. Waiting for one of them to come and take this little message away. But they don't come.

I press down on the knob that lets a trickle of water escape the faucet and wet the paper until the ink runs. Then I shred it and throw it in the toilet.

I have no idea what *Be ready* means, but I'm fucking ready for whatever it is. I can only assume it's a message from Case or Linc. Or maybe Molly. One of them is coming for me and hell yeah, I'm ready.

I'm a patient guy. I can withstand a lot of things. But enough is enough. A month, goddammit. A month is more than enough. And I'm gonna rip Linc and Case a new one when they finally do show up for leaving me here to rot for so long.

After I finish being grateful, of course.

Fucking emotions.

I turn away from the camera so they can't see me smile.

Fucking smiles. I never used to smile, now I find everything funny.

A buzzer sounds out in the hallway. I wait, wondering if that's what I'm supposed to be ready for. But no. Nothing happens afterward. So I sit and stare at the SpyGlass on the wall.

It's disabled. Ever since that shit went down a couple months ago—the same shit that got me locked up in here—they've disabled them all over the city. It's created a mess because Case's little public alert system was built in almost everything over the course of the last year.

Now they have to do things the old-fashioned way again. People have to come to my room and use a chart to determine which medications I get. Nothing is automated anymore. No friendly voice comes through that speaker telling me it's time for food, or sleep, or therapy. They don't trust us. Of all the people not to trust in this city, me and my friends shouldn't even make the top five. Top ten, sure. But not top five. And since they do still trust Yasmine and she's number one on my list, well, just proves how fucking stupid they are, I guess.

Footsteps. Ah, there they are. A little late, but still paying attention.

But this time, instead of just the slot opening, the whole door opens. Yasmine is standing at the threshold with three armed guards pointing their weapons at me.

"Can I help you?" I ask.

"You have visitors," she says.

I nod and walk towards the approaching guards. One shackles my ankles, another cuffs my hands, and the third points his electrodart gun at my head.

God, they're a bunch of idiots. They still haven't figured out that a ToyBox subsidiary makes those weapons.

I want to tell them they won't work on me, but eh. They'll figure it out eventually. And since I'm supposed to *be ready*, I'm pretty sure this isn't the time to fill them in on how ignorant they are.

"Who came to see me?" I ask, looking Yasmine in the eyes.

"Your friends," she practically purrs.

"I have lots of friends," I say.

"Clearly," Yasmine shoots back. "Since I have an order from the governor to let them have thirty minutes with you today. But you know which friends, I'm sure."

I shrug. I'll know either way soon enough, so whatever.

Handcuff guy loops a chain around my waist and attaches my cuffs to it, and once that's done, Yasmine waves me out of the room.

There is a fourth guard waiting in the hallway. I follow him. The other two are directly behind me, and Yasmine, presumably, takes up the rear. The visitors' center is actually the dayroom on the ground floor. It's a nice big room with couches and tables so family members can come play checkers with their crazy aunt or uncle. And a big-screen TV mounted on the wall which perpetually plays daytime television. Not the trashy talk shows. Those get the inmates—excuse me, *patients*—riled up. They play old movies. Mostly westerns.

Someone blew up the old asylum last year. It might've been my brother Atticus. Or my mother, since they were both escaping at the same time. But maybe not. You just never know in this town.

But anyway, the whole building is brand new. Bright and shiny.

When we get to the hallway that leads to the dayroom, Yasmine calls out, "See you in thirty, Thomas?"

I don't bother answering. I don't usually see her twice in one day, but it does no good to wonder about it. If she's got plans for me after this, nothing I can do about it. Besides, the message said, *Be ready.* I'm ready to get the fuck out of here so an out-of-the-ordinary second session with Yasmine is not going to happen anyway.

We move forward to the door where patients enter the day room and one of the guards behind me takes off my shackles, but not my cuffs.

"Come on," I say, smiling at him. "Give a guy a break."

He doesn't even look at me. The door opens and I'm pushed forward.

"Do anything stupid, Brooks, and we'll set you straight," one guard says. He waves his electrodart gun at me.

I find enough will to look properly frightened by his threat, but he doesn't buy it. If I were the old me I'd say I'm not capable of being frightened. But I'm not the old me. I'm the new me, thanks to fucking Case and that bullshit he shot me up with last spring.

I'm ticked off about that. But I'm handling it. I'm dealing. I can do emotions. I had them once, I can wait this out. The drug has to wear off, right? Or I'll get out of here and get back to work on a replacement. Sheila has dozens of trials going back in Linc's lab. We'll figure it out. I'm not worried.

Speaking of Case and Linc, I look around for them, scanning the dozens and dozens of tables and chairs. The couches. But... they're not here.

"Hey," I say, turning towards a nurse holding a clipboard. "I'm supposed to have a visitor?"

"What's your name?" she asks.

"Brooks," I reply. "Thomas Brooks."

"Oh, you're in there," she says, pointing to a door on the far side of the room. "Private."

"I didn't call for a lawyer," I say, irritated. I really was expecting Case and Linc to be here.

"Not lawyers, sweetie." The woman says in her practiced, patient tone.

"Sweetie?" I sneer.

"You'll see soon enough. Now I'm real busy, hun. So let me do my job, OK?" She says all this in a sing-songy voice intended for children—or mentally ill adults—then turns her back to me and looks down at her clipboard.

I walk towards the room with a door. There's no window, so I'm standing in the threshold when I see who requires a private visit with me.

"Randy Shits," I say, mimicking Case's nickname for the guy. "And Chief O'Neil. Well." I laugh as I enter the room. "When'd they let you out, old man?"

"He was pardoned by the governor last week," Randy chimes in. "He's back in charge, if you can believe it."

"Sit, Brooks," the chief says. "We've got business and even though it's a waste of time and the governor knows that, we're gonna check you off our list today so I'm just going to get to the point. We need a statement, Brooks. We know you and your friends are guilty as hell and the governor needs to keep the peace before people start burning things down again. So you're gonna admit to what you and your buddies did last spring and then we're gonna cut a deal with you and let you out."

"Are you ready?" Randy asks.

I look at him. Warily. Did he send me that note? God. Please, no. I've been patient. I really have. I've been waiting for Case and Linc to get their shit together all month, but honestly, I'm about done with this place. I can't stay here.

"Tell me what I need to be ready for," I say. "And I'll let you know."

"Ready to get the fuck out, right? I'm sure you miss the outside. Your SkyEye business isn't doing too well. Have you seen the stock reports?" Randy Shits laughs. "So just play nice, sign the papers, and we'll send someone to get your suit."

My suit. My own fucking suit. It's a good start as far as negotiations go. At least for me. I hate these scrubs. I hate that room. I hate these people.

Well, I hate all people, but these people are at the top of the list at the moment.

"Sorry," I say. "I won't be signing anything today."

"You sure about that?" Chief says. "I'm gonna need you to be very sure about that, Brooks. Because if you say no to me now, there won't be a second chance. Just think of all that money you're losing while we keep SkyEye shut down. Just think of your future. You can walk out of here right now."

"You don't even have to ride home with us," Randy says. "I'll call you a cab."

"But the point is," the chief says, "you will go home. Today. By tonight this place will be nothing but a bad dream."

"His answer is no." We all look up to see Yasmine standing in the open door. "I'm afraid he's not interested in your little deal, gentlemen. He's much too loyal for that. But you can tell the governor that I will have what he needs by tonight." She winks at me. "Thomas and I have a date this afternoon. I tried to do this the easy way, but he's resistant."

"Ma'am," Randy says, "the governor told us—"

"The governor told you to try and I told the governor I'd give you one chance. You had your chance. He's refused your offer. Now it's time to go and let me finish the job."

Yasmine looks like a prowling lioness who hasn't eaten in weeks. The hunger for me lingers in her eyes, even as Randy and O'Neil go silent, then recover and start peppering her with questions.

"On whose authority?"

"We just talked to the governor. He told us to make the deal happen."

Yasmine holds her gaze on me for another pregnant second, then turns her head and smiles at them. "You failed. So he's mine now. Guards, take Mr. Brooks up to my office and prep him."

"Prep him for what?" Randy asks.

I'd like to hear her answer—I'd really, *really* like to hear that answer—but I'm tugged away just as an alarm sounds, sending the whole day room into chaos.

CHAPTER FOUR

The brand-new Cathedral City Asylum is beautiful in a way only buildings can be. It's not tall, only six stories, and stretches out into east and west wings. It's not institutional in design, either. Even though the front gate leading onto the property is all gothic archway with pitted stones covered in lichen that remind you of ancient battles in places that are much wetter than here.

It's last-century modern with long panes of glass near the roofline, accentuated with strips of metal gleaming from a stray ray of sun.

I stop the truck and wait my turn at the gate, acutely aware of the timer on my vision screen, ready and waiting to begin counting up once I initialize the trip.

When it's my turn, I start the illusion and the timer, but they wave me through, so it only gets up to three seconds before I drop the trip and it resets.

My power is very limited. Five seconds is the average time it takes a person to do a double-take and reassess what they're seeing. If I need it to last five seconds, it's perfect. I can go up to nine if I have to. But anything past ten is almost unheard of.

It's a hitch, and nothing more. A moment when you're looking out across the hot desert and you see… something. But then it's gone. What I do is not a mirage. It's something in between hallucination and delusion. Something people want to see. Something people expect to see. But then quickly realize it cannot be.

It works on everyone except my Prodigy handlers. Nothing works on them. My inhibitor keeps them immune. Each Prodigy child has their own unique inhibitor and mine is coded into my DNA through periodic manipulation. It will last for months before it degrades and has to be reinitialized.

I won't be out in the real world for months. I know this. The assignment is scheduled to last four hours and one and a half of those hours has already passed. When I finish, I will be rewarded with bliss once again. The dream in my head will become real. I will shut down, and then everything will be perfect until the next time they wake me for a job.

But I am special. They almost never let me outside. I like it this way and I'm anxious to complete this mission so I can return to what I do best.

The map on screen tells me where to park. A worker dressed in the white uniform with the asylum logo approaches me. His name tag says Grant.

This is when things become tricky.

Almost any illusionist can manage what I've done so far, but no one but me can manage what I'm about to do now.

The timer starts as I throw the trip. A wave of energy flows out of my head in concentric circles with me at the center.

My net catches almost two dozen people. And the wave is powerful, something that calls me to attention. But they don't see me. They see what they want to see. What they expect to see. I open the door at two seconds, smile, but don't talk to anyone because that will cancel out the illusion, and walk straight for the back loading dock. Some of them call out. "Hey, Jane!" or, "Hi, Mike! Are you going bowling tonight?" One says, "Sarah, you look great today. Is that a new haircut?"

I become—whoever. I become the person they expect to see.

At seven seconds I'm pulling the door open, at eight seconds I'm walking down a dimly lit hallway as it closes behind me. At nine seconds I am Sadie again. But it doesn't matter. These people don't know I'm supposed to be the laundry truck driver. They're not even looking at me as my recovery timer counts up the seconds I will need to make a new trip.

It's a small power. I'll admit that. It's fleeting. Nine seconds is not enough time to do much, but I have perfected my art. I can do so much with nine seconds. I can create havoc with nine seconds. I can become a dead child in a mother's eyes. I can become the husband they lost in the war. I can become a celebrity. I never become a celebrity or any of those other things. The point is to go unnoticed. Getting people to notice me defeats the purpose.

I essentially become invisible. Hidden in plain sight.

No one but me can pull this off *en masse*.

The bright red path in my vision screen leads me to a locker room as an alarm sounds off in the building. I punch in the code to enter, find the place empty—my handlers taking care of me now with that fake emergency—and go to locker number 818 where there is a gray uniform waiting for me. I pull the loose top on over my existing uniform, then drag the extra-large pants up my legs. Looking down at my chest I see a name tag. I am Phil now. There's a picture of him inside the locker. Him and his wife. Poor woman. Her husband is probably dead. Well—I chuckle— she's probably dead too.

I slam the locker shut and follow the lighted path out of the room and into a stairwell, climbing to the fifth floor, home to one escaped Prodigy child called Thomas Brooks.

I access his personal file to get familiar with him. His power is… well, that's interesting.

My feet are still climbing up the stairs as I read.

Thomas Brooks—Level Ten Mentalist. Level Ten Aggressionist. Level Ten Manipulist. Level Ten Capturist. Use extreme caution. Non-lethal intervention advised at all times.

It's a unique combination, but it all adds up to one thing. Mind thief. Mentalist combined with capturist means he can steal memories, especially from people who die in his vicinity. Aggressionist combined with manipulist means he can force people to do things against their will.

All together these things mean that unless he's drugged, he's always the one in control.

My vision screen has a flashing red caution sign next to his name, and there's a yellow tag attached to it which reads: *Active.*

Well, he won't be active for long. My hand unconsciously pats the outline of a syringe in my pocket underneath my asylum uniform. I have what I need to deactivate him.

When I get to the fifth floor, I enter the hallway. People are insanely—no pun intended—busy because of the blaring alarm Prodigy triggered to help me get in the building, and take no notice of me. So I don't even have to bother with a trip. There's a nurse's station along the far end of the hallway, but there's no way to get into that computer, so I head to my left, push through another door, and try for one of the empty offices.

The third one on the right is unlocked when I turn the knob, so I slip in, close the door behind me, and take a seat at the desk just as a passcode flashes on my vision screen.

I type it in, get access to the database, then go looking for my target.

There he is. Thomas Brooks, level three, room seven, solitary housing.

Level three, though. That's not what I have on my screen—my vision screen updates, changing level five to level three.

Hmmm. They don't usually get this stuff wrong.

I shrug as I stand, then head back out. The chaos is dying down now that people realize the alarm was a bug in the system, so I have to throw a trip, make my face and body look like poor Phil, to get past a few people and back into the stairwell. It only lasts a few seconds, so recovery is a non-issue by the time I'm back on track.

Level three is empty.

It's also very… prison-like. Nothing at all like level five. There's no nurse's station, for one. And there's no tile on the floor. Just bare concrete. The rooms look more like cells. Small, high windows. Slots in the doors for… what? Food? Yes, definitely more like a prison.

I walk cautiously along the corridor until I get to the one door with no window.

Number seven.

And it's open.

Empty.

What the fuck? I type out to my handlers. There's a little camera in my iris that shoots footage back to them, so they see what I'm seeing.

Check the computer.

What computer?

End of the hall, turn left. Second door on the right. Code to get in…

It lists the sequence to enter that door.

I punch it in, ready to throw a trip if anyone's in there—even though I have no idea who I should become if that happens—and push it open.

Dark and empty. Just the faint light from a sleeping screen off to the left.

I take a look behind me, checking for people, then slip inside and close the door.

How do I get in? I type.

What is presumably a password flashes across my vision.

I take a seat, type it in, gain access, then go searching for Brooks.

Sixth floor, it says. Dr. Yasmine Bates' office. Room six-nineteen. Scheduled for… It doesn't say what he's scheduled for. It says, 'Classified.'

Hold, is Prodigy's reply.

I wait, nervously looking over my shoulder at the door. If anyone comes in I will fail. I don't have a face to trip into. Not one that will have security clearance to get into this room. Phil was presumably a low-level employee, a janitor or something. And there are no pictures in here to steal a face. I tap my fingers on the desktop, forcing myself not to start counting seconds.

And then they're back.

Abort mission and return to Prodigy.

"What?" I say, then type it with my mind, since they can't hear me. *What?*

You will abort mission immediately and return to Prodigy for storage.

Motherfuckers. I was just getting excited about this shit.

The chair slides underneath me as I stand and make for the door. I open it, peek out, then type, *Send me a face to steal in case I'm seen.* Assholes. I can't use any of the faces from before. Those people clearly do not belong on this floor.

A picture flashes on my vision screen and I memorize it, slipping back out into the corridor at the same time.

I go back the way I came, looking around. A face appears in a window, the man's hand slapping against the shatterproof glass. I do not jump or scream. But he definitely makes my heart skip a beat.

This hallway is creepy as fuck.

A loud buzzer blares and the doorway leading to the stairs opens. I trip into the face Prodigy sent, but the woman scowls at me when it… fucking *fails to take*.

What the hell?

"Who are you?" she demands. "What are you doing on this floor?"

Abort, abort, abort, my vision screen is flashing.

No shit, assholes. I *am* aborting.

Three things happen, almost all at once. First, the woman leans into her shoulder, clearly about to speak into a radio. Second, I move forward with speed, reacting out of instinct now. Third, she says, "We—"

But she doesn't get any farther than that because I've snapped her neck.

Her body slumps to the floor as her radio squeaks static, then words. "Say again, Mona?"

I'm Mona now. I grab her face, tuck it away in my memory for later, and enter the stairs.

Footsteps below me. Running up.

Shit.

My stupid screen is still flashing, *Abort, abort, abort.*

"Mona?" someone calls.

I am frozen in place. I cannot call back. I cannot capture voices. So I'll have to wait until they reach me, or risk going down to meet them, in order to start a new trip. And even then—fuck—it hits me then. My trip didn't work. What the hell?

But I'm saved again by another blaring alarm. I pray that it does the job, since we just used that tactic a few minutes ago.

"Forget Mona," another voice says, one floor below me. "We've got a riot on three."

Their footsteps recede, going down again. I take my chances and go up to the top floor just as more people enter the stairwell down below.

What's happening? I type.

You were told to abort.

I am aborting! But if you want me to get out of here unseen, then I have to take the long way back.

Proceed to the garage level.

Fuck them, I decide. I'm on six. But there has to be another stairwell. Probably on the other side of the building. I have Mona's face now. I can be her on my way out. *If* I can manage to get a clear path. And—I don't want to think about this part, because it unsettles me—if I can make the trip work.

What the hell happened back there? It was like… I was… normal. I don't want to be normal. I do not do normal. I am Sadie Scott, the best motherfucking illusionist this world has ever seen.

I like it that way.

I open the door for the sixth floor and peek out. It's quiet and silent. I slip out, walk casually, Mona's face at the ready so I can throw a trip. But then I see the room I'm almost looking for. Six-nineteen. Dr. Yasmine Bates.

Inside that room is my objective, Thomas Brooks.

CHAPTER FIVE

It's not being strapped to a table that starts the panic. It's not the injection, or the way reality begins to expand almost instantaneously as the burning liquid makes its way up my arm towards my heart. It's not even the second alarm. I can only see a slice of reality through the nearly shut lids of my eyes, but everyone in this room ignores that alarm.

It's the memories that come flooding back as they open me up. Not my body, but my mind.

Panic for me has unique consequences. And these people have no idea what they've started.

"Thomas," Yasmine says. Her voice is far away and echo-y. I can't see her, but I can feel her. Smell her. Sense her in other ways too. There is a spongy aura surrounding her body. Everyone's body. But all I see is hers, because she is closest to me. "Can you hear me?"

I have known Yasmine since we were small. She was probably my best friend at one time. My only friend for a long time. Her hair was always dark—unless she was standing in front of a window and the sunlight could catch the ends and highlight her head in gold. And it was always long. She was a lot like Molly, I think. Except Molly is a lot younger. She wasn't even born yet when I knew Yasmine.

"Can you hear me?" she repeats.

It's dangerous to answer her. I remember this much. Especially under the drugs. She's a level eight mentalist.

Not a ten, like me. But she is a level ten manipulist. And a level ten capturist.

She can steal minds under the right conditions.

She's wrong if she thinks this is "right conditions," but I don't tell her that.

"Thomas," she tries again.

My very first memory was in my nursery. I was four, maybe. Five, at the most. It doesn't help to describe the nursery, because the nursery was perfect. Everything was new and high-quality. A finely polished sleigh bed, sized for a small child, with bright white linens, soft pillows and blankets, and stuffed animals.

There were toys to engage my mind and a rocking chair that reminded me of the nurse who cared for me. There was a large mobile in front of the window, just above where I would lay my head at night. It was a flock of flying birds. They would swing and bob on their wire tethers, each one weighted slightly differently to simulate natural behavior. If birds flying in a perpetual circle are considered natural.

"Do I have to dose you again?" Yasmine asks in the now.

She can give me more, but I can't be responsible for what happens if she does.

The memory of the nursery is always where things start. Something pretty bad happened in there. And when you're four or five, pretty bad can mean a whole plethora of things that have no real consequence whatsoever.

But that's not how this memory shakes out because this isn't a real memory. Oh, the nursery was real. The nurse too. All the things in there. But this... what's happening to me right now... this is a trigger.

Oh, no. Yasmine is not going to like this at all.

If I had better control of my facial muscles I'd smile. Give her a little peek. A little jolt. A little glimpse into what's coming.

A chance to escape, maybe. I have never actually hated her. I just… dislike her a lot. Still, I'd let her get away if she could manage it. I'm loyal like that, even though she doesn't deserve it. She helped me once. We were friends. But then they took her away and she never came back.

She's not paying enough attention right now. She thinks she's got me. She thinks she's the one in control. She thinks a whole lot of things that aren't really happening.

And why is that?

I'll tell you. If you can keep a secret, I'll let you in.

"Come closer." I don't mean to speak, but the whisper comes out anyway. This is the part I can't control. But you understand, right? You're me, so you must.

"What is it?" Yasmine asks, leaning in. Closer. Then closer still.

"You're not," I whisper. Again, not meaning to.

"I'm not what?" she asks.

I don't think Yasmine hates me either. I think she's just… one of those women. The controlling types. As least she thinks she is. But no matter how many straps are holding me down to this table, and no matter how many syringes she empties into my bloodstream… she will *never* control me. I made sure of it.

"Aggressive enough." There. I said it. A small, weak chuckle escapes my lips. She's a level two aggressionist, which means she cannot really force people to do things against their will.

"Fuck you," she whispers back. Her lips are so close to my cheek I can feel her breath.

She hates that. The reminder that they never finished her. They left her incomplete. "I would've killed you," I growl, my voice clear and strong now. "When I killed all the others, you know."

"Fuck you," she says again.

"But only to put you out of your misery." His—*my*— laughter bursts forth.

"Give him another dose," Yasmine barks to her team. "We'll see who's aggressive enough."

See, this is her whole problem. She still lives in the nursery. She still thinks she's one of the favorites. She still buys into the lies they weaved into our tiny minds—day after day. Until the days turned into months and the months turned into years.

I'm sure plenty of people think Yasmine Bates is aggressive. But that's not what I'm talking about and she knows it. I'm talking about the modifications they did to us. The manipulations they subjected us to when we were small. Before we left that nursery we were complete and she was missing something. Something I had plenty of.

Aggression.

Not aggression, as in the desire to fight. But aggression as in the ability to hurt. Not with my hands, but my mind.

I told you. I told you there's anarchy up there. I told you it's inside me. I told you this over and over and over and over and—

"That's the second dose," one of her helpers says.

"Gimme more." I laugh. "Gimme all of it. I can take it. I can take it and you know it. Nothing you do to me will ever change who you aren't."

Level ten aggressionist is part of what I am. Just one tiny part, really. But it makes all the difference and Yasmine knows this. She sees what I can do. She sees what I'm capable of. And she knows she can't compete.

She's just missing something.

Her soft hand touches my throat and when I force my eyes open to see my little sliver of reality, she's baring her teeth at me.

"If only you had fangs, darling, then you could suck it out of me like a leech."

She squeezes my windpipe. Chokes me. I'd still be laughing if she wasn't cutting off my airway.

I mentally push against her spongy aura, testing things out.

Not yet. Not quite. But almost.

I don't want to do it. I've taken great care of the past fifteen years to keep it in check. But then fucking Case had to go shoot me with that poison.

You want to kill him for that.

No. I correct the voice inside me. I want to kill *someone* for that, but it's not Case. He didn't do this to me. He didn't turn me into this fucking freak show. He didn't strap me down as a child and force me to change.

"You're wrong, Mr. Brooks," Yasmine seethes into my ear. "So, so very wrong." But I'm not. And when she barks, "Give him another one," I know this for certain.

This is it, Thomas. This is the end of you. One more syringe will be enough. One more syringe will trigger it. One more goddamned syringe and I will finally be free because I'll be dead.

"Do it." But this time it's not out loud. That anarchy chained up in my head knows better than to beg. It knows she will get suspicious and put a stop to it. It knows I will die quietly instead of the way it was always planned.

So she doesn't hear my warning.

I feel the push in my vein. I feel the burn travel up my arm. I feel it entering the right atrium of my heart. And then a contraction. *Thump.* It's in. *Thump.* It's out. *Thump,*

thump. Into the lungs. Back to the heart. *Thump, thump.* That quick… everything has changed.

Her aura is no longer spongy. It's a wall. And walls can be knocked down. Walls are breakable. Walls are *meant* to be broken.

My eyes open. I see the operating room light. Yasmine off to my right, still partially bending over, her hand still on my throat in a gesture of aggression she knows she can't use against me.

Oh, she can choke my throat all she wants. But that's not the part of me she needs to hold in her hand.

She needs my mind.

But now we know who's up there. You. You're up there. Holding me close. Keeping me safe. Making me the monster I was meant to be.

Hello, *you.*

Did you miss me?

The last dose of drug has now flowed through my whole body. It's been absorbed by the muscles and that's it, people.

Time to go.

The gathering is not something I like to describe. It's a contraction of my whole body. I seize up on the table. My back arching. My hands pinned to my sides with straps. My legs bound to the table.

My mouth opens, but I don't scream. Not with my voice, anyway.

I scream with my mind.

Imagine throwing a pebble into a puddle. Imagine those harmless little circles that radiate out, getting bigger and bigger and bigger the farther away they travel.

You want to be far away from me right now, take my word on that. Because the mental scream that comes out of my mind is a force of nature.

People fly backwards in front of the supersonic shock wave. The wind that comes from the explosion blows past them, taking everything around me with it.

Walls disappear. Windows shatter.

And then there is silence and I'm alone.

I'm free. At least from the restraints holding me down on this table. But I retreat back into my head.

You're back now, right? This is what you wanted. This was your plan all along.

So fuck you. I don't wanna be in control anymore. Just fuck you. Take over then. I don't care.

"What the... fuck?"

I open my eyes and see a girl. Dark hair, olive skin, unknown color eyes. About five nine. Maybe five ten. She's wearing a uniform but that's not the part that bothers me.

What bothers me is she's still *standing*.

I sit up, the useless bindings falling away from my body. "Who the fuck are you?"

She squints at me. Frowns. Looks down at the floor. Then behind her. Yasmine's body is visible, but she's underneath one of her team members. Looking lifeless.

The dark chick shakes her head, then opens her eyes wide, like she's clearing her vision.

Amber, I see. Her eyes are amber.

"What the hell was that, Brooks?" She says my name with confidence, but it fades quickly. Her eyes dart back and forth for a few seconds. Not focused on me. Not really. Just like... they're searching for something they can't find. "You are Brooks, right?"

I swing my legs over the side of the table and step down. My feet are bare, and there's shards of glass and metal everywhere. It crunches under my soles. I ignore it, but the girl winces for me.

"Yes," I say, straightening up. She's kinda pretty. I might want to make a good impression. "Thomas Brooks. Who, might I ask, are you?"

"Did you..." She looks around again. Very confused, this one. "Did you just explode?"

"No," I say, patting down my chest, just to make sure. That's when I notice the IV needle sticking out of my arm. I give it a tug and throw it aside. "I seem fine."

"What was *that*? This whole place is... gone!"

"Oh," I say, noticing the side of the building is missing. Car alarms are going off outside. "Well, shit. They just got this building up and now look what I've done." I smile as I take my attention back to the pretty female. "Do you have a name?"

She's confused again.

"Darling?" I say. "A name?"

She shakes her head.

"You don't have a name?"

"I do," she says, letting out a sigh at the same time. "But I don't understand what's happening. I... can't remember why I'm here."

"You... presumably work here?" I ask, trying to be helpful. "You're wearing a uniform." Her name tag says Phil, but she's definitely not a Phil.

She looks down at her clothes in horror. "What the hell?" Her wide eyes meet mine again. Yes. A very pretty yellow-brown color. Strikingly unusual. "Am I bleeding? Do I have a concussion? Am I halluci—" She stops. "Halluci—"

"Hallucinating?" I offer, again. Just trying to be helpful.

She takes a deep breath. Her lips move, silently counting to three. Then she lets the breath out.

"You're not bleeding. I don't know why you're not bleeding, since everyone else in this room was knocked to the floor. But you seem fine to me."

Something changes in her. A panic. A moment of pure... fear. "I need to get the fuck out of here. I have no idea what I'm doing. I have no clue how I got here. I don't even know my name!"

I step forward and take her hand. "Now, now. Don't worry. We can leave if you want. I just need to grab something from the other room."

"The other room?" She turns to look behind her.

"Oh." I'm genuinely disappointed. The other room is mostly gone. Blown to bits. "I was hoping to grab that suit."

"Who *are* you?"

"Thomas," I say, placing her hand on my arm. "You just said my name."

"No," she says. "*No.*" More forcefully this time.

Well, she's one of the inmates, obviously. That's too bad. I haven't been laid in months. I had a little spark of hope there for a second. But clearly, I will be leaving and she will be staying behind.

"It was nice meeting you, whatever your name is. But look, I'm sorta busy today. So I gotta run. Cops are gonna come and—"

Sure enough, there's sirens downstairs.

When I look back at the girl she's... flickering. Like... seriously, flickering into *other people* before my eyes.

One second she's a man, then she's an old woman. A few flickers of that and she's a young woman wearing a different uniform.

"What the fuck?" I ask.

She shakes her head and rubs her eyes.

"What was that?" I ask.

She stares at her feet for a moment, then slowly brings her eyes up to meet mine. "I'm a level ten."

"Are you?" I ask, jutting my head back in surprise. "A level ten what, exactly?"

"Hallucinal—" She shakes her head again. "Delusional."

I laugh. "Yes, darling. I think you are quite right about that. You are definitely level ten delusional. Now, as much as I'd like to hang out with you, possibly fuck you crazy and then drop you off somewhere, never to see you again, I'm gonna have to move along now. I'm not into the psychotic ones. They're more trouble than they're worth."

"Illusional," she spits out with some effort. "No. Illusion*ist*." She smiles with relief. Like she just solved the biggest puzzle ever. "Yes. I'm an *illusionist*."

"A level ten… illusionist?" I raise an eyebrow at her. "Not possible."

But then she flickers. And for five whole seconds, she becomes me.

CHAPTER SIX

If I wasn't scared out of my mind, I'd laugh at the man's shock. Thomas, he called himself. It feels familiar. I look around at the total destruction in this room. I can see *outside*. A hole has been blown into the wall.

That is not familiar, but the other side—the side with a door, complete with frame, still standing amid the missing wall—that side seems familiar.

How did I get here? Why can't I remember anything?

"Where," Thomas says, bringing my attention back to him, "the fuck did you just come from?"

I open my mouth. Clearly about to say something. But my mind is… blank.

And everything, I mean everything, about my blank mind is wrong.

"What's happening?" I ask.

"I think you're the one with the answer to that question. You just appeared here. You're not a patient, are you?"

He's pointing at my clothes again. Why am I wearing this ridiculous uniform? "No, I'm not a patient. I'm here for you!" It comes from somewhere, but I have no idea where.

"Me?"

The sirens downstairs are louder now. I can hear people shouting.

"I need to go, sweetheart."

I don't bother answering him. I just whirl around and make for what used to be the hallway. There's no one up here but us right now. But there will be soon. And whatever is happening, the last place on Earth I want to be stuck is inside this hospital.

Thomas catches up to me, grabbing hold of my hand. "Look. We can help each other out. How about that? I need to get out of here. You need to get out of here. Do that illusionist thing again so we can slip by everyone."

"I'm not a patient," I say, looking him up and down as I pick my way through piles of debris, making my way towards the sign that says exit.

Exit.

Yes, this feels right. For whatever reason, this exit sign is exactly where I need to go. "I have no idea who you are."

"That's not saying much." He laughs. "You don't know who you are either."

We both start jogging down the stairs towards the ground floor. "Well, I do know I'm not a patient. And you clearly are."

"I'm here by mistake. Just like you."

But that doesn't ring true. Not the part about him. The part about me. I am here for a reason. I just don't remember it.

He squeezes my hand tighter, making me acutely aware that he's still got a hold of it. "Just get us out, OK? We can put all the pieces together once we're away from here. I promise, I'll take you somewhere safe so you can figure it out. Sound good?"

I want to put up a big fight right now, but I don't have many choices. What if I am a patient? What if they stop us downstairs and try to take me... *prisoner?*

When we get to the third floor, the stairwell becomes clogged with people. Nurses and patients. There's screaming and pushing. Panic, I realize. People are about to panic.

Thomas pulls me close to him, leaning into to whisper in my year. "Just be calm. We're gonna flow right out of the building with everyone else. When we get outside, we'll head to the parking lot. You disguise us as… whoever the fuck you want. Just not the real us, got it?"

I say nothing.

"Then I'll get us a car and we'll drive out amid the chaos."

I'm still too busy concentrating on the mass hysteria around me to answer.

"Listen to me, trippy chick," Thomas says, squeezing my hand hard. "Do you understand me?"

People are pressing up against me. I hate it. I hate them touching me. I want to be away from this chaos more than anything. "Yes," I finally say. "OK. Just get me away from here."

"Follow my lead."

We take our turn shuffling down the stairs towards the ground level. An old man who smells like stale bread and mold is too close to me. I want to be sick. But then there's the door being held open by firemen. There's a few nurses and doctors, but mostly we are just patients.

No. I'm not a patient. I do not belong here.

"When we get outside, make us look like visitors. Can you do that?"

Can I? "I'm not sure," I say, deciding it's better to be truthful.

"You can, OK? You just told me you're a level ten illusionist. If that's true, then I know what you can do. Just find the faces of two people in plain clothes and change us into them. OK?"

I stare at the daylight pouring through the open door. I want to be outside so bad.

"OK?" Thomas asks again, shaking my arm to jolt me to attention.

"OK," I agree. I don't know if I can really do what he just said, but it won't hurt to believe in it. Just get me outside and away from all these smelly people.

We approach the firemen, and just when I think I won't have to throw a trip—trip?—and we'll be able to make our way to safety, there's a whole army of nurses and doctors, rounding up each and every patient as we file out through the stairwell.

Thomas sees them at the same time, because he says, "Fuck."

"Fuck," I echo.

"Do it now, OK? Make us anyone but who we are now."

"I don't know if I can."

"You can. I know you can. Just do it *now!*"

I find two people far out in the parking lot, both clearly hospital employees by the way they're dressed, and I just... steal their faces. Thomas still has my hand. And it's only when I throw the trip—trip?—that I wonder if I can change him as well as me.

But I feel the shudder, in my mind and his, in the same moment.

When I look over at him again, I almost let go of his hand in shock.

So this is what it feels like to see a trip. Where am I getting that word from?

I shake my head and concentrate on keeping the illusion in place. We walk, hand in hand still, right through the door. Several nurses are herding patients as we emerge, but they yell right past us.

We walk faster. Walking off towards a large parking lot. We're not the only people doing that, either. Several dozen others are right alongside us.

When we get to the parking lot, Thomas steers me towards a car. "You can drop it now," he says. His illusion falls away as soon as he speaks, becoming Thomas again. "No one is looking. They are way too busy back there."

"Is this your car?" I ask, feeling the illusion drop away.

"Sure." He laughs as he takes his shirt off.

I lift an eyebrow at him.

"I need one to break the glass without fucking up my hand. And I don't want to take yours. Yet." He smiles at his innuendo.

I look down at myself. Horrified. Again. What the hell did I put on this morning? Where was I this morning? I search back, trying to find something about my day that makes sense. A cup of coffee, maybe. Or checking email. *Something.*

Thomas wraps his shirt around his hand, then punches the glass, making it shatter into a million shards that fall harmlessly down to the ground.

I go still, almost in a panic. Who am I? I know my name, but that's not enough. Who am I?

"Hey, trip chick," he growls in my ear. "Snap the fuck out of it and get with the program. We need to leave."

"Sadie," I say.

"What?"

"My name is Sadie. So stop calling me that stupid name."

He smiles at me. All the way up to his eyes. "Fine. Sadie it is. Now, do you want to get the fuck out of here or not? Because the longer we hang around the greater the chances that these people will get their shit together and stop us on the way out."

45

I blink, realizing something. "It's not supposed to work like that."

"What are you talking about now?"

"The illusion. It took us at least five minutes to walk over here. I should not be able to throw a trip for more than a few seconds."

He cocks another eyebrow at me. "Really?"

I nod. "I know I seem... confused. I get it. I don't make much sense right now, but I know this. I just know this. It's not supposed to last that long."

"Well, Sadie," he says, taking both my hands and giving them a squeeze, "I tell you what. As soon as we get out of here I'll help you figure it all out. OK? But first, we have to get the fuck away from this place before they figure out I'm missing."

"They want you," I say. "They're looking for you."

"Yes," he says. "But I swear, I'm not as crazy as they think."

"Just a little bit crazy?" I ask.

He smiles again. And I don't know why I find his smile so reassuring, but I do. So I wait. Holding my breath until he speaks. "Just a little, I promise." He reaches inside the car, opens the door, then slips into the driver's seat.

"How will you—"

But he's already got it started before I can finish that sentence.

When he looks up at me from under his unruly head of dark hair, he winks. "I've got talents too. Now get the fuck in the car. We're out of here."

I walk around the other side, get in, and close the door behind me. Thomas is already backing the car out before I can say anything else. Like what if they recognize us on the way out? But it's clear, there's no one at the front gates to the asylum long before we get there.

We pass through unnoticed and drive south towards Cathedral City looming in the distance. After several nervous minutes of looking behind us, Thomas finally relaxes. "Thank you," he says. "You saved my ass, Sadie. So I owe you one."

He reaches over, places his hand on my leg, and squeezes. But oddly, it's not creepy. It's... comforting.

"And hey," he says. "Don't worry. Whatever's happening to you, we'll figure it out."

"Where are we going?" I ask as I remove his hand from my thigh. It's not creepy. That's not why I removed it. It's just... not something I allow. I might not remember much, but I'm a hundred percent sure I don't let strange men touch my legs.

"Well." Thomas sighs as he gets on the freeway going south. If he takes my rebuke personally, he doesn't show it. "We can't go to my place." He looks over at me and smiles. "Obviously. And I'm pretty sure your place is also a very bad idea. We can't go to my friends'. They'll look there first. So I guess we're stuck with a tower. It's the only place I can think of right now."

"A tower?" I ask. This day is so confusing.

"Yeah," he says, pointing at the tower at the southern edge of the city. "I own those towers. They're mine. And they have basements that weren't in the plans, so no one knows about them but us."

"Who is us?" I ask.

"So they won't find us there," he says, ignoring my question. "We'll be safe until we figure out what to do."

I slump back in my seat. The tower he's pointing at feels far, far away. And I am way too tired to think for another second.

"Hey," Thomas says, grabbing my shoulder to jolt me awake. "I don't think you should sleep. You might've been hit after all." He reaches up to tap my head. "Amnesia, right? You lost your memory."

"No, I didn't," I say. Groggily.

"I think you have a concussion. Don't sleep. It's not safe."

"I'm not even bleeding," I say through a yawn. "Nothing hit me."

"Yes, Sadie. Something *did* hit you. You just didn't see it."

"You're crazy." But I smile as I say it, then open one eye to look at him.

He's nodding. Which is not a good sign when you call someone crazy. Especially when you just helped him escape from an insane asylum. "I know. But not the way you think. Trust me, something hit you back there and fucked with your head. I'm sorry that happened. So don't sleep. Not yet."

My eyes just cannot stay open. I can't even fight it. They are heavy. Like my mind. And they are out of my control. So no amount of shaking from Thomas or calling my name can make me stop what happens next.

I'm out.

CHAPTER SEVEN

I can't stop… *looking at her.* There's something there. Like I know her. Which is impossible. I have never seen this girl before in my life. I'd have remembered those eyes. For sure. I'm positive.

I try to wake her again, but she's out. I think she really does have a concussion. If I was smart I'd drop her off at a hospital, but I can't.

Well, I could.

But I won't.

There's just no way I'm not taking her with me. Fuck dropping her off. I need to know who this girl is.

Illusionist. Now that is some big news right there. And it can only mean one thing. She's Prodigy.

But it can't be. We blew Prodigy up fifteen years ago. More than fifteen now. And she can't be that old. I'd bet not even twenty-five. Probably even younger than Molly.

I wonder if Molly knows her?

But again… we blew that place up. And this Sadie girl was not there.

The inner voice is cautioning me. *Don't go there, Thomas.*

Because if she's Prodigy and we've never seen her, then… fuck.

I shake my head. I don't want to think about it. I just want to get her some place where I have her full attention.

I want to ask her every question I can think of. I want to... *know* her.

The tower I'm heading to is on the southern outskirts of Cathedral City but I have to pass the remnants of ToyBox to get there. And that brings me back to why I was locked up in the first place.

And Yasmine.

Bitch. That fucking bitch.

But I got even, didn't I? I have a private moment of satisfaction at that thought. She thought she had me. Stupid. Didn't they tell her how they made me? Didn't they tell her me and my drugs, all these years, were the only thing keeping me in check? And yeah, it was Case who started this process. But I was still in control until Yasmine went and fucked it all up.

Look out, motherfuckers. Because I'm back and I'm better than ever.

I smile as I look over at Sadie. I have a level ten illusionist sitting not two feet away from me.

Could things get any more ironic?

Well, I could ask myself why she was there in the first place.

Obviously, I need to face the fact that Prodigy School is alive and well. And the reason Sadie was standing in the vicinity of my mind wave was because they sent her to eliminate me. Or capture me. Steal me away from Yasmine.

But the really fucked-up thing here—for them, at least—is that they're not on the same side. No way would Prodigy let a level ten illusionist in my general vicinity if they knew what Yasmine was planning. No fucking way. Because the two of us together—Good God. I have to chuckle as I shake my head in disbelief. The two of us together are what you call an unstoppable force.

I cannot wait to tell Lincoln and Case.

Too bad I can't do that now. Not yet. If I go up to Lincoln's they'll definitely come looking for me. Same with Case. But they can wait. At least until I crack Little Miss Trip Chick here.

And crack her I will.

I haven't felt this sure of myself in ten years. We will put an end to this Cathedral City bullshit once and for all as soon as I get Sadie on my side. Hashtag, done deal.

God. Happiness does weird things to me. I feel like I'm in a state of manic euphoria.

I get off the freeway and turn onto the dirt road that leads to the tower. I only finished them last month. Which is the whole reason we're in this fucked-up position in the first place.

Shit got a little… well, let's just say… complicated last month the day the towers went live. I think the electromagnetic force was what did it. But people won't care what I was doing when they locked me up once I get my revenge, because I will take care of all the Cathedral City scum at the same time.

The tower disappears from view as I weave my way around the mountain, but I can feel that fucker. It's a hum. A vibration. A wave of power. My power.

And when it finally comes back into view, my whole body is electric. I am on fire. But not the way Case and Linc heat up. I am raw and ready for battle.

I glance over at my new sidekick and smile. And if I were to see this smile in a mirror, I'd see what everyone sees.

Evil.

That's right, motherfuckers. I'm about to let everyone know just exactly what I am. I'm about to make everyone pay.

I don't park in front of the tower. I drive right into the ponderosa pines and stop under the cover of a two-hundred-year-old tree. They'll see this car for sure once they realize I'm gone and put out an alert.

They'll get out their drones and their helicopters and scour this city. In fact, I'm damn lucky I own all the satellites, or they'd track me that way too.

Dumbasses. What did they think I was gonna do with a satellite network? Phones? Really?

Insert evil laugh here.

They won't find us. Not until we come out of hiding. And I won't do that until this girl is on my side. I will do anything to keep her with me. Make her part of my plan.

Yes.

Me alone. Now that's something people really need to fear. But me and her together?

That's some apocalyptic shit right there.

I cut the engine and look over at my prize. Shake her shoulder. "Sadie," I say. "Wake up. We're home."

I'm really in a goddamned good mood.

She doesn't wake up. So I get out, walk around to her side, and open her door. "Come on, partner. We've got plans to make." I shake her again.

Nothing.

Fuck. Is she sweating? I feel her forehead and realize she's burning up.

Dammit. She can't die now. I just got her. Fuck that.

So I pick her up, kick the door closed with my foot, and take her to the secret entrance to the tower.

It's tricky trying to enter the security code, and I almost drop her a few times as I juggle her body and punch in the numbers. But I manage. The door clicks, opens a few inches, and I push my way through, using my body to slam it closed and lock us in.

Lights near the floor flick on when I step forward, then flick out, so the next one a few feet forward can take its place. This would be creepy as fuck if I didn't know these towers so well. But I do. So they're not.

I like the feeling of being in the spotlight. Like I'm in command of them, even though they're just on motion sensors. I stop at the top of the stairs, adjust Sadie's body in my arms, and then descend. Each step has a light. And each time my foot falls, it lights up.

Case came up with this little improvement after Lulu complained about Lincoln's dungeon stairs being too dark, so of course, I had to upgrade as well.

When I get to the bottom of the stairs I say, "Lights," and the whole room illuminates.

I might not have giant jellyfish tanks, but I make up for it with computer monitors.

Sixteen seventy-two-inch monitors to be exact. All mounted and starting up so they can feed me satellite info on command.

I place Sadie on one of the couches near the back of the room, then walk over and take a seat at the command center to enter the codes to see the city.

Then I go back to Sadie. "Hey," I say, bending down to touch her forehead again. "Can you wake up?"

She really needs to wake up. I cannot take her to a hospital. If I had a Sheila, we'd be all set. But after Steve went a little crazy when the Red Robber hacked into him at Case's house made of SpyGlass, we put the whole sentient house program on hold except for Sheila.

I had one called Mitch. But he was very elementary. Couldn't even do things Steve could, let alone Sheila. So I didn't lose much when we quarantined him.

No, I might not have a Sheila. But I have something almost as good.

I walk over to the small kitchen and open the fridge where I keep all the drugs. Hundreds of little vials are neatly stacked in their proper places. I look around until I find the one labeled REGENERATION, take it out, slam the door, and go looking for a syringe.

This is a special healing enzyme that Linc and Sheila cook up down in that dungeon of theirs. It does exactly what it sounds like. Well, with the exception of Case. But it only went weird for him because Molly poisoned him with something the Blue Boar gave her before we killed him.

I open the syringe, draw out the viscous goop, then flick it with my finger to get rid of air bubbles.

There is a slight risk to using this. She could have an allergic reaction, which would make things significantly worse very quickly. But it's unlikely so I feel the benefits of not having to take Sadie to a hospital outweigh them. She's Prodigy. Which means they did things to her as a child, just like they did with me, Linc, and Case. Which means she's probably had this before anyway. Lots of times. If she was allergic she wouldn't be here. She'd already be dead.

So I lift her floppy arm and stab her in the vein, pushing the goop in with one quick motion.

She hisses through her teeth. Probably because that shit burns going in, but it's a good sign. It means she's still in there. She's not really unconscious. She's probably just exhausted.

"Sadie," I say, slapping the skin on her arm. "Wake up."

The goop must hit her bloodstream at just that moment, because her eyes fly open and she sits up, panic on her face.

"Shhh," I say, putting a hand on her shoulder. "It's just me. Remember? Thomas Brooks? We met at the insane asylum. You fell for my charming good looks and now we're living together down in a dungeon?"

I smile at my joke. It's something new for me. Joking.

She doesn't find me funny. She yanks her arm away from me and looks around. "Where the hell am I? How did I get here?"

"We're in one of my towers," I say, pointing up towards the ceiling. "You know, those giant metal things on the edge of town?"

"No," she says, eyes searching the room like she's desperate for something familiar.

"Yeah," I correct her. "You're just confused. You can't miss those towers. I've been building them for like a year."

She places a hand on her head, like she's got a migraine. "I have *never* seen any towers," she insists. "And how did I get here?"

"I brought you, remember? We had that whole daring escape from the asylum and—"

"Oh, my God. I forgot. You're crazy. I need to go." She stands up, but staggers over sideways so fast, I have to make a mad grab for her waist to stop her from falling to the floor.

"Whoa, there, tripper. Just take it easy."

"What did you call me?" she snarls.

"Tripper? You know. That's what we call illusionists in my neck of the woods."

"What I *mean*," she sneers, "is how did you know I was an illusionist?" She enunciates each word carefully.

"Level ten," I say, shooting my finger at her. "You told me, remember?"

"I'd *never* tell you that." Her eyes pin mine to hers. Her attention stabs me with an intensity I've only ever seen in a few people. Lincoln Wade and Case Reider.

Alphas.

"OK," I say, shoving her towards the couch so she'll fall over in that direction and not hurt herself. "Fine. I can see you need a little more time to adjust. So just take a seat while I pull up the hospital on the maps and take a look at how much damage I did up north."

"That's right," she says, pinching the bridge of her nose to stave off pain. "You…" She opens her eyes and looks up at me. "What exactly happened back there?"

"Sorry about that," I say with a shrug. "You just got caught in one of my infamous mind blasts. But you didn't get injured. At least not by the shock wave. I'm still thinking about that head injury you have." Her fingertips go to her scalp, searching for a wound. "Don't worry. It didn't cut you. At least on the outside."

"What's that mean?" But just as the last word comes out of her mouth, she winces, like the pain is still shooting through her mind.

I got her good. I don't know why she didn't fall over with the blast like everyone else. I don't know why her injuries aren't worse. But that's only because I haven't had time to think about it too hard. It'll make sense soon. But first… I really need to figure out what's happening in the city. So I'll give her some lame excuse and leave her alone to sort it out.

"Well, I'm just guessing here," I say in my most amicable tone of voice. "But I think what I did knocked something loose in your head. You know, because you're an illusionist. You're Prodigy, Sadie. Like me," I add. "We've probably had some of the same modifications."

She just stares at me. For several very long seconds. Then shakes her head. "I don't know what's happening."

"My mind blast knocked your memory out of whack. That's all. It'll come back, I promise you. Just give it a day."

"Should I know what a mind blast is?" And it's such an honest question, I smile.

"No," I say, shaking my head at her. "Not really. It's not important. You didn't get hurt too bad, just a few screws loose up there. I promise, it wears off. Your memory will come back."

Her fingertips gingerly pat the side of her head where she thinks there should be an injury. She draws them back, looks at them, unable to believe there's no blood, then sighs heavily. "What if it doesn't?"

"I'll call my friends and let Sheila do a work-up on you. K?"

"Who's Sheila?"

"It's not important right now. But she's capable of fixing pretty much anything. So don't worry."

"Then why don't you take me there *now*?"

"We'll be caught if we go now. So we're here. But I swear, you'll be fine. I gave you something. It's the same thing Sheila would've given you anyway. Where she'd start, at least. We're just gonna roll with it, OK? One step at a time. Besides, I can just call her and she can tell me what to do if anything goes wrong. I have almost everything here they have there."

This seems to mollify her, because she sinks back into the couch cushions.

"Now just rest up. We'll figure it out. But right now, I need to see what's going on up north OK?"

She doesn't answer. Just stares at me.

I take that as a yes and go back over to my control panel and take a seat. All the screens are live now, and I zoom in and out, looking all over the city for anything that could help me understand what's happening.

Obviously, this was an attack. And now that I know what this Sadie girl is… it means it was an attack on me and my friends. She has to have come from Prodigy School. I don't want to admit what that means. That the school still exists. That we didn't end things when we blew it up fifteen years ago. But I have to. Because she's real.

She didn't come to kill me. She *can't* kill me. And they know that. But they sent her for something.

And Yasmine. What the hell was she up to back at the hospital? Obviously, she knows what I am. I think she was trying to draw out Sullivan. But why?

I fucked up pretty bad last month when shit got… out of hand. Funny thing about that… Yasmine did manage to get rid of the voices in my head. And they're not back.

Yet.

So maybe our luck is changing all the way round? Maybe we have the perfect team now? Linc, me, Case, Molly, Lulu, Sheila… and—I look over my shoulder to see Sadie, lying down on the couch, her hands tucked under her cheek as she stares back at me—*her*. Yeah. She's exactly what we need to finish this city once and for all.

"Go to sleep," I say over my shoulder. "I'll keep watch while you rest. That stuff I gave you is gonna kick in soon and you're gonna need rest. Lots of rest. Don't fight it. You can't win."

All I gotta do is keep her happy until we figure out what to do next.

I take one last look at the satellite images and swivel my chair around to look at her properly. We blew up Prodigy School fifteen years ago, so her mere existence is a mystery I'd like to solve.

She's very young. Older than fifteen, for sure. But not by much. Barely legal if I had to guess. No way can she walk into a bar and order a drink. Way too young for me.

But… there's always a *but*.

She's pretty. And she survived my mind blast with nothing more than a headache. I'm exaggerating, obviously, since it wiped her memory. But she was still standing. That in itself is practically unheard of.

So she's one of us. And that's the only thing that matters.

Because now that I found her, it makes her mine.

CHAPTER EIGHT

He's not someone I should trust. I feel that. My memory might be fucked, but I know this to be true. Somewhere deep inside my mind is my missing reality. And if I know anything, above all, I know that this man—this Thomas Brooks—he's not one of the good guys.

"Stop it," I say.

"Stop what?"

"Looking at me that way."

"I'm just..." He stops, thinking. "I'm just admiring you, Sadie. Your... strength. I've never seen anyone withstand a mind blast like that. Granted," he says, putting his hands up as if to enunciate this exception, "I haven't blasted anyone like that in a long-ass time. They drugged it out of me before I left school and I kept up the protocol—albeit a modified one—because I like to be in control. So I don't have a lot of recent experience on what my mind blasts are capable of these days. But just look at Yasmine. She took a direct hit and it did her in."

"Who's Yasmine?" I ask.

"The woman," he says. "The doctor. She was on the floor. Pinned underneath one of her cohorts."

"Was she dead?" I ask.

"One could hope." He laughs, then stops abruptly. "She's not one of the good guys."

"Neither are you," I shoot back.

He nods. "No. I'm not either. But there's worse than me out there. For sure."

"What are you going to do with me?" I ask.

"I'm helping you, that's all."

"Why?"

"Because you intrigue me, Sadie. You shouldn't exist and yet you do. And regardless of what side we're each on now, if we both came from Prodigy, and we both did, then we started out the same. We could be a team."

"I work alone."

"Do you?"

It came out so fast I didn't have time to think. But I feel that to be true as well. "Yes," I say. "I do. I'm confused now and I don't quite know what's happening. But I can feel it coming back. I will understand soon."

"Good," he says. "That's what I want too. But you're going to get very tired very fast. That's the nature of the drug I gave you. So why not let it come back when it's good and ready, hmm? Close your eyes and relax."

I want to resist him. Like *really* want to. But he's right. I can't fight it. I can feel my body becoming heavy.

"It's almost night, anyway," Thomas continues to persuade.

My eyelids fall and that one simple action is like a trigger. Like a switch. Like a signal to just let go.

Can't fight it.

"Don't make this hard."

The voice is unfamiliar. A hand is pressed hard against my mouth. My eyes are desperate to open, but they can't. Or won't.

"If you fight, I'll win," the voice continues. "So be a good girl and just go along."

I wiggle and realize my wrists are tied with some kind of thick scratchy rope that scrapes my skin as I resist, making it burn.

"You think you're here to kill me, little girl?"

"Who…" I try to say. *Who are you?* But my words—word—is thick and my tongue won't work.

"Just be still and quiet, little Sadie. Be good, like you've been taught. They spent a lot of years forcing you to obey, didn't they?"

My mind responds with a yes. But there is no hope of speech. It's like my mind and my body are two separate entities.

Then… who was forcing me to obey? I don't know that's true even though the *yes* formed in my mind automatically.

"I won't hurt you," he says. "Not if you're good."

How does one *be good?*

"But if you cross me I'll have to react. You understand, right?"

I understand nothing.

"Say yes, Sadie." A hand pets my hair. I realize I'm wet with sweat when he leans in and his soft breath creates a coolness across my neck.

I can't even open my mouth, but a stinging slap across my face makes me try.

"Whoaaaaaaa…" leaks out from between my lips.

"Don't worry. I'm not unreasonable. I know you can't properly talk just yet. So I won't require much speech from you. Believe me"—he laughs—"I'm not interested in you for your intellectual prowess."

Then what? I ask myself. What does this man want? Who is he?

Thomas, you idiot. My brain is catching up with the situation. My body is heavy and my senses are dull. But it's beginning to wear off. This man is Thomas Brooks. The one who… well, I'm still not sure what happened back at that hospital. But he was the one responsible for it.

"You like me, don't you?" he whispers against the heat of my neck.

I like the coolness he brings to my skin. But that's about all I'm capable of understanding at the moment.

"You want me, don't you?"

I want to know what the fuck is happening to me. I arch my back, just barely lifting off the table, since my muscles are so uncoordinated.

"Don't fight," he warns. And now his mouth is right over mine. His lips brush along my cheek. He smells like the woods.

What?

His hand rests on my hip. Just enough pressure for me to understand he's there. He's touching me. And then a kiss. A soft flutter of lips on my lips. His mouth pressing against mine. His tongue… then his hand leaves my hip and slides right between my legs.

I have no clothes on, I realize. The same scratchy rope is burning my ankles. My legs are tied open.

My back arches again when his fingers find what they're looking for.

"What did I just say?" he whispers into my mouth. "Don't fight it. You won't be able to stop me and you'll make everything harder."

His finger is inside me. Probing, pushing. And I realize, with much horror, that I'm slick down there. I'm responding to him.

"See how nice that is, Sadie?" He's still kissing me. His finger is pressing inside me. In and out. A soft—very soft—slow—very slow—in and out. With each stroke the friction decreases as I become wet.

"You like it, don't you?"

"Yes," I say. And this time the word is very clear.

"They always do," he growls against my mouth.

They? *What the fuck are you doing, Sadie Scott? You're letting a man touch you!* "Stop," I say, just as clear as the yes.

"No," he insists, back to kissing my mouth. "You already gave me permission."

I buck my back again. The feeling in my limbs is coming back. My muscles begin to respond. Not quite at the level I'll need to fight this guy off—not that I really could, since I'm tied down—but enough for him to take notice.

Another slap across my face. Harder this time. More than a sting. A burn. A hot smack of heat across my cheek.

"You don't control me, little Sadie." His kiss is stronger now. More insistent. Not gentle and soft like it was a few seconds ago. "It's the other way around. I'm the one in charge here. You belong to me." He growls the words into my mouth. Claiming me.

"No," I say, sucking in a breath when he draws back. I try to open my eyes but they refuse to respond. I realize they're taped shut.

Panic.

"Stop," I groan. My whole body wiggles under the restraints. My wrists and ankles are burning from the rope. My heart is beating fast. *Thump, thump, thump, thump* in my chest. I can't breathe. I can't suck in enough air because his mouth is there. Pressing me for a kiss.

His hand grabs my face, thumb and forefinger digging into my jawbone hard enough to feel the bruise forming. "If you fight," he says, pulling back momentarily to speak, "you'll lose."

I realize with horror that his fingers are still inside me. Still stimulating me. And the moment I let that sensation back into the front of my mind, I begin to climax.

"No," I say, frantically wiggling. Desperate to make him stop his stimulation. Desperate to not respond the way he wants me to.

But it's no use.

I come.

I moan, and my back arches again, only this time it's from pleasure.

His mouth is on mine again. Kissing. And even if I wanted to—and I don't—I can't stop myself from kissing him back.

I let him overpower me. I let him kiss me and finger me. I kiss him back. He presses his groin against my clenched fist at my side and my hand opens. I find him hard and ready, my fingers grabbing him, closing around his thick cock beneath his pants.

"See," he says, his mouth still hovering over mine. "What did I tell you?"

My orgasm is subsiding and the realization of what I just did comes rushing back.

I let go of his dick and clench my fist again.

"No," I say.

"It's too late, Sadie. It's simply too late."

A sharp prick in my neck makes me *scream*. He pushes something inside me. Some drug that burns like fuck as it enters my bloodstream. I can feel it making its way through my body. And the moment it hits my heart—that moment when the *thump, thump, thump, thump* delivers it to every cell in my body—everything goes black.

I sit up in bed, breathing hard and sweating profusely. I am covered in heat. I kick off the covers, panic setting in as I check my body.

I am dressed. In the same weird clothes I was in earlier. The bed is soft and comfortable, the blanket a thick down comforter. I turn around and find several pillows—all damp from my body—stacked against a headboard.

What the fuck?

Did I hallucinate?

Which makes me laugh out loud. Because that's what I make other people do, right? It's my superpower.

"You're awake?" Thomas calls from another room. The door is open, so I can hear him clearly. His fingers are tapping out something on a keyboard.

I just stare at the open door, trying to figure out what's real.

"Sadie?" he calls again. "Are you awake in there?"

"Yes," I manage to croak out.

"Take your time. You've been out for a while. Almost twelve hours."

Out. I was sleeping. That was a dream—nightmare—I correct myself. I reach up to wipe the sweat from my forehead and stop.

There's a rope burn ringing my wrist. I check my other hand and find the same leftover evidence of... my nightmare. I lean down, pull up my pant leg, and look at the matching burn on my ankle.

It was real. He did that to me. He drugged me, took off my clothes, tied me down, and then... violated me.

"When you're feeling OK, come out here. I think I know what's happening," Thomas calls.

Was it him? Maybe it was someone else. I didn't see him, did I?

No, he taped your fucking eyes closed so you couldn't open them, remember?

I swing my legs over the side of the bed and lean my elbows on my knees, head in hands.

"Hey," he says from the open door. "You still feel off?"

I look up at him from underneath my sweat-soaked hair. "Off?" I snarl.

"You look better though. A little flushed. You might have a fever. I have something for that." He turns to leave, presumably to go get some drug that will put me out again.

"No," I say, making him turn back to me. "No. I was just..." I turn to look at the bed. "I was under that heavy blanket, that's all."

"You're probably hungry," Thomas says. "We've got emergency food here. But we can go shopping. Pick up stuff for a good meal. The kitchen isn't anything special, but there's an oven and a cooktop."

Is he for real right now? He practically raped me. While I was drugged unconscious. "What the fuck?" I yell.

His head instinctively retreats backwards, like my outburst took him by surprise. "What's wrong?"

"You—" I stop. Because it's so... unthinkable. That he would do that and then just... pretend it didn't happen.

Maybe it didn't happen?

"I have rope burns," I say, holding up my wrists. "And on my ankles too." I mean the words to be an accusation but they come out weak and confused.

Thomas walks over to me and sits down on the bed very close to me. So close I have to lean into him when the mattress sags. "Let me see," he says, taking my wrist in his hand. His eyes meet mine. "I'm sorry they did that shit to you."

"They?" I ask. "What shit?"

He shrugs, nothing but sympathy in his eyes. Pity, I think. That's a much better word for what's in his eyes. "I don't know what they did." He sighs. "But I can imagine. They did a lot of shit to me too when I was young. So I'm sorry. I have ointment that might help. Take the sting away, at least."

I squint my eyes, unsure of what to make of this. He's certainly not acting like he's the one who did this to me. In fact, he's insinuating that I came here with these rope burns.

Did I?

His hand squeezes mine. "Sadie," he says. "It's OK. Whatever they were doing, it's over now. You're with me. I know it's not much since we're complete strangers. But I've been there. I've been where you are now. The weeks and months after I left Prodigy were the worst time in my life. I was on my own because my friends and I had to split up. It was a very fucked-up time. I get it."

I just stare up at his dark eyes. He's definitely handsome. He's got one of those faces that say—dashing. Square jaw with a light coat of shadowed stubble. He's wearing a t-shirt now. His shoulders are broad and his arms well-muscled. His hand is big, completely covering mine.

"Did you… have nightmares?" I ask. "When you left?"

A slow nod of affirmation. "For years. I know we weren't in the same school." He looks away, like this is something he takes personally. "I didn't know they had more than one school, you understand, right?"

I don't know. I don't think I understand anything right now.

"I would've blown up all of them if I had known there were more. I would've saved you." His eyes dart away from mine, but return in almost the same instant. "Killed you, at least."

"Killed me?" I ask, almost out of breath.

He shrugs. "To save you from what they were doing. So I'm sorry. I didn't know."

I feel… defeated. And sad. And stupid. "I don't know what's happening to me," I finally manage to say.

"I know," he says softly. "But it'll get better. I promise."

"When?" I ask. "I don't even have my memories. I don't even know what they did. They're going to come back and—"

"Shhh," he says, putting an arm around me. Holding me close to him. "We can worry about that later. I'll try to prepare you as best I can. I imagine it won't take long for the effects of my blast to wear off, so we'll talk about it today. But not now."

"You have something to show me?" I ask. The panic has faded. The uncertainty is still there, but I don't think he's the kind of man who'd drug a woman and violate her. He seems concerned. It was a dream. A nightmare. A hallucination.

"Later, huh?" he says, smiling. "We're going to go grocery shopping and then we'll stop by a store and get you things to wear. When we get back, I'll show you then. We can talk then." He gets up and walks out of the room, only to return a few minutes later with a little bag in his hands. "Here," he says, putting the bag down on the bed beside me. "There's some stuff in there to help you freshen up. Toothbrush, washcloth, soap. You can take a real shower when we get back with clothes."

He turns and walks out. Cool as can be.

It was a dream. That's all.

"Don't make this hard."

The voice is unfamiliar. A hand is pressed hard against my mouth. My eyes are desperate to open, but they can't. Or won't.

"If you fight, I'll win," the voice continues. "So be a good girl and just go along."

CHAPTER NINE

"Sadie," I say as we drive out of the forest and back onto the roads. "What's your last name?"

"What?" She's nervous. Very nervous. And she's got a confused look on her face.

"Relax. I'm just making conversation since you're so quiet. What's your last name?"

"Scott," she says. "And sorry. I'm pretty sure I'm not a very good socializer. Are you sure it's safe to go into town?"

"It's the edge of town. Barely counts."

"You don't think they're looking for us?"

"They probably are. Maybe even seriously. But they don't have this vehicle on their radar. It's not registered to me. And we came out the tunnel, so even if they're watching the towers, and I doubt they are because no one in their right mind builds a Batcave under a tower, they won't know what car we're in. I left the one we came in back in the forest. It's covered up so they can't fly a drone over and spot it."

The confused look is even more pronounced. Like I was just speaking a foreign language. "How long have you been out?" I ask.

"Out?"

"Of the school, Sadie. How long have you been away from them?"

"I have no idea what you're even talking about, Thomas. I really don't."

Hmmm. I reach over her lap, open the glove box, and pull out a map of Cathedral City. "Here. Can you read this?"

She takes the map from my fingertips with an annoyed huff. "I know how to read a map."

"OK. So tell me where we are." I point to an upcoming sign, just before the entrance to the freeway. "This is Meadowlark Boulevard and that's the Ninth Street Freeway. Find it on the map."

She knows what I'm doing. But she also knows how to read a map. So she takes a few seconds to orient herself and points. "Here. We're right here."

"OK. So they at least taught you things."

"I'm not stupid, either."

"Sadie," I say, cocking an eyebrow at her. "Don't be so damn defensive. I can't ask you anything because you don't remember. I'm just trying to form an opinion on things. You don't know anything but your name. Which I find interesting. Because most amnesiacs lose all memories."

She frowns. "Do you think I'm lying?"

"Not at all." I laugh. "If you knew who you were we would definitely not be going out to breakfast right now."

"Why?" She's still scowling. "And you never said anything about going out to breakfast."

"Because they sent you to kill me, Sadie. And I'm pretty sure if you were faking it, you'd have completed that mission last night. And I did say we were going out to eat. I just changed my mind on how to go about getting food. You look like you need a meal now. We can shop after."

She laughs this time, which is a nice change. "Why the hell would anyone send me to kill you?"

"Because we're Prodigy, right? You didn't come to that hospital to check me out and take me home." I waggle my eyebrows at her. "If you know what I mean. You came to kill me or take me back to them so they could do it themselves."

She sighs and shakes her head, but she doesn't deny it. She feels it to be true, even if she's not a hundred percent sure. "I don't know," she finally says. "I know I'm different. I know what *illusionist* means. I know I can make people hallucinate, so I know I'm not normal." She pauses for a second. "I know I'm not supposed to talk about that. I know my name." She looks at me. "I know your name."

"And deep down you know they sent you to finish me. It's OK. I'm not taking it personally. It's my fault you got left behind anyway. I can't blame you for what they did after I failed to save you."

She practically snorts. "I don't know why you think I needed saving."

"Because it's Prodigy School, Sadie. They are evil incarnate." It comes out rougher than I intended. Which makes her look at me, then quickly look away. "Have you come up with any ideas about why you're blocking your memories?"

"Blocking?" She huffs again.

"I'm not saying it's on purpose. But the chances are high that you lost your memory due to... what they put you through."

She looks out the window at the last part. Stays silent.

"I know what they put me through. My friends through. My brother and..."—it takes me a second to spit out the word—"sister too. And none of it's good."

"You have a brother and sister?" she asks, taking the conversation in a new direction.

"Yes. Sort of. My brother, Atticus, and I were in Prodigy together. My sister, Molly, was there too, but she and I were never close."

"They're... still alive? You saved them?"

"No," I say, changing lanes on the freeway to get off at the next exit. "No. Atticus never needed saving. Our father didn't want him in the program like me. He was the... *heir*, right?"

Her lips make a tiny o. "And your sister?"

"I tried to kill her but Lincoln, my friend, he was... attached. So he helped her escape. She made it. Barely, but she did. She's still around, at any rate."

She's quiet after that. Even when we get to the restaurant. She looks at the menu like she's never eaten at a restaurant before, but orders pancakes by pointing at the picture. I expect her to scarf them down since she's obviously in need of food, but she doesn't. She eats slowly. Watching me. Almost mimicking my motions. She says no to coffee, tea, and juice, but drinks the ice water they have on the table.

When we get to the mall a few miles closer to town, she looks utterly lost and doesn't protest when I take her hand and place it on my arm as we walk across the parking lot. When we step through the door, she grips me. Tight.

I don't bother asking what kind of clothes she prefers. She obviously has no idea. Instead, I take her to the women's department and begin to choose. A salesperson helps us, a young girl who looks at Sadie like she's a homeless person who just walked in off the street. But then she looks at me, and pastes the fake smile on her face as she helps her make decisions.

The two of them disappear into a dressing room and an hour later she's wrapping up the packages.

We leave the mall with Sadie clutching my arm again.

"Well," I ask. "How was it?"

Sadie takes a deep breath as she looks over her shoulder at the department store entrance. "Frightening."

"You did good though," I say, holding up the packages. She got a few shirts, a few pairs of jeans, and a new pair of shoes. Sneakers. Which is almost cute. But she refused to change into anything new, so she's still wearing her uniform.

"That lady called me Phil the entire time."

"Your name tag says Phil."

"It does?" she says, looking down at her shirt. "Oh. It does."

"Did you correct her? Tell her it's your boyfriend's shirt?"

When I look down, her eyebrows are all scrunched together. Like she's thinking about this very hard. "No."

"It's OK. Work shirts are kind of... in vogue."

She bites her lip, making me smile, but only says, "Mmm-hmmm."

Grocery shopping is a similar experience. Sadie is wide-eyed with either fascination or fear, I'm not sure which. She walks alongside me as I push the cart, grabbing things off shelves and placing them inside. I wait for her to grab her favorite foods, but the only item that catches her attention are the oranges stacked in a neat pyramid in the fresh food section.

We buy a whole bag of them.

"You didn't want juice at breakfast but you like oranges?" I ask, fishing for insight.

She doesn't answer. In fact, she's silent the whole time I check out at the little kiosk in the front of the store. She watches me scan items one at a time with such intensity, I find myself smiling.

I should not let my guard down. In a few hours she will get her memory back and want to finish her job. In a few hours I might have to kill her.

But I like her.

I decide I don't want to kill her. She cannot kill me, so I'm not even worried about that. But she might be a whole other animal when those memories come rushing back. I need to keep that in mind.

When we get off the freeway at Meadowlark Boulevard again, the morning is gone. She hasn't said a word to me since that comment about her name tag in the mall parking lot. But when I pull into the long tunnel that leads to the tower, she seems to relax. Her shoulders press into the seat back and drop.

"Thank you," she whispers in the dark. "You've been really nice to me."

Yes. I really have. I'm not called nice often, but I am being extremely nice to her.

The drugs, I decide. Or lack thereof. It's been a long time—very long time—since I was this person she's seeing today.

I think it has something to do with the mind blast back at the hospital. It was a rush of relief when I finally let go and unleashed my power. Like a dam breaking.

It scares me a little. I'm not sure what kind of consequences I'll have to face. Everything has consequences. You can't bottle up your emotions for more than a decade and not expect there to be consequences.

Not to mention the drug Yasmine injected me with just before all that shit happened. I think I know what it was. Some kind of antagonist that counteracts all the drugs in my system. Ever since Case shot me with—whatever the fuck it was—back at his house a few months ago, I've been different. I've had *feelings*.

But it's different now. It's like… I feel almost… *normal*.

Not that I know what normal is. But it feels good. And Sadie. She's something good, I think. Killer instincts aside. It's not her fault she's a product of her environment.

We could make a good team. Case has Lulu and Lincoln has Molly.

It's almost a natural progression of things that I should get someone too.

I've been telling myself that since yesterday. I deserve a partner too. And I don't have many options. Case is lucky he found Lulu. She's not Prodigy but she gets him. Completely. And Molly and Lincoln were genetically made to be partners. Literally. Molly is bonded to him and he is bonded to her. Even if they ever stopped being in love, they are meant to be together because he is her Alpha and she is his Omega. They complete each other.

I don't have an Omega. I killed them all a long time ago before they could kill me first. Lincoln is lucky, I decide. I almost feel envy.

"Good God." I laugh. I cannot believe I'm envious of *Lincoln*.

"What?" Sadie asks as I stop the car and turn off the engine. "What's funny?"

"Nothing," I say. "Just irony, I guess."

CHAPTER TEN

I only know a few things to be true at this point.

First, I came from Prodigy School. I feel this. The name means something to me. Obviously, Thomas came from there too, which makes us... somewhat similar. He wasn't lying about that stuff. I really do believe I was sent to kill him.

Second, I'm an illusionist. Which makes me... abnormal. But I don't seem bothered by it.

Third, I feel calm. It's weird because there is some kind of cell or muscle memory inside me that knows... I'm not usually a calm person.

This is the part that's bothering me. Because I get the feeling that Thomas isn't normally this calm either.

There's a dark side to us both.

And then the memory of the nightmare is back. His lips on my lips. His hand on my hip. How it slipped between my legs and made me wet—

"Are you getting out of the car?"

I look up and find Thomas standing at my side, the passenger door open, two thick brown paper bags in his arms filled with our food.

"Yes," I say, letting the dark side drift away as I step out of the car, grab the bags of clothes, bump the door closed with my hip, and follow him down the long, dark hallway to the bunker entrance.

That's what this is. A bunker. Real end-of-the-world type stuff.

"Do you think something bad is going to happen?" I ask, following Thomas into the corner of the large open room that acts like a kitchen. There's one long counter, a cooktop stove, and a refrigerator. It's all new, but nothing matches. Like he pieced this place together from leftovers.

He empties the two large bags and puts things away. "I've never done this before," I say, mostly to myself.

"How do you know?" Thomas asks, not looking at me.

"I just know."

"Are your memories coming back?"

"No."

I catch him looking at me from the corner of his eye. I don't think he believes me. "You're very quiet, Sadie. It worries me."

"Why?" I ask

"Because quiet people are often thinkers. So you're thinking right now. What are you thinking about?"

"The nightmare," I say, then wonder why I said it.

"Tell me about it," he says, finishing up with the groceries and walking over to the large bank of screens. They are all maps. Satellite maps. He sits in his chair and nods his head at me. "Pull that one up so I can try to explain a few things."

I look over at an office chair along the wall, walk over to it, and wheel it back to his desk. I sit. Breathe through the silence as I watch him pull up new maps.

"Do you know what this is?" he asks, pointing to the center screen.

"Cathedral City," I say. "City Park."

"How do you know that?" he asks.

I point to the screen. "The town towers. I recognize them now. I know I said I didn't during our escape, but I do now. It's coming back, I think. My memory."

"Interesting," he says. "That you recognize them but not a grocery store."

"Look," I say, becoming frustrated and maybe even a little mad. "I don't know how, OK? I don't understand anything that's happening to me. If you don't want me here—if you don't trust me—then I'll leave. I'll figure it out on my own."

"Settle down," he says, still working with the maps. "I'm not saying that at all. I'm just trying to make you think about things. You can't kill me, Sadie. So let's just get that out in the open right now. If you try, you'll die. I don't want to hurt you, so I'd prefer that you don't try."

"You don't know that."

"Which part don't I know? Because I'm the one with all the memories, Sadie. I'm the one with perfect recall of what they did to me. What they made me. What I'm capable of. And you saw it back there at the hospital. You saw what I can do."

"It had no effect on me." I shrug.

"No effect?" He laughs. "I knocked your fucking programming right out of your mind. Wiped it away. You're a shell right now. I did that to you."

I look up at him. He's staring at me with an intensity I haven't seen before. Granted, I've known him like one day. But so far he's been calm, collected, and completely in control. This new look says he might not stay that way. "It's only temporary."

"My point is," he growls, "you don't stand a chance against me one on one. That's all. I'm not worried about you killing me. But I don't want you to get hurt."

I don't need his protection, I decide. I have nothing to back up this feeling, but I know it. I'm surer about this guess than anything else.

I am something unique. Special. Capable, and strong, and... deadly.

I don't need his protection.

"I thought we were talking about maps," I say in a cool, calm voice. "You had something to tell me."

He lets out a long, frustrated exhale. "OK, so you know this is City Park in Cathedral City and these are the City Towers. But do you know what they do?"

I shrug. "Broadcast," I say. "Some kind of wave. Obviously. That's why one builds towers."

"Yes," Thomas says, his eyes brightening at my deduction. "Yes. My towers broadcast signals."

"What kind of signals?" I ask.

He doesn't look at me, but I can see the corner of his mouth turn up in a smile. "Dangerous things."

"Like radiation?"

"No," he says, turning his head slightly so I can see him in profile. "Like... well, it's complicated. Sound and light are strange things, Sadie. Powerful things. We're just at the very early stages of understanding them. But they are weak in some respects. You need a receiving device. Like a phone. And..." He turns his head to hide his smile. "A tablet, in our situation."

"Whose situation?" I ask.

"My friends and me. Do you remember—" Then he stops. "No, you wouldn't. Several months ago, terrorists blew up all the cell phone towers around Cathedral City. But lucky for the citizens of this great city, I had others in place. What I didn't have was a cell phone company. I deal in satellite phones, you see. So in order to restore wireless phones to the area, I gave everyone in the city one of my sat phones and put them on my network."

"Sounds pretty ominous, Thomas."

"Oh"—he laughs—"it gets much better than this. You see, in order for a phone to be useful you have to have access to the satellite and you have to have a way to communicate with the satellite. Which is why I gave everyone in the city a free terminal."

"You're going to hurt these people?" I ask. He hesitates, and in those few seconds I realize—even if he says yes, I won't be bothered by this admission.

Why do I feel this way?

"Not really," he says. A noncommittal answer if ever there was one. "I am trying to hurt certain people. But not all people."

"Which people?" I ask.

"Who do you think?"

"Prodigy people," I say.

"Yes." He turns to fully face me and the smile is back. "I'm going to hurt them, Sadie. And I'd like your help."

I sigh. "I'm not much use like this. I know I have certain capabilities. But I get the feeling I have certain parameters that contain me as well."

"Oh, I'm sure you do," he says, chuckling. "But I can fix that. I can fix you, Sadie. I can take the parts they own and set them free. Wouldn't that be nice?"

It's my turn to laugh. "Maybe you're just one more really bad guy and I should leave all of you behind and find my own way in the world."

"That's one option, for sure. But if you stick it out with me we can rip the world apart and put it back together. Make it new, Sadie. Make it ours."

"You realize you sound like a madman, right? This calm demeanor isn't fooling me one bit."

"I'm quite mad, yes. But not any more than the people who control you."

"I'm not on your side," I say.

"You can be on your own side. What a novel idea, right?"

"Why were you in that hospital?" I ask. There's something really wrong with this man. Really wrong.

"They... compromised me. A few months back. When the cell towers were blown up. I have a unique body chemistry that requires careful manipulation."

"Your mentalist capabilities?"

"Exactly. But they compromised my friends. One of them shot me with a drug that disrupted my brain chemistry. I went... a little mad. And then they had me locked up. It was the perfect opportunity for them to try to get the upper hand."

"Who?" I ask. "Who did all this?"

"Yasmine, I think. But I'm not sure."

"The doctor?"

"Her. And others I haven't identified yet. You see, there are two sides to this story. Us and them. But both sides are trying to do the same thing. Albeit for very different reasons."

"Why do you want me?"

"Because you're special, Sadie. So obviously special." His hand comes up to my cheek, petting it. The way he—whoever—was petting my hair last night. It was him. I'm sure of it. Thomas Brooks drugged me and touched me, then tried to pass it off as a nightmare.

"Don't," I say, slapping his hand away. "Don't do that. I know what you did."

He pulls his hand back. Chastised. "I'm just trying to give you options."

"By taking off all my clothes and tying me up? By... violating me?"

"What?" He laughs. This time the smile is different. Real. Not on the verge of diabolic. "I didn't tie you up. When the fuck would I have done that? You were sleeping for twelve hours."

"While I was sleeping," I say, angry at his manipulation. "You *touched* me."

His eyebrows knit together as he squints at me. "Touched you... where?"

Asshole.

But I stay silent. I'm not going to describe what happened last night and give him a thrill. I refuse.

"It was a nightmare, Sadie. I'm sure those things probably did happen at some point in our past, but I wasn't the one who did them."

Could it be true? I have no idea. Was it him? Was it just a sad, lost memory floating to the surface under trauma?

The fact that I'm considering this—that I'm so confused about it—leads me to believe him when he says the Prodigy people are cruel and mean. I know that, just as I know the few other things about myself without actually remembering them.

Could my experience have happened in my head last night, and nowhere else? Am I nothing more than the residual effects of my life that came before Thomas?

I decide to change the subject. "Why was *I* at the hospital?"

"To kill me," he says.

"But you already said I can't kill you. Wouldn't these people know that?"

"I'm sure they figured they had a way past my protection. My power. Perhaps Yasmine's drug wasn't in their plans."

"But if she's on their side—"

He points his finger at me. "Maybe she's not. Maybe we have two enemies, Sadie? Ever think of that? Maybe what Yasmine did was not part of their plan. And that drug she gave me unleashed the power of my mind. A power I've held tightly in control since I walked out of that burning Prodigy building fifteen years ago? Maybe," he says, "what Yasmine did went against what they were doing."

A flashing red alert races through my mind. *Abort! Abort! Abort!* I put my hands to my head, trying to make it go away.

"You remember something?" Thomas asks, a gentle hand on my shoulder.

"Yes," I whisper. "Something flashing across my eyes. The word 'abort' in red letters."

"See," he says, like I just confirmed his theory. "Prodigy sent you, but they didn't expect Yasmine to unleash me. Maybe you *can* kill me, Sadie. Or could, I should say. Maybe before Yasmine released my mind from the grip of the drugs I've used to hold it prisoner, you had that power. But it's gone now. I assure you. It's gone now. I am the most powerful weapon to ever come out of a Prodigy School."

Until me, I think.

And I have no idea where that came from.

But like everything else popping into my head today— I know it to be true.

"We'd make a good team," he says, grabbing the arm of my office chair and pulling me closer to him. "Think about it. They wouldn't send you if you weren't powerful. Mentalist is the most powerful weapon they can produce from the kids. But illusionist is pretty powerful too. We're perfect, Sadie. We're practically meant for each other."

His hand is back on my cheek. Softly stroking me as he looks down into my eyes. When I don't stop him, he leans in. His soft lips brush against mine, just like in the nightmare last night.

I kiss him back this time too. I wait for his wandering hand to slip between my legs and make me feel the pressure of his fingers against my sex.

But he just pulls back. Smiling. "See," he says in a soft, low voice. "See how perfect we are?"

I bite my lip and inhale deeply.

"We can change things, Sadie. We can make them pay for turning us into little science projects. For stealing our childhoods away. Taking our innocence. Us," he whispers as his mouth covers mine once again. "We are the enemy they've been waiting for."

I give in. Hell, who am I kidding? I practically melt against him. I want more. I want him to touch me again. I want him to take what he wants and not ask for permission. I want him to control me the way they did. I want my submission to set me free.

"I need it," I whisper.

"What?" he answers back. Kissing me one more time. "What do you need?"

But I can't say it out loud. I can't admit what I really want. So I say, "A friend."

"I'll be your friend, Sadie. Just trust me. We'll be good together, I promise."

CHAPTER ELEVEN

My face is still right up next to hers. I can hear her heart beating. Feel her chest rising and falling as she considers my offer.

"I don't even know you," she finally says.

"What more do you need?" I ask. And I'm serious. "We're products, Sadie. We were created. Molded into what they wanted us to be. We've been through the same things. Were brought up by the same people."

"You don't know that," she says. "We came from two totally different places. You have no idea how I grew up."

"Neither do you," I retort. It's kind of a low blow, but that doesn't make it untrue.

"Right," she says, placing a hand on my chair so she can push away and create some distance. "But I will soon. You said so. I'll remember and I have a feeling that there's a very good reason they sent me to confront you."

"Confront me?" I laugh. "That's a nice way to put it. They sent you on a suicide mission."

"I don't care about that right now."

"You should."

"Like I said, I'll remember eventually. It would be stupid for me to make that kind of promise to you before I know all the facts. You're not a good guy, Thomas. And before you say the same thing right back to me, I'm not the one trying to manipulate the entire town. And I'm not the one hiding things. I don't remember who and what I am.

91

But you know exactly who and what you are. And you won't tell me. There's something... wrong with you, I think. Something big."

"Like what?" I laugh.

"I don't know," she says, standing up from her chair. "I don't know. But I think I'm going to leave now."

"No," I say, getting to my feet so fast, my chair goes sliding across the floor.

"You don't own me, Mr. Brooks." But she's not moving towards the door. She wants a reason to stay and so far I haven't given her one.

"What do you need to know?" I ask. "What can I tell you to make you stay? I think if you just wait it out, Sadie, if you just give yourself a chance to stabilize, you'll see that I'm right. They want you dead. I want you alive."

"You want to use me just like they do."

"No," I say, frustrated. "That's not what I want. I want a partner in this."

"In your world domination plans? No, thank you!"

We stare at each other for a few seconds. I take her in. She hasn't changed yet. And she hasn't showered. She's a mess. There's still a smudge on her arm from the destruction I caused at the hospital yesterday. There's a rip in her stolen shirt proclaiming her name to be Phil. She has those stupid work boots on.

I want to see her. Really see her. And I know she'd feel better if she just cleaned up and took a breath. Got a good night's sleep.

"I want the truth from you. I want to know why you were in that hospital. Because I think you were there for a very good reason. I think you're crazy."

"Look, I want to know all about you too, Sadie. I want that as well. But you're still wearing that stupid uniform. And you need a shower. How about you clean up, put on something else, and then come back out here and I'll make us lunch. After lunch, if you still want to leave, I'll take you wherever you want to go."

She hesitates. She's close to a yes. I know this because her eyes dart to the bathroom door on the other side of the room. But something is holding her back.

"Sadie," I say, walking towards her. "Come on. You can't just walk out of here on your own. We're in the forest. You have no car. Just take a breath, for fuck's sake. Relax."

"I want to know why you were there," she insists.

"Fine," I say, putting my hands up. "Fine. You clean up, we'll have lunch, and we'll talk. Fair?"

I smile at her indecision. It's not exactly fake. I really do think she'd rather leave. But something is holding her here. Maybe it's me?

I walk over to the bathroom, flick the light on, and run the water for the shower. "Come on," I say, beckoning her with a finger. "You've been here for two days almost. What's thirty more minutes?"

She looks longingly at the steam rising up around me. Her hair is dark, her skin is probably olive when she's feeling good, but right now, it's a little gray. And there are the beginnings of dark circles under her eyes. She really does need rest. She's pretty now, but cleaning up and wearing something that actually fits would go a long way towards making her beautiful.

"I'll get your clothes," I say, walking back over to the kitchen where her bags are.

When I turn around, she's inside the bathroom. Crisis averted.

But it won't be enough. I can't tell her more about me until I know more about her. So what else could I do to put all those flashing red flags running through her mind to rest?

Well… there's always the oldest trick in the book.

I follow her into the bathroom with her bags, set them down in the corner, and grab two towels from the shelf and place them on the vanity.

She stares at me. Says, "Thank you." Stares some more.

I reach behind my neck and drag my t-shirt over my head. Drop the shirt to the floor.

She's staring at me. "What are you doing?"

"I need a shower too. And we only have so much water."

She starts shaking her head, but I walk over to her and start unbuttoning that stupid work shirt.

Her chest is rising and falling rapidly again. Just like it was when I kissed her.

"Stop me if you don't want it, Sadie. I'm not gonna force you."

Her eyes dart up to mine. "You did last night."

"That was a fucking nightmare." I sneer. "That wasn't me. You need to get your head around reality."

"It felt real."

I finish unbuttoning her shirt and open it up, revealing a tight sports bra. God, I bet her tits are spectacular once I take that awful binding off. Two soft flicks of my fingers make the shirt slide down her arms. It drops to the floor at our feet.

I wait to see if she'll stop me, but she just stares up into my eyes with something that might be a mixture of fear and longing.

I grab the edge of the thick stretchy fabric of her sports bra, but her hands clamp down on my wrists before I can pull it up and expose her tits.

"Wait," she says in a weak voice.

"Why?" I ask.

"I don't know if I want to do this," she says, almost breathless.

"You do," I say. "There are as many ways to say no as there are to say yes, Sadie. If you didn't want this, you'd have stopped it before it started. I won't fuck you if you don't want it. But I'd like to look at you, at least."

She's silent again, so I take that as permission and finish what I started. The bra comes over her head. I absently throw it aside as I stare at her body. "Now the pants," I say, going for her button.

She lets me this time. No argument. They're barely being held up by that button and the moment it's released, they fall over the curve of her hips and join the shirt on the floor.

I grin at her body. "You're very pretty."

She says nothing so I kick off my boots, release the button on my jeans, and step out of them. I'm not hard, but she stares at my cock. I can almost feel her want. And then she blushes. Color rushes back into her cheeks in an instant.

I place my hand on her flushed face and say, "I like that reaction."

She turns away from me and steps into the running water.

I won't fuck her.

I'll try not to fuck her.

Who am I kidding? I'm totally gonna fuck her.

I step in beside her, letting her have the water first. She closes her eyes and wets her hair, letting the water stream down her face. The heat takes the rest of her gray pallor away, flushing her cheeks with pink, and she looks a hundred times better immediately.

When she's wet, she steps out of the shower stream and I take her place.

I cannot stop the grin as she watches me. I'm a nice specimen of a man. No one can deny that. My body is hard and lean. My shoulders broad and strong.

She doesn't even try to stop her stare.

"We would make a great couple, Sadie."

"Couple," she says with a frown. "I thought you said team?"

"Same thing," I reply, picking up the soap and washing my arms. She misses nothing as I drag the bar up and down my muscles, leaving behind a froth of bubbles. "I'd rather be washing you, but…" I shrug. "I said I wasn't gonna fuck you if you don't want me to, and if I got my hands on those breasts of yours, I don't know if I could stop myself."

I think she wants me. Pretty bad. But she's not giving in that easy. And I'm not going to take that decision away from her. I want her to work for it, anyway. I might even want her to beg. Beg me to fuck her. To squeeze those tits. To push my cock deep inside her pussy until she screams my name. I want her to open her legs for me of her own volition. I want her to place her hands on the top of my head and guide my mouth to her clit. I want her to say, *Lick me, Thomas.*

"You're hard," she says.

"I'm thinking about you," I say, reaching for my growing cock. I fist it, squeeze it hard as I move my palm up and down my shaft. Masturbating in front of her.

Ten minutes ago, this was not even in the realm of possible outcomes. But she likes to submit, I realize. She will let me lead her along. She wants me to fuck her and she wants me to make her say yes.

But I won't. I want her to give in.

"You can touch yourself," I say. "I'd love to watch that."

Her mouth parts in surprise. Her nipples bunch up before my eyes and I realize she's probably cold. "You want the water?" I ask.

She nods. Stays silent.

That's her default setting, I realize. Silent.

I move out of the water and let her take my place. I lean back and watch her as she reaches for shampoo. I am mesmerized as she lathers up her hair. My hand is still on my cock. My breath is coming quicker. Louder.

"Touch yourself," I say. "And not your hair."

She bites her lip and shakes her head no.

"I'll come without you. I can come right now."

"Go ahead," she says, her words barely audible over the sound of the water. "I'm not playing this game with you."

"I'm not playing a game. I'm just enjoying the view. You are as well. But you're just a bundle of inhibitions and reasons to say no. Which makes no sense because we both know you want to say yes."

She turns her back to me and rinses the shampoo from her hair.

I stare at her ass. The hourglass shape of her body. Who knew underneath Phil's work shirt she had a body like this?

It's definitely a nice surprise, but not the reason I've decided to keep this girl for myself.

When she turns around again, she has the conditioner. She massages it into her long locks. Eyes on my eyes. Not my dick, which is where they should be. But slow progress is still progress.

She rinses that too. I lean back against the cold tile wall. Pressing my back against it. Tilting my head and letting my eyelids fall to half-mast as I continue to masturbate.

When she turns around and drags the soap over her breasts, I pump harder. Her nipples are all bunched up into peaks. I want to suck them. I want to twist them between my fingertips. My hand on my cock makes a slapping sound in the echo chamber of the shower stall. I begin to grunt a little. She can't help herself now. She stares openly at my erotic display.

Her soapy hand creeps down her abdomen. I almost die waiting for it to slip between her legs. And she makes me wait for it too. Teases me as she lathers the lower part of her belly. Coming so close to that little sweet spot between her legs, I have to close my eyes for a moment.

When I open them, I stare at her face. She's staring back at me. Her hand is very busy between her legs. Her mouth slightly open. Her breathing rapid and coming faster and faster with each passing second.

"I want to touch you," I say. "I want to bend you over in front of me and fuck your pussy from behind."

"Then do it," she says.

I grab her so quickly she gasps in surprise. One second is all it takes for me to place a hand on her back and push her forward. She bends to my will, reaching down to place her hands on the tiled floor of the shower. Her pussy is peeking at me. Practically winking. Practically begging me to stick my fat cock inside her.

I start with my fingers. I trace the outline of her pussy. She moans, rises up a little, then places her palms flat against the wall to keep her steady.

"I'm gonna fuck you, Sadie Scott. Right now."

She looks over her shoulder at me. Her eyes are drooping, like she wants it.

But I want her to beg. "Do you want me to do that?"

"Mmm," she says. But it's not enough for me.

"Then tell me you want it. I like to talk, if you haven't noticed. It turns me on to talk dirty to you. But I like it back just as much. Tell me what to do, Sadie."

I expect her to blush. She's young. Maybe too young to have much sexual experience. But she doesn't even hesitate. "I'm bent over, Thomas Brooks. My pussy is staring you in the face. Fuck it."

I laugh so loud, it echoes off the ceiling of the shower stall. I grab her arms, bending them until her hands are crossed at the small of her back. Then I ease forward, my cock poking her entrance. "Do you want it?" I ask, smiling.

"I'm going to rescind my offer if you—"

I ram into her. She gasps, standing up, which allows me to push even deeper inside her. I keep her arms behind her back and push her forward until she has to press her cheek against the hard tile wall. She leans her head into my neck. An invitation to kiss her, if ever there was one. I lick the water streaming down her neck and then pull her skin into my mouth with my teeth. She hisses in a breath, holds it until I let go and then lets it rush out in a moan.

I let go of her hands, reaching around to fondle her breasts. "I'd make sure it was as good for you as it is for me right now, Miss Scott. But I'm too fucking horny to care. So come right now or I'll leave you hanging."

"You wouldn't dare."

I pull out and come as she finishes that sentence. My cock spews out semen in a long arc of white that pulses, over and over again, spilling all over her back.

"You fucking dick!"

I back away and lean against the wall, grinning like a dumbass. "Your turn," I say. "Next time I tell you to do something, you better do it. I'll always take the dare."

She turns to face me. Still and silent. The default setting, I remind myself. I wait for her to get angry. To make a quick escape and pretend this never happened.

But she stands her ground. God, I love that.

Then her hand is between her legs. Stimulating her clit in small, slow circles. Her other hand goes to her breast. They are nice. Her tits are big, I realize. Bigger now that I see one in the grip of her small hand. She closes her eyes. Starts moaning. I might be getting hard again, but I think cold shower thoughts to keep it at bay. This is her moment and I don't want her thinking she can take control of me, because she can't.

No woman has control of my cock.

Her moaning increase as she brings herself towards climax. And then, just as she's about to come, she opens her eyes. Smiles. And then closes them again, her whole body shuddering with release.

I watch her as she enjoys the moment. She's a lot more sexual than I thought she'd be.

"Hey, Sadie," I growl out in my deep post-coital voice.

"What?" she replies, not even bothering to open her eyes.

"The next time I tell you to do something you should do it. Because when I give orders, I mean them. No second chances."

I reach for her arm, pull her to her feet, push her gently aside, then rinse off under the shower. When I'm done she's watching me. Nothing to say.

"And Sadie, this whole deer-in-the-headlights thing is over now. You're no innocent schoolgirl, so stop the facade."

I step out of the shower, grabbing one of the towels off the counter and wrapping it around my waist, and just barely catch her response as I exit the bathroom.

"Fuck you, Thomas."

She will let me lead her along.
wants me to fuck her and she wants me to
make her say yes.

But I won't. I want her to give in.

"You can touch yourself" I say. "I'd love to
watch that.

CHAPTER TWELVE

Just fuck him. I watch Thomas walk out of the bathroom, irritated for being talked to like that and angry for putting myself in this position in the first place.

A bolt of electricity shoots through my head, making my vision flash red. "What the fuck?" I mumble, doubling over from the pain.

But then it's gone. Just as quick as it came.

What the hell was that?

I lean against the tile wall and soak up the steam. The shower water is spraying down on my legs, beckoning me into the stream of heat. I want to go home. But sadly, I don't know where home is. I don't even know if the place I came from could even be called home. I just don't understand what's happening.

I had a life. I'm pretty sure of it. I have a lingering feeling that my world was... was... what?

What the fuck is wrong with me?

I turn the water off and grab a towel, wrap it around my body, then lean over the vanity and wipe a circle of steam from the mirror.

"Who are you?" I ask the girl staring back.

She has olive-colored skin, dark hair, amber eyes—darkened by the hair framing my face—and she looks sad.

Do I feel sad?

I'm not sure. It's hard to put a label on my emotions right now. I just know I don't want to be *here*. I don't think I want to know this man.

But I don't want to be alone, either.

I want whatever it was I *had*.

It's stupid, I understand that. It's stupid because I don't even know what I had. But this... this place, this guy, this situation. It all feels wrong.

I sigh, then turn away from the stranger in the mirror and grab some clothes out of the bags and start pulling tags off things.

It's just clothes, but I don't want to wear them.

And yet I have to. I have no choice unless I want to put that stupid uniform back on. At least that's something I came with.

They're not mine either, though. Clearly, I am not Phil.

I allow myself to smile at that because it's all I can do.

Another sharp pain shoots though my head, but this time it's so severe, I double over and sink to my knees.

Sadie, Sadie, Sadie, Sadie...

There's a voice in my mind, but it's not my voice.

My vision flashes. Like static across a screen. A bolt of electricity that comes with crackling sound. I feel like a receiver trying to accept a transmission.

Sadie, Sadie, Sadie, Sadie...

"What?" I yell. "Who are you?"

But there's no answer. Just static.

Transmission failed.

The word blips across my eyes, but disappears so fast, I'm not sure if it was real, or I made it up.

"What's going on?"

I look up to find Thomas in the doorway.

"I'm leaving," I say. "I'm leaving here. I don't care if I have to walk back to the city, I'm not staying here with you."

"Why? You don't like the consequences of disobedience during sex?" He laughs.

"You did something to me," I say, sucking in a breath of air as another spark of electricity shoots through my brain. "With your stupid mind blast." I lean over again, staring at the tiles on the floor, as a wave of nausea cramps my stomach.

"It's not my fault," he says. "I didn't shoot me with a drug that counteracted all my careful planning. I didn't put myself in that insane asylum. I didn't tell Yasmine to use that drug that unleashed my mind. And I didn't fucking send you to that hospital, Sadie. None of this is my fucking fault."

"No," I whisper, a little relieved that the nausea is subsiding. "I guess not." I stand up, clutching the towel to my body. "You don't seem like the kind of guy who takes much personal responsibility."

He laughs. More of a huff, actually. "Why should I? Why should I be the one responsible for this fucked-up world? I didn't start that school. I didn't experiment on my own body. All I've ever done is *deal*, Sadie. I deal with their actions, that's all. If anyone is innocent in this goddamned city, it's me."

He points to his chest to emphasize his convictions.

"If you say so," I add.

"I do say so. I'm not Lincoln, looking to turn myself into a supervillain. I'm not Case, trying to pretend nothing's happening. I'm the only one who faces reality. I'm the only one who took the necessary steps to rein in the damage they did. I'm the only thing standing between good and evil right now."

It's my turn to laugh. "You're insane. That's why you were in that asylum. You're crazier than all of them."

He shrugs. "If what I'm doing is insane, then what level of crazy would you like to label your handlers? Don't you realize what you are?"

"You don't know anything about me," I snap.

"I know you showed up on someone's command. I know my mind blast wiped your programming. And I know how to set things right."

"With revenge?" I ask, sneering the word. "That's what you call setting things right?"

"Why not revenge? Why not take them all down and get even in the process? You should want that too. Which is why we need to stay together. We could do it together, Sadie."

"Is that really what you think?" I ask, shaking my head. "That your… plan is what will set things right? I highly doubt that."

"You don't even know the plan."

"I don't need to know the plan. I might not know a lot right now, but I know evil when I see it. You've got big problems, Thomas."

He smiles. It sends a shiver up my spine. And then the electric shock is back. Only this time it's so painful, I grab my head and stumble backwards, trip over the rug and fall on my ass.

Sadie, Sadie, Sadie, Sadie…

"What do you want?" I yell.

Thomas is talking, but I can't hear him. I hear nothing but, *Sadie, Sadie, Sadie, Sadie…*

"I'm here, goddammit! Tell me what you want!"

His hand grips my upper arm and brings me to my feet. "Who are you talking to?" he says, shaking me with enough force, my mind feels like it's slipping. "Who the fuck are you talking to?"

I close my eyes, trying to will the pain away. The flash of light flickers across my vision again.

"Go away!" I scream.

Thomas is pulling me out of the bathroom. He shoves me towards the couch and I fall against the cushions.

Then it stops. The pain, the flashes of light, the sickening hum of white noise static.

Find us, the voice says. Clear as fucking day. *Find us, Sadie. We're waiting for you.*

"How?" I yell. "How do I find you? How do I get out of this—"

The sharp prick of a needle stops my screams.

My eyes fly open and see Thomas standing over me, syringe delivering more drugs into my neck.

He's not smiling when his mouth moves. But his words are slow. Warped. Eerily deep and hypnotic. "*Sleeeeeeeeep.*"

It's not a shiver or a tremble. It's not a quiver, or a quake, or a shudder. That's not what my body is doing.

I am convulsing.

I am cold.

I am tied down.

I am blind.

I am naked.

My legs are open and his hands are *right there*. Caressing my lower abdomen. Slipping right between my legs to play with the fleshy part of my pussy that makes me whine and try to draw my legs up.

This is not pretending. This is not practice to get me ready. This is not an exercise.

This is execution.

"Sadie," the dark voice says.

"What?" I ask, feeling breathless. My reply is weak.

"Did you forget who's in charge?'

"Thomas—"

"I'm not Thomas. Do not fucking call me Thomas."

It is Thomas. It is. "I recognize—" A sharp slap across my face cuts my words off.

"We've never properly met. So don't go thinking for yourself. Not after all this time." He chuckles a little. Right next to my ear. So I can feel his warm breath.

"I'm cold," I say in response. "Cover me up."

Another slap, only this time it's my breast. "Are you in charge, Sadie?"

What the fuck is going on?

"Answer me." He pinches my nipple and I let out a cry of pain.

"You. You. You. You," I moan.

"Yeeeeessssss," he says, releasing his grip. "Now listen closely." Another sharp pinch, only this time it's the needle. He sticks me in the neck. I wince away and he's pinching my nipple again. "Do you want to piss me off?" he asks. "Hold still."

The needle he is using to inject me stabs again. There is hot blood running down my neck.

"Why are you doing this?" I say through my heavy breathing.

"Because you're mine now, Sadie. They made a mistake letting you out of that little prison they keep you in."

"What the hell are you talking about?"

"What year is it, darling?"

"What?"

"Tell me. What year it is."

"It's… it's…" But I have no idea. None. "I can't remember," I say.

"Do you know why you can't remember?"

"Because you blasted me with that mind fuck!"

"No," he says, withdrawing the needle from my neck. He wipes it with something scratchy. Gauze maybe. "You don't remember because they've had you in *training* for years."

The sizzle of static is back in my eyes. They are taped shut again, so the bright red letters are clearly outlined across my blackened blindness.

Abort! Abort! Abort!

"What the fuck?"

"What do you see, little Sadie?"

"What are you doing?"

He slips a finger inside me. I gasp, then moan. I can't stop that moan. He's pushing his fingers inside me. Stretching me. I start breathing faster. The air I draw in has almost no time to fulfill its purpose before I exhale. I am panting. I am panting and I do not want to think about *why*.

"I'm reprogramming you, Sadie."

"Oh, God." But my response isn't about what he just said. It's to what he just *did*. His fingers are still pressing up inside me. But they draw back, then press again. He's fucking me. Then his thumb presses on my clit. He pushes all my buttons and I moan.

"Tell me what you seeeeeeeeee…."

"'Abort,'" I say. "It's spelling out the word 'abort.'"

"Goooooood," he says. And I know he's smiling. "I see that too. It's flashing across the monitor."

"What are you talking about?"

"Your *commands*, Sadie." The slow, soft voice he's been using is gone now. His words are sharp. Clipped. And angry. "They run commands through software in your head."

"You fucking freak! You're lying! You're the one doing this to me! You're the one with the drugs. You're the one—"

Sharp, stinging slap across my face.

"Shut up and listen." He pinches my nipple again, making me cry out. His hand leaves my pussy and covers my mouth. The other one pinches my nose closed and I panic.

"Hold still. Be silent." He whispers this next to my ear. "And I'll let you breathe. But if you continue to piss me off, I'll let you pass out. But I won't let you die, Sadie. You're worth far too much to let you die. I'll find very interesting ways to torture you with fear. I'll bring you to the brink of death and then pull you back. Over, and over, and over again. So make a decision. Accept the fact that I'm in charge *right now*, or let me have some fun with you first."

I go very, *very* still.

He lets me breathe. "See how easy that is?"

I suck in air, trying my best not to cry. But that last bit… that was some kind of line for me. He crossed it and I'm no longer in control. I start to sob, then wonder if that will piss him off more, and try to hold it in.

"Are you ready to listen, Sadie?"

I nod my head. "Yes. I'm listening."

"Good. They have an implant in your brain. I know how this implant works, because I helped them develop it. I have one too. That's how we get these abilities, Sadie. That's how we have the powers we do. And if I do just the right things, if I pump you with just the right concoction… I can read your mind. We will be linked. Now," he says, switching to matter-of-fact mode. "I can't read most minds. And this stuff has some weird side effects. One being you can collect thoughts from dying people. It's not a pretty side effect if you collect the wrong thoughts. Does that make sense?"

I nod in affirmation. But none of this makes any sense.

"There's more. Things like…" He sighs. "Like corruption. Like I'm doing to you. Your mind can be hijacked. Just like mine." He laughs. "But if you think you can hijack me the way I just did you, think again. No one has the formula for that particular chemical reaction. I made sure of that before we blew up the Prodigy School fifteen years ago. I injected Thomas with those drugs. Well"—he chuckles, as if this is funny—"I persuaded him, to put it simply."

He is insane. He is fucking insane.

"But he went along and that's all you need to know. He is incorruptible. I am incorruptible. I can make you incorruptible too." More laughter. "But why would I? When I can link up to you and read your commands."

His hand is back between my legs. Caressing me. Soothing me. I don't want it to feel good, but I can't help it. His touch is soft and my desire builds.

"We're going to do this together, Sadie. Do you understand? We make a great team, you and I."

"Thomas," I say, breathless now, not because of the fear, but because of the way he's still playing with my pussy.

"I'm. Not. Thomas," he growls. His denial is animalistic. A threat. And he withdraws his hand from between my legs.

He *is* Thomas. How stupid does he think I am? I recognize his voice. It's not exactly the same, but it's *him*.

"OK," I say. "I'm sorry. Just tell me what you want from me." I don't want him angry. I don't want more slaps.

I just want him to stop what he's doing. Give me a chance to think about things.

"We're a team now. Partners. You're going to feed me information about your handlers at Prodigy and I'm going to use it to destroy them."

"Fine," I say, giving in. "I'll help you. But I don't want to be tied down. I don't want to be blind. I'll go along, I swear. I'll help."

He caresses my forehead with his hand, dragging sweat-soaked hair from my forehead. I can smell my sex on his fingers. "I know you will. Because you have no choice. I own your mind now. The drug I injected you with has you under my control. I can make you do things, Sadie. Would you like an example?"

"No," I gasp. "I believe you."

But his response is the jingle of his belt. The unzipping of his pants. The shuffling of a hand beneath fabric. And then the sound of a hand caressing a cock. *Open your mouth* prints across my field of vision.

I do open my mouth, but not for the reason he thinks. Except... the words *fuck you* aren't what come out. Nothing comes out. I can't speak. I can't move. I can barely think, because the only thing I see is his command, blinking now, in bright letters. Flashing white, then red, then white, then red.

Suck. My. Cock.

I wait for it. I wait for him to make me do this.

But he just laughs. "See," he says, unable to hide his amusement. "I could make you do that, Sadie. I can make you do anything I want now."

The words stop flashing and the control is released. My world is black again.

"But I won't. Not yet."

I can *feel* his smile. My body—which had stopped convulsing—begins to shiver again.

"Would you like to see me, sweet Sadie?" he asks. "Meet me? Finally? After all this time?"

I shake my head no. I really wouldn't.

But he peels the tape off my eyelids, pulling gently on the tissue-paper thin, sensitive skin until my blinders are off.

"Open your eyes," he says.

I shake my head again. *No, no, no. This isn't real. I'm not here. This is a nightmare. He's some ghost. Some distant memory. I'm not here.*

The red and white letters flash across my still-blackened blindness.

Open. Your. Eyes.

I open them. His face is handsome. Slight scruff on his jaw and chin. Dark eyes flashing with mischievousness. Corners of his lips upturned in a smile. "Thomas?" I ask, unsure, but yet still very, very sure who this man is.

"No." He laughs, shaking his head. "I'm Sullivan, sweet Sadie. But *shhhhhh*." He chuckles through his whisper. "Don't tell him about me. He doesn't like me. If you tell him, Sadie, he will go insane!"

The last word comes out as an evil laugh. He stops. Smiles down at me. "He can't help you anyway. When I'm in charge, I'm in charge." He laughs again. "But the important thing now, Sadie, is that we're a team. We can be a team. Just the three of us."

"The three of us?" I ask, feeling sick at what he's saying.

"You. Me. And Thomas. Do you know what they call that in comic books?" More sinister chuckling.

I shake my head. Not at his question, which makes no sense to me at all, but at... everything. No. This is not happening.

Red and white letters flash across my field of vision. *THIS. IS. HAPPENING.*

"They call it a power trio. He wants to get revenge." Thomas—Sullivan—whoever this insane freak is—waves a hand in the air like that doesn't matter. "We can get his silly revenge. Why not? But Sadie," he says, slipping his hand between my legs once again as he leans down to press his soft lips against mine. "We could get so much more. You and I?" he says, pointing to me, then himself. "We could rule the world."

I should know better by now. I should know better than to take my eyes off his hands. Because another needle stabs me in the neck. This is different than the last thing he gave me. It's the thing he uses to put me to sleep. I feel the sting in my veins. I feel it hit my heart. *Thump, thump, thump, thump.* And then it's in my bloodstream.

My eyes get heavy, even as he continues to kiss me.

I might kiss him back, I'm not sure. I'd like to think I don't, but I'm not sure.

"Don't tell him about me, sweet Sadie. Because if you think he's insane now..." Sullivan laughs. "Just wait until he finds out I'm back in control without his permission."

I sit straight up when I wake. Just like last time. "Holy fucking shit!"

"Sadie?" Thomas calls from the other room.

I'm on the bed again.

Where the fuck does that freak take me when he gives me the drugs? Not the bedroom. It's not the bedroom. I was not on a bed. I was on like... a table. Something hard.

"Sadie?" Thomas calls, sterner now.

"What?" I call back. Habit, maybe. Or just still responding to the commands his crazy alter-ego was feeding me in my… *real-life nightmare.*

Good God. What's happening?

"I didn't want to drug you but you were crazy. Talking shit about hearing voices. I think you're going insane."

He says it so matter-of-factly I want to laugh.

I'm the only one who faces reality. I'm the only thing standing between good and evil right now.

Does he really think that?

I need to get the fuck out of here. I mean, maybe he's right. Maybe wherever it was I came from was a pretty dark place. But he is the insane one.

Split personality? Is that even a real thing?

"We need to come up with a plan," Thomas says from the doorway. He's got no shirt on and his jeans are low on his hips, showing off the cut muscles of his abdomen.

"No," I say, swinging my legs over the bed. "I'm leaving."

"There's something wrong with you."

"Something wrong with *me*?" I huff, mind blown.

"I think I should take you to see Sheila after all. It's been five days already, so—"

"Five days?" What the fuck? How the hell did five days go by?

"— I don't think they're still looking for us. At any rate, we need to meet up with Lincoln and Case. Make sure the plan's still on track."

"What fucking plan? The one where we all admit we're insane and we're out to destroy the world?"

His face screws up. "Maybe you should rest a little longer? You're not all here."

Again. Mind blown. Incredulous isn't a strong enough word to describe how I feel.

I take a deep breath, hold it in for the count of three, and let it out. "I'm going to leave now. No need to worry about me anymore. No need to drop me off somewhere." I get up and straighten the new shirt he bought me. "And thank you for the hospitality and clothes. I appreciate it. A lot," I add, trying to be as congenial as possible so I don't set him off and drag that psycho alter-ego out of that fucked-up head of his.

"You can't just… leave, Sadie. We need to see Sheila. I'm sorry, OK?"

"Sorry for what?" I ask. Picturing his hands on my body. His lips on my mouth. His grip on my mind.

"The mind blast. I didn't realize, I guess."

"Realize what?"

"I mean, I couldn't know. I had no idea you'd be in the direct path of the blast. I did it out of instinct, I guess. It wasn't conscious, not at all. So if you're worried I'll do it again—well." He laughs. "I don't even know how to do it again. I think it was just the perfect set of circumstances."

Yeah, the perfect moment is right. The moment when his insane double personality took over and hijacked his body.

"And I'm sorry for leaving you hanging in the shower." He laughs again, but this time it might be genuine. "I just kinda…"

I wait for the rest of that, but he shakes his head and smiles. His eyes aren't as dark when he smiles. Not this smile, at least. "Just kinda what?"

"Like to be in control."

Control? He's so not in control.

"You're cute, you know? And I'm not just saying that because I've been locked in a hospital for a month. You're just… pretty. And a little too young," he adds, shrugging. "Which I like… but probably shouldn't. In fact, I should just stop fucking talking because I'm digging my hole deeper with every word."

I laugh. Because he's… different. Not that cocky asshole he was before he drugged me this last time. He's definitely nothing like the nightmare version. He's just a guy right now. Just a guy trying to figure shit out.

"Let me take you to Sheila, OK? I swear to God, she will hook you up to Lincoln's diagnostic shit and come up with a plan in less than a day. She can fix it."

He has no clue. None. If that wasn't a nightmare. If that other him—that Sullivan guy—if he's real and what he said is true… then I'm compromised from within. I have something inside me. Something in my brain. Something that will let people control me.

"Maybe I don't need to know my memories. Maybe it's just better to start over. A new day, so to speak."

"That's not gonna help." He says, stern look on his face. "You can't live in denial. It always comes back to haunt you. Better to deal with reality than push it down into some dark crevice of your mind, ya know?"

I don't know how much to tell him. What if he does go insane if I let him know his second personality is back? What if he loses his mind for real? What if I'm locked down here and can't get out? I don't even know how to get out!

So I decide on half-truths. "I had a flash of memory just now."

"What'd you remember?" he asks, walking towards me. He sits down on the bed. Not too close. Not so close so we're touching.

"Do you think we have these powers—this mentalist and illusionist stuff—because they did something to our brains?"

Thomas nods. "For sure."

"And you think I was sent to kill you? How do you think they got me to do that?"

"Programming," he says. "You don't know anything, Sadie. It's pretty evident you've been under their control your whole life."

"Yeah," I say. "Programming. Maybe they put something inside me? Like a computer?"

"There's an interface inside my brain, so you probably have one too. You're not as developed as I am. I'm pretty sure of that. My hardware was for Alpha testing and you"—he laughs—"are clearly not an Alpha."

"Can you see words?" I ask. I wish I knew what this was.

"Words?"

"Like across your eyes. Messages?"

"No," he says. "That's some real science-fiction shit right there. The interface is just impulses. It triggers neuronal pathways in your brain. Gives you... urges."

Urges. None of this is good.

"Let me take you to Sheila. She'll know—"

But an alarm goes off. A deep, prolonged buzzer. *Ent. Ent. Ent.* Something ominous. Lights begin to flash.

Thomas looks up at the ceiling as I cover my ears. "Time to go," he says. But I can't hear him over the repeating buzzer. I only see his lips. He leans down in my ear and says, "They've found us. Follow me."

CHAPTER THIRTEEN

I grab her and walk out of the room. This is just a perimeter alarm, so they're not inside yet. I take her over to the monitors and study them.

"What's happening?" she yells over the alarm.

I turn the alarm off. No need to broadcast what I already know. I let the buzzer ring in my ears for several seconds before I talk.

"Look," I say, pointing to the security monitor. "They're here."

"Who?"

"Prodigy, most likely. Maybe Yasmine's people. If she had those kinds of resources."

"How will we get out?"

"Well," I say, scratching my chin and looking around. "First I need to blow this shit up."

"What?"

We might have an unhealthy obsession with blowing things up. I smile. "Just the hard drives. I need this fucking tower, so we'll leave all the rest intact. They won't blow it up. They'll need to study it. But they'll never figure it out. I'm the only one around here with eyes in the sky."

I exit all the satellite programs, transfer ownership of the data to the other three towers, open the security panel, and type in the code for self-destruct.

"We've got five minutes before the air becomes unbreathable. If they come down here, they won't go back up."

"But where will we go?" Sadie asks, looking around in what might become panic if I don't rein her in.

"Don't worry. Do you really think I didn't build this place with an escape hatch?"

She takes a deep breath and nods. "Fine, I'll go with you."

I almost snort. "Like you have a choice, sweet Sadie."

Her whole body stiffens at my words. But I just grin and take her hand. "Come on, it's this way."

I lead her down a hallway, which leads to a two-foot-thick door made of reinforced steel. I key in the combination, heave it open, and wave her through.

"It's dark," she whispers into the blackness as I close and lock the door behind us.

"It's this way," I say, calmly taking the lead. She keeps hold of my hand, trips a few times over the uneven concrete below our feet, then bumps into my back when I stop at the next door.

"How can you see?" she whispers.

"No one can hear you. And I just have an excellent sense of direction, that's all."

There is another alarm, which makes her jump in surprise. "Why is it going off again?"

"The gas," I say. "It's releasing the gas now."

"That was fast," she says. "There wasn't even a second warning. What if we were still in there?"

"I don't make mistakes, Sadie. So why give the bad guys an opportunity? If you're gonna do something, do it with winning in mind. I never half-ass my shit. If I make a security protocol, there's no room for fuck-ups because I don't fuck up. Here's the car."

"Car?"

"Train car, Sadie. Please get inside. We're on a deadline."

I code in the password into the security panel and the doors open, soft green lights barely illuminating the train we'll be leaving in.

Sadie steps in. I step in after her, and then I type in the code to make the doors shut.

Another alarm screeches outside the car and green gas starts to fill the tunnel.

"Well, that was a little too close," she snaps. "We almost got gassed!"

"Relax," I say. "I got this. We're fine, right?"

"Two seconds, Thomas. That's all the time we had to spare."

"I told you we had to be quick. Just do what I say, the way I tell you to, and you'll be fine."

She doesn't like that answer, I can tell. But she doesn't say anything else.

There's two seats up front for a driver and passenger, even though once I program the car, it will drive itself. I take a seat in the driver's side and start punching in codes to wake it up.

Sadie sits down in the passenger seat and looks out the window. "What if the gas seeps in?"

I roll my eyes. "I think of everything, Sadie. Just relax and enjoy the ride."

She mutters curses under her breath, but I ignore it. Just start up the computer and get things going.

"Where are we going?"

"To the west tower. The north tower is too close to the asylum for my taste. And there's nothing over on the east side, so I'd rather not be there unless we have to. So west it is. At least we'll be closer to Lincoln. When we get there,

I'll contact him and have Sheila come pick us up in the helicopter. Then we'll just go up to his mansion in the mountains and try to figure out what's going on with you."

She huffs out some air. "Better order a double of that. You're not exactly in your right mind either."

"What?" I laugh.

"Forget it. How long will it take?"

I look up at her and smile. "About eight minutes."

She looks impressed, if I do say so myself. "How the hell did you build a fucking high-speed train down here without anyone knowing?"

"Who said no one knew about it?"

"Oh," she says, taking her attention to the window again.

"I hired workers from out of town. They each worked on different phases. Phase one did the tunnel, phase two the track and so on. So it is secret. As secret as something like this can be, anyway."

She just stares out the window at the green gas. It's all around the car now, the thick cloud falling down the windows like slow, twisting tentacles of an octopus.

I study her for a moment as I wait for the operating system to run through all the necessary checks before we get going. She's not looking much better than the first day I found her. Her skin is still slightly pale and she's hardly eaten at all.

"We'll get some real food when we get to Lincoln's. I'm sure you're starving."

She shrugs. "I don't think I eat much. I'm not really hungry."

Right. "Well, generally speaking, people need to eat."

The system checks are over and the engine starts. Less than a minute later we move forward. It's not like a regular train. It's quiet for one. Sadie leans forward in her seat, then glances over at me. "Are you driving?"

"I don't need to drive. It's only one stop."

She leans forward again, just as we begin to really pick up speed. "What's that?"

She's pointing to the first of many metal gates that will spiral closed like an iris less than a second after we pass through.

"Security," I say. "In case anyone thinks they can follow us."

We're only going about a hundred miles an hour, but it's fast and the iris begins to close before we even get there.

Sadie stands up, her hands braced on the dashboard. "It's gonna close before we get there! It's gonna cut us in half!"

"You have no trust."

But she doesn't hear me because we fly through the gate and her head whips around to look out the back window to watch the iris close with a bang.

Before she even looks back we pass through another one. *Bang!*

Then another.

Bang!

Then the final gate on this end.

Bang!

"Holy fucking shit!" she says, holding her hand over her heart. She looks at me and says, "You're fucking insane! Those things barely missed us! Was that... was that a blade in the center of the gate?"

I grin and soak up the impressive display of my genius. "We made it, didn't we?"

She shakes her head and sits back down in her chair. "That's dangerous. How does it know we're through? We were like milliseconds from being sliced like salami!"

"Relax," I say, easing back in my chair and putting my feet up on the dash. "It's all math, Sadie. The physical laws of nature never let you down. Life is predictable and boring if you know the right equations."

"Right." She snorts, blowing up the hair that's fallen over her face. "Because all that weird mental shit follows the laws of nature."

"Well, what you do is just tricks."

She huffs more air. "Whatever. I'm pretty talented."

"I'm sure you are, but it's a trick. Like a magician. What I do is command a force of nature."

"What kind of force?"

"You know... like... wind, right?"

"Wind?" Everything I say seems to make her scoff. "How the hell do you get wind from that freak show of a display back at the asylum?"

"Well, wind is caused by the sun heating the earth. The air moving around it too. So it creates this force, right? You can't see it, but it's there. And it's all based on natural properties because the earth has different topography so it heats unevenly. Which creates wind, or moving currents of air. When I use that mentalist power I'm creating uneven heating of things around me, which creates a force. Like wind, only... on an extreme scale. So there's heat and air and then pressure, which makes the blast."

"Freak," she says again. "No one's supposed to be able to do that with their mind."

"Yeah, but it makes a whole lot more sense to have my power controlled by my mind than it does to have it controlled by two non-sentient forms of energy, don't you think?"

"Whatever you say."

"But you... you really have some kind of *link*, right?"

She stares out the front window for a few seconds. Mulling it over.

"To people's minds. That shit makes no sense at all, thus it's a trick."

She rolls her eyes. "A better trick than yours. I can make people hallucinate."

"But how long does it last?"

She shrugs. "About ten seconds."

"Bullshit," I say. "You have three to five good seconds if you're lucky. You're a mirage, Sadie. Nothing more. A trick."

"Well, as fun as this whole my-superpower-is-better-than-your-superpower shit is, I'm tired of it. Let's move on to something else. Like why you were in the crazy house to begin with."

I catch her smirking reflection in the front window, her face lit up by the dim green dashboard lights.

"I tried to kill myself," I say. I figure I'd have to tell her eventually.

"What?" She sits up in her chair and looks straight at me. "Why?"

I let out a long breath of air. It's my turn to stare out the window. "I haven't thought about it much. Things just got... crazy about a month back. My friends and I were... doing... shit."

"What kind of shit?"

"Evil supervillain shit."

This makes her smile. "Like what?"

"It's not important. The important part is what went down a few months back. When my friend, Case, also a Prodigy student, shot me with a drug that disrupted a carefully concocted protocol I've been using for more than fifteen years to rein in this stupid mentalist bullshit."

"Hmm," she mutters, then stays silent for a few seconds. "So you don't like your power?"

"My power is a force of nature. I could do without blasting people like a bomb when the wrong set of circumstances randomly happens. So no. I don't enjoy what they made me into."

"So you were... what? At the end of your rope? You had like a... breakdown?"

"Sure. You can call it that."

"Who cares what I call it. What do you call it?"

"Temporary insanity, I guess."

"But why?" she asks. "What triggered that?"

I'm not even remotely interesting in talking about what went down *that* day. Not to her. Not to Case or Lincoln. Hell, not even to myself. So I give her the only part I am willing to talk about. "This mentalist shit. It's a mind fuck, right? For me it is, anyway. I never asked to be this guy. I never wanted to have that power. So I've been taking drugs for a long time to keep the emotions at bay. I think it's triggered by emotions. Brain chemistry and all that bullshit. But Case shot me with an inhibitor or something. None of the drugs worked after that. It was one emotion after another. A constant stream of fucking feelings."

I stop. Because I'm getting dangerously close to the end of that train of thought.

"What's it like to live without emotions?"

"It's bliss," I say. "Pure motherfucking bliss."

"Sounds sad to me."

"Says the girl who doesn't even know where she came from."

"I just lost my memory. From that stupid power of yours. I'll get it back. I can feel it coming, anyway. There's static in my head."

"What kind of static?" I'm happy to switch the conversation back to her.

"Like electricity. Like… static. I don't know. Flashes of light and… words."

"Words?" I ask. "You said that before. Messages across your eyes."

"Do you know anything about that?" she asks.

When I look over at her, she's staring at me intently.

I shake my head. "Nope. Never heard of that shit before. Prodigy must've really upped their game if they've invented a vision screen overlay."

"Vision screen overlay?"

I stare back at her, looking right at her eyes. "I can't really tell in this light but once we get up top again, I'll see if I can detect a lens. If they have invented an overlay, I'll be able to see it."

"Hmm," is all she says.

"You're probably a pretty dangerous girl, you know that?"

"Says the pretty dangerous guy."

I smile. "Which is why we're gonna make an awesome team once Sheila and Linc figure out what they did to you."

"What makes you think I want to be on your team?"

"Why wouldn't you?" I ask, glancing at her for a second before looking ahead again. "What could you possibly have to look forward to going back to Prodigy? You're nothing but a slave to them, Sadie. They keep you like a pet. Like a project. They'll use you again, you know."

"So will you."

"I said T-E-A-M. I never said I'd use you for anything."

"You'll use me for a friend."

I laugh. "Since when is friendship using someone?"

"Since we discovered we're pretty equal opposites. Who understands you, Thomas?"

"Case," I say. "Lincoln. Sheila. Probably Molly. Lulu, maybe. One day. That's more than most people have, I bet. I'm not using you. I don't need you. I just want you."

I smile at her, but she's not smiling. "Lots of people probably want me. I'll take 'need me' any day of the week over 'want me.'"

I shake my head and roll my eyes. "There's the next gate. We're almost to the tower."

"Will it close behind us again?"

"Yup. Just like clockwork. The ones on the other side will close too. So they won't be able to get inside the underground rooms from the tunnel."

"It's quite the set-up you have here—"

But she stops talking, stands up, and looks out the back window as we pass through the gate. "Fuck!" she says, holding her head like she's in pain. Then she drops to the floor and screams, "Fuck!" again.

Bang! The gate spirals closed.

Then the next one.

Bang!

"What the fuck is wrong with you?" I ask.

But then the power goes out. The train slows and the next gate—*BANG!*—comes so close to cutting the ass-end of the car off, I forget about her and take my attention to the next gate.

We're still going fast—but not fast enough. It starts to close too soon.

"Shit!" I grab her by the arm and lift her up. But she's unconscious. Dead, heavy weight. "Sadie, get up! We need to move to the back! Now!"

She's not moving, so I throw her over my shoulder and run to the back of the car just as the final gate slams down on the roof. A deafening crushing sound of metal on metal. Screeching as the magnetic field under the car collapses and the car—at least the part we're in because the fucking thing has been cut in half—wobbles for a split second, before it flies backwards from the blast force of… my fucking mind!

We roll with what's left of the car as it spirals through the air. I lose hold of Sadie's arm and she goes tumbling out in front of me, hitting her head on the ceiling. Metal collapses in on top of us. Pinning her, me, everything to the floor as the car spins wildly—tossing us both like rag dolls against sharp edges and jagged pieces of ripped interior.

We slam into the concrete walls of the tunnel and everything goes black.

I come to groaning, but obviously still alive. I'm hurt, but not dead. Never dead.

My skin has a grid of mesh embedded underneath it that will heal most wounds instantly. I don't know how long I was out, but it was definitely longer than instantly.

But I can feel it working. It makes me sick to my stomach to know that shit is inside my body. Makes me want to hurl. Makes me want to rip my flesh off. Makes me want to… die.

"Sadie," I croak out, the crash coming back to me. We are both encased in a coffin of train parts. "Sadie," I say again.

I hear moaning from off to my left. But I can't see her. Everything is dark and it feels like there's a mountain of steel on top of me.

"Sadie," I say again. More moaning.

I grab a long piece of twisted metal pinning my leg to the floor (roof?) of the car and push until I can bend my leg. I pull out my phone, thankfully still mostly intact, tabbing it awake so I can find my flashlight app.

There is an open gash in my leg. I'm talking visible bone.

But I can also see the little mesh framework doing its best to patch me up.

My fucking head spins just looking at it.

Case and Lincoln think I wear armor under my suits all the time because I'm paranoid.

I'm not fucking paranoid. Not about getting killed, at least. I don't want to get *hurt*. I don't want to be cut. I don't want people to know what I am. What they did to me. And most of all—I do not want to see or feel this healing shit happening in real fucking time.

I force myself not to think about it. I force myself to ignore it. I force myself to move all the metal around me, bending it with my Prodigy-provided superhuman strength, until I'm free.

Then I go looking for Sadie.

She's only a few feet away. The car—what's left of the fucking car—wasn't cut in half. We are in a section about eight feet long.

I think about Sadie's suspicions about the gates. I'm gonna have to apologize to her. She was right. Nothing about us or our lives follows the laws of nature.

I pull the metal off her too and stop. Sickened at what I see.

She is... mending. Healing herself. The minuscule criss-crossed wires underneath her skin doing to her exactly what they do to me.

We are so much more alike than I ever thought possible.

Later. You can think about that later when she's out of this tin can of a train car.

I lift each piece of metal, extracting her like one of those game pieces in that wooden puzzle tower, until she's free.

She's pale. Paler than I've ever seen her. Her face is cut, bleeding still. The little machines inside her—just little dots of charcoal-black, not even the size of a pin prick—slide along the mesh as they knit her biological components back together. Her dark hair is covered in a thin layer of white dust and debris. Her clothes are ripped, one of her legs is even more fucked up than mine.

But she will live.

If there's one thing I won't have to worry about, it's that.

She will live. Because those fucking sickos at Prodigy did the same thing to her that they did to me. They fed little monsters into her bloodstream. They spent months torturing her with pain to get the framework established.

I have wanted to kill those Prodigy assholes for as long as I can remember. I have wanted to torture them the way they tortured me.

But the rage I feel right now…

It comes out as a mind blast that creates a wind of power. Pieces of hot, twisted metal move aside as I stumble forward.

Everything but her moves.

She is immune to me because we are the same model of monster. We cancel each other out—or, if we're lucky, build to synergy.

I pick her up in my arms, carefully, even though I know I can't hurt her. And I carry her. I create another mind blast—smaller this time, because I'm not very good at this. It never works great when I need it most. Just enough to clear debris away so I can slide my back down the concrete wall and cradle her in my lap.

There's more to this girl than I realize. There has to be more. Otherwise she'd be conscious right now, just like me.

But that's the only reason our body parts aren't cut in half right now. That's the only reason our limbs aren't strewn about in pieces, inching their way towards one another, desperate to put themselves back together.

Something happened in her head to make the car stop.

She shut a maglev train down with her *mind*.

Who is this girl?

I want to think about that for a while. Mull it over good in my head. Roll it around in my hand, see it from all angles. But exhaustion overtakes me.

I'm not used to this, I realize.

I need her help.

But before I can even wonder what kind of help that might be, the blackness comes to take me away.

CHAPTER FOURTEEN

Sadie, Sadie, Sadie.

The words are in my head but they are flashing across my eyes too. My closed eyes.

Where are you? Where are you? Where are you?

It must be them. It must be Prodigy School. They're looking for me. Or maybe hunting me.

They're trying to communicate with me with some kind of link. Mentally? I don't think so. I think there's something inside me. Some kind of computer or—

Sadie, Sadie, Sadie, "Sadie!"

I open my eyes and see Thomas. His face is right up next to mine, eyes searching me—filled with questions. He smells like charred metal.

"You had me worried." His voice is low and deep. Some kind of flashlight is illuminating his face from below. There's black soot on his cheeks, giving him a hollowed near-death appearance. Like he just walked through fire.

"Thomas," I whisper.

He strokes my head softly, moving my hair out of my eyes. "Try again."

Shit.

And this time I'm not asleep. I know that for sure. This is real. "Sullivan?" I say, trying out the name.

"Ding. Ding. Ding." He says the words slowly, pausing between each one. "You're gonna be OK. You seem to be… working the way you're supposed to."

"What the hell happened?"

"You tell me. You're the one who did it."

"What?"

"You grabbed your head, Sadie. You and Thomas were talking about things you shouldn't be talking about. Then you grabbed your head and the fucking train just *shut down*."

"We were coming up on the gates."

"Correct again. If this was a game show, you'd be two for three. What the hell did you do?"

He's got a very stern look on his face. But it's so different from the other times I've met him. This is real. And clearly those times were real too. He really had me tied up. He really did touch me that way. "I don't understand."

"That's because," he says, letting out a long sigh. "It's because you have no idea what you are."

"What am I?"

"How the fuck should I know? But look." He points to my body. I'm lying down with my head resting on this thigh. So I have to sit up a little to see what he's pointing at.

My leg is... disgusting. My jeans are ripped open. But that's not all that's ripped open. The denim is covered in blood and the wound is gaping and huge. But it's... "Oh, my God. There's little things moving around. Are those bugs inside my leg?"

"No," Sullivan says. "They're little fucking computer fuckers. Nanites, but like... supernanites. Globs of them. Gross, isn't it?"

"What the hell is a nanite?"

"What part of little fucking computer fuckers didn't you understand?"

Dick. "What are they doing?" I try to sit up to get a better look, but Sullivan's hand is on my shoulder, pushing me back down.

"Don't get up. Just let them work. They fix you, Sadie. They repair you. Prodigy put a scaffolding mesh of healing... whatever the fuck it is. I don't know what it is. But Thomas and I have it too. It repairs tissue damage."

It's weird hearing Sullivan refer to Thomas and him as separate people.

"You were hurt pretty bad but they were already working by the time I got out from under all that goddamned steel and found you. We'll be fine. Eventually."

"Who? You and Thomas? Or me and you?"

"All of us," he says, waving a hand in the air. "It just takes a little while."

"Where are we? Can we get out of here?"

"Well." He laughs. "As if things couldn't get any worse, we're on the other fucking side of the gate about a mile from the west tower."

"How do we get through the gate?"

He shrugs. "We don't."

"Then how can we get out of this stupid tunnel?"

He sighs again. "We can't."

I just stare up at him. "Surely there is a door? There's always a door. Some secret access point or something?"

"Yeah," Sullivan says, absently stroking my head again. "If this were a normal tunnel there would be. But it's not, so there isn't. We could walk back, but we're still on the other side of the south tower gate. And the walk back..." He shakes his head. "I'm not even sure that's possible. My leg is fucked up just as bad as yours. It's going to take the better part of a day for it to really heal. At least to make a walk like that. It's sixty miles to the south tower. There's a tunnel that connects to the other towers somewhere in that blackness. But the east tower is probably a hundred miles away. And the other tower even farther than that. Besides," he says, exhaling loudly. "My phone battery will die and then we'd be in total darkness."

I picture that whole scenario in my head as he's talking. The distance, the state of my leg, the darkness. "So we're fucked."

"Good. And fucked."

I let out a breath and close my eyes. "I'm going to die down here."

"No," he says. "We can't die. We'll starve. And we'll go crazy from lack of water. But we're not going to die. There was an emergency kit in the train car with water and rations. But—" This time his laugh is curt. "It's gone now. The whole car is gone thanks to your little *trick*."

"I didn't stop the damn train car, Sullivan. Don't be ridiculous."

"Then who did?"

"How should I know. Maybe something is happening up top? Maybe the power went out or something?"

"This tunnel is powered by the towers. And if they weren't still standing there'd be green gas in here. We have it set up to self-destruct."

"Wait," I say, realization hitting me in the face. "If you guys set it up so the green gas releases when anyone breaches—we're going to die anyway!"

"Was I speaking a foreign language just now? I told you, you can't die."

"So that green gas can't hurt me?"

"No." He laughs. "It can't hurt *me*. Because Thomas had Lincoln code it for our DNA."

"Well, aren't the two of you just a couple of fucking Wondertwins. This is just great. I'm gonna *not-die*—whatever the hell that means—and you're gonna be just fine. Just wonderful. Does this shit get any better?"

"Well, there was plenty of antidote in the fucking train car, just like there was plenty of water and rations. But not anymore. It's not my fault we're here," he says.

"I didn't do it," I say, getting pissed off about his accusation. "Maybe it *is* your fault. Maybe you're the one who wrecked the train? Ever think of that, Mental Man?"

"Wasn't me, Trip Chick."

"Why not you? You're the one with all that weird mentalist shit inside your head. *I'm the wind, Sadie. I'm a force.* Well, OK. Fine. But it's more likely that the stupid force of nature inside your head got out of hand and… and…"

"And what?" He laughs. "I don't know how to stop electricity. The train car wrecked because the power went out and we slowed down as we approached the gates. And that was all you. I saw it. I might not be able to talk when Thomas is in control, but unlike him, I see everything."

"I didn't do it."

"Messages inside your head? Remember that little conversation?"

"That was you!"

"Yeah. Back at the tower. But I wasn't in your head when the car stopped. And just before you woke up you were talking to people. Mumbling, 'Who are you. Who are you?'"

I think about that for a little bit. Because he's right. My head did hurt. "There's static in there," I say.

"What kind?" he asks. Like people say this all the time and he just needs a little clarification to understand it better.

"Are there different *kinds*?" I ask.

"Describe it," he practically snarls.

Dick. "Like… like an in-between radio signal. Static like that. And lights flashing. There were words too."

"What do they say?"

"Just… 'Sadie, Sadie, Sadie.' Calling me. You know."

"Prodigy?" he asks.

"Probably. But then, just before I woke up, they said, 'Where are you, where are you, where are you?' Three times. Just like that."

"They're looking for you."

"Obviously." I roll my eyes.

"It's some kind of transmission. And now that I know that—thanks for the punctual update, by the way—that's probably who came to the tower. You were broadcasting to them. You're probably still broadcasting to them. So hey, bright side." He fake-laughs. "Looks like we'll be rescued. Too bad it's gonna be a bunch of mad scientists who come looking for us."

We think about that for a long, long time. Time in the dark passes in strange ways and I spend it thinking about the green gas. Then not-dying, whatever that means. And probably going unconscious, at least. Waking up back wherever it was I came from, I guess.

It *might* all be my fault.

And just then, when I think it can't possibly get any worse, the flashlight is flickering. Which means the phone is dying.

We really are stuck here. We really are fucked.

"I'm sorry," I whisper. "I didn't mean to mess things up. I don't understand anything and I don't know what I'm doing but I don't want to go back there. I don't know what I want, but I don't want to go back there."

"Well, Thomas and I don't agree on much. But we are both one hundred percent on board with staying the fuck out of the grip of Prodigy School." He sucks in some air and pauses. "We were so fucking close, too. So fucking close."

"Close to what?" I ask, tipping my head up so I can see his face. It's still lit up from below. Reflecting eerie shadows onto his cheeks.

"Revenge. We have the perfect plan. And even though I scared the fuck out of Thomas last month when all that shit went down and he tried to blow his fucking head off with a goddamned gun—as if that would make things better—just to get rid of me again…" He stops to sigh. "I was only there to help. That's all. I just wanted to be there when it all finally went down. And now look. I'm stuck in a grave I made myself. With a girl who has no idea what's going on. With a plan that can't even be implemented because my satellites—well, technically, they belong to Thomas, but anyway, our satellites are the trigger that starts the ball rolling and Case won't be able to initiate Lincoln's program without them." He pauses again. More in control when he speaks. "In case you're wondering what all that has to do with anything, I'm the only one who can initiate the satellites. Irony can suck my dick."

I almost find him funny. Almost. "Well, maybe next time you should consider letting your team in on your secrets. Then they can carry on without you. And you sure do swear a lot more than Thomas. I think he's the good twin."

"Fuck off."

I laugh. I should be insulted, but he's frustrated and defeated. And this is the asshole who tied me up and touched me twice. This is the asshole who made himself out to be a god who had all the answers.

His depression lifts my spirits.

"So let me see if I can put all this together. Thomas used drugs to keep you away for all these years. Locked you up in his head by eliminating his emotions. Then that Case dude shot him with something that messed up all his perfectly laid plans. That released you from your prison. And when Thomas figured out you were back, he tried to blow you out of his mind with a gun. Stop me when I get it wrong."

"Ding. Ding. Ding," he says, mocking me with his slow words.

"Why did you tie me up? Kiss me? Touch me?"

He shrugs. "Why not? You're pretty. And young. You didn't know anything about anything."

I tilt my head up to see him again.

He's smiling when he looks down at me. "Besides, you'd want to touch you too if you were me. I was locked up in that head of his for fifteen years."

"You're a pervert."

"You liked it."

I say nothing. Because I did.

I look up again and now he's grinning like a boy. "Thomas made a move on me too," I say.

"I saw," he grumbles.

"He kinda frustrated me. After… you." A chuckle from Sullivan. "You just take. But Thomas doesn't."

"He's dumb like that."

It's my turn to grin and chuckle. "I thought you were an everyday run-of-the-mill asshole, but I'm reevaluating."

"I'm not an asshole?"

"You're the definition of asshole. But I like your diabolical side."

"Well, that's awesome. I can waste away to pathetic weakness waiting for Prodigy to come take me back, knowing you prefer me to him." He looks down at me, not smiling. "I appreciate the gesture."

"There has to be a way out."

"There isn't. Not without explosives. It might take them a while to blast through the doors back at the southern tower, but they will. And then they'll blast through these too. Or maybe they know there's a tunnel over here and they'll say fuck those southern doors and just head west." He lifts his arm. Like he's pointing to something. "They'll come right though that gate there. Or you know what's even better than that?" He pauses to see if I'll play along, then just continues when I don't. "They might figure out that there's a tunnel connecting to this one up north or out east. Maybe they'll just sneak up from the south and surprise us."

Dick. "Optimist you are not."

"What's there to be optimistic about? We're stuck in the goddamned tunnel. This is all Thomas's fault. We'll get out of here eventually. We might spend the next twenty years as Prodigy prisoners, but eventually we'll get out of that too. And I tell you what... the next time I see an opportunity to get rid of that asshole, I'm gonna take it."

SULLIVAN
MENTAL MAN 2

CHAPTER FIFTEEN

I sigh into the encroaching blackness. Thinking, thinking, thinking.

"Do you hate him?" she asks.

I think about this question for a little bit. The light on the phone flickers, then dims, flickers a few more times until the battery finally dies. I tried to call Case and Lincoln while I was waiting for Sadie to wake up. But no luck. No satellite signal down here in the fucking earth.

"Well?" Sadie finally says. "Do you or don't you?"

"Hate is a strong word. Do you hate people?"

She laughs. "I don't know. I don't remember."

"Well, I don't hate him. He's me, for fuck's sake."

"But you'd like him to be the...what do you call it? Like... secondary personality? Instead of you?"

"He *is* the secondary personality, Sadie. I'm the one who was born in that body."

"Then why was he in control for so long?"

"Because they tricked me."

"Who? Prodigy?"

"Who else."

"What happened?" she asks.

I stay silent.

Sadie turns her body a little. Her head is resting on my thigh. She was sweating profusely while she was sleeping, but she's cooling off now. I wonder what they did to her to make her this way?

143

"If I knew what they did to me, I'd tell you."

"Are you a mind-reader too? I thought that was my job."

"Can you read my mind?" she asks.

"A little bit. I can read most people. Thomas can't. He only reads them when they die for some reason. And only when he's not on the drugs. Like now. Which is why he was off his game that morning you showed up. Someone died and he caught all those thoughts. Which gave me an opportunity to get a better hold on him. Quick tip. The inner ramblings of crazy people will make you crazy. So if your superpower is collecting the thoughts of the dead, try not to get yourself locked up in an insane asylum. I never understood any of it when I was younger. And I barely understand much more now. But I do know I can't read your mind unless I'm... inside you."

"What's in there?" she whispers into the dark. "In my head? What did they do to me?"

"It's computer shit. I told you that. Nanites and some kind of interface. We have one too."

"What kind of interface?"

"I don't know. They locked me out, obviously. If they hadn't we wouldn't be here. I'd have taken over again. You know. The way it's supposed to be."

"So that's your plan? Take over Thomas. Become him?"

"Kick him out, you mean? Hell, yes, that's my plan. I mean, I'm not against his little revenge scheme. My life only gets easier with Prodigy gone for good. But he's the one who stole my body. Fucking body-snatcher."

She thinks about this for a little bit. "So there must be a link, right? Between us?"

"I can only assume, since I can access your interface."

"Hmm," she says. Then silence.

I let that linger until I can't stand it anymore. "You're forming an opinion about me."

"I suppose."

More silence.

"Well, what is it?"

"Do you care?"

"Why not? We're stuck here for the duration. Let it all out, Sadie. Hit me with your opinion."

"Well," she says, pushing herself up until she's on her elbows. I can't see her leg in the darkness, but I decide she's probably well enough along her little healing journey to sit up. So I help her until she's got her back against the hard stone wall. Our shoulders are touching, which I find oddly comforting. "I think," she continues, breathing hard from the effort, once she's settled. "I think we might be parts of something, you and I."

"Yes. It's the most likely answer. But definitely the worst-case scenario."

"Why?"

"Because they only do that for one reason, Sadie. They pair us up to keep us in control. Have you ever heard of the Alpha-Omega Program?"

"No," she says. "Not that I remember, anyway."

"It was a genetic program at my Prodigy school. Maybe they did that at your school too. I don't know. But the basics go something like this. If your goal is to make a superhuman you're gonna need a way to control them. There's only so many ways to control a genius like Lincoln Wade, right? He has super-strength on top of that giant brain of his. Same with the rest of us, although Linc was always the leader in the superpower shit. Thomas kept him in check with the planning, but Lincoln was, is, and always will be the most dangerous Alpha to come out of that school. Regardless of what they think of me and Thomas.

"So you have to have something to hold over him. A threat. They did that by genetically engineering each of us a counterpart. The Omegas were created with one thing in mind. To be able to kill us if we got out of hand. They coded something called inhibition poisoning into our DNA. So if we tried to hurt the Omega, we'd get sick immediately. Like, crippling sickness that makes you double over, fall to the floor, and hug yourself."

"But couldn't you kill all the Prodigy people?"

"No," I say. "They gave us drugs so we'd experience the same effect if we tried to hurt them. Those drugs wear off, but not the Omega bond. That one is forever."

"Do you think I'm your Omega?"

I shake my head. "No again. This is why I tied you up that first time. I was testing it. Even today, Lincoln can't physically hurt Molly. She is, and will always be, his worst weakness. But when I tied you up, I felt nothing. So you can't be my Omega."

"Well, that's good, right?"

"You could be something even more dangerous. There's just no way to tell. I have no clue what they did to you. And you don't either."

"But Thomas said my memories will come back."

"It's been almost a week, Sadie. I don't think they're coming back."

She ponders this for a few moments. "So... who am I?"

I shrug. "No clue."

More silent thinking.

"I realize this... past of mine can't be ideal."

"Pfft." I laugh. "Understatement."

"But it is *my* past, right?"

"I get it, Sadie. I do. I'm missing parts of my past too. Lots and lots of years. Almost more are missing than I remember. So it sucks to lose something of yourself like that. But do I really need to know what they did to us back when Thomas was in control and I was suppressed? Do you really want to remember those things?"

She huffs out some air. "Yes."

"Well, I tried," I say with a sigh. "I don't entirely believe me, either. I'm pissed as hell about all the years since Prodigy School. The years when Thomas had me locked away while he was off living his life. But it does me no good to dwell."

"So why do you want to get rid of him?"

"He pretty much stole my fucking body, Sadie. I'm *me*. Not him. *I'm me*."

"Maybe you're both you?"

"We're not both *me*," I say, almost hissing the words out from between my teeth. "There's only one me. If there were two of us, well, we'd be an *us* then, wouldn't we?"

"Hmmm," she says again.

"What's that *hmmm* for?"

"I'm just thinking. Wondering, really. I get it, Sullivan. I'm not saying your feelings are invalid or anything. It was just a question. Mostly because it's true what you say. And it's also pretty likely that I have some kind of link in me. To you, obviously. But it feels like…"

I wait for her to finish. Not patiently. And when the pause drags out for several seconds with no continuation, I say, "Feels like what?"

"Like some part of me is missing." Her body turns towards me, her arm pressing against mine. I wish that stupid fucking phone was still working so I could look at her. "Do you think they split me in half too?"

Split me in half. God. Those words make me sick to my stomach.

"I mean… What if I have some other personality inside me too.? What if… Oh, fuck."

"What?" I ask, placing my hand on her arm.

"What if the reason I can't remember things is because I'm the *other me*? God, that makes no sense."

"No," I say. "It does. It makes perfect sense. What if they did the same thing to you that they did to me? And now you're…"

"Thomas. I'm the Thomas in this scenario. The body-snatcher."

I wonder what the other her is like?

Then I feel guilty for thinking that.

"So…" she continues after a short pause. "So they're gonna come get me."

"And me," I add.

"Yes, and you. Which, from what Thomas says, was the whole reason I was at the hospital that day. To get you. So if they get us both, that means…"

I don't wait this time. It just needs to be said so she knows what she's up against. "That means they're gonna switch you off again. Put you back in that dark room where they've been keeping you for however long. And let the other you take over."

She leans her whole body against mine now. Defeat, that move says. "I don't want that, Sullivan."

"Me either, Sadie. I kinda like you, odd as that is, since it's so fucking obvious you *are* my Omega. Not in the traditional sense, obviously. But somehow, some way, they linked us. If I go down, you will be the reason why."

We sit in the dark for a long time after that.

I have so much more to talk about, but none of it is good. None of it needs to be said now. So I let the itchy feeling of healing nanites preoccupy me. That's enough to make me sick—the thought of all those little fuckers inside my body, just running off a program that I never asked for and have no control over. The only bright side to it is they will be finished soon. And then they will retreat to that little corner where they hide when not needed.

"Sullivan?" Sadie says, breaking my thoughts.

"Yeah," I answer.

"If they break the tunnel and the green gas comes and makes me not-dead... Don't let them take me back."

Fuck. *Fuck*. I scream it in my head. Why do I have to like her? Why do I have this connection with her? Why does she have to be pretty?

Back at Prodigy Thomas was relentless. He killed every Omega they sent us. He laughed at Lincoln when they sent him little Molly. We all knew why they switched from boys to girls. To make us love them. Make us even more vulnerable. And Thomas was so cocky. So sure he didn't have a little Molly Omega hiding in the school somewhere.

Well, he was right about that. She was in a different school.

"I'll do my best, Sadie," I whisper, answering her question. "But I'm pretty sure it won't be enough. Now try to get some rest so you can heal. If we have any chance of getting out of this you need to be able to walk."

CHAPTER SIXTEEN

I lean against Sullivan and sigh. What a crazy week it's been.

But then I realize I have nothing to compare it to. Maybe all my weeks are crazy?

He leans forward and puts his arm around me. "Stop thinking about it and just rest."

"What if I wake up and you're gone?"

A soft laugh at that comment from Sullivan. "Are you falling in love with me, Sadie? Got a little Stockholm Syndrome going?"

I smile. But then frown. "You didn't kidnap me. I mean, Thomas didn't kidnap me. God, this is very confusing. I just feel like I know you better. That's all. And I've been through enough change for a whole lifetime these past few days. I could use a little more of the same."

"I get it," he says, rubbing my shoulder.

"But you didn't answer me. If I close my eyes and rest… will you still be here when I wake up?"

A shrug is all I get for an answer. He has nothing.

"Can you try?" I ask, unwilling to give up. "Just try? What if Thomas comes back and he's confused? Or… thinks I crashed the train on purpose? What if…"

"Stop it," Sullivan says. "I can't control it. Not really. When he sleeps he's weak because of all the drugs, maybe. And I think the crash had something to do with me returning. Or maybe it's the dark. At any rate, we can't control that. Let's focus on what we can control. Healing. Let's focus on healing. And the best way to do that is sleep."

I let out a long breath of air and try to let it go. We really are stuck. Until someone comes bursting through that gate or ambushes us from behind, we're just stuck.

So I close my eyes and will myself to let it go. I enjoy his warm body, at least. We're pressed up against each other. It's freezing down here. We could use that emergency kit. We'd have options. But that's dumb too. If we didn't crash we'd already be in the west tower. Safe and sound.

Eventually Sullivan relaxes and his breathing becomes softer. Slower. His head is against mine. And I'm pretty sure he's asleep.

How long will he sleep? Which one of them will wake up? Who is coming for me?

Who? I ask my head. *Who are you?*

Electricity shoots through my brain, making me gasp for air and press my hands up to my temples.

Sadie, Sadie, Sadie, flashes across my closed eyelids like a neon sign. *Where are you? I'm coming. I won't let you die down there.*

Who are you? I ask the message in my head. *I don't know who you are.*

Nothing. No answer. No static. No flashing words. Just nothing.

I'm here, I mentally whisper back. *I'm in the tunnel near the west gate. I'm stuck. I can't get out. I'm stuck.*

It's probably a huge mistake to tell them this. But if we're fucked, and we clearly are, then why not just get it over with? Face it, deal with it, and then—figure out a way to fight them. Right now, we don't even know who they are. What their weaknesses are. We need to see them to know those things.

We're friends, my vision overlay suddenly messages. *We're friends and we're coming to get you out of there. Just hold tight.*

"Yes," I whisper. Thomas's friends are coming. I debate waking up Sullivan and telling him about the message. But then… he might fight them. He might think they're here to put him back in the dark. And I get it. I get him. He wants his control back. I don't want to be put to sleep, either. And I'm probably not even the primary personality.

But fuck that. I want my life back even if it means whoever I stole this body from gets locked up in the dark instead.

I don't want Sullivan to go away, I decide. I don't want Thomas to go away either. But if I have to make a choice…

Well, I don't. It's not my choice to make. I just don't want to lose Sullivan. Not yet.

I like him. And when these partners of his get here I'm sure they'll have some remedy—some weird fucking drug they can give Sullivan to get Thomas back.

So I let him sleep. I enjoy him just a little bit longer.

My wound is itching like crazy. Probably from those— *don't think about it, Sadie. It's sick in a very diabolical way*— nanites as they heal my leg.

But eventually I let that go too. I give in. Give up. Same thing.

I rest my head against Sullivan's shoulder and let myself relax.

Sadie, Sadie, Sadie.

He is tall, muscular, and intimidating. His arms are crossed across his bare chest. They are huge. Bulging to the point of being grotesque. Like cannons. His body is covered in tattoos. Birds, I realize. Indigo blue ravens and midnight black jays. Raptors and songbirds too. But when I sweep my eyes up to his face, his frown is all I see.

He turns his back to me and walks to a doorway, his body forming a black silhouette against the bright light streaming through the opening, then disappears into it, taking the light with him.

Sadie, Sadie, Sadie.

"Sadie."

I try to open my eyes, but they are still heavy with sleep and in my dream, I'm calling for the big man to come back.

"Sadie!" The urgent whisper comes with a shake this time.

"What?" I manage through dry, thirsty lips.

"Do you hear that?"

I open my eyes and find… "Thomas?" I ask the voice.

"No," Sullivan says. "You're still stuck with me. But listen. Am I hearing things? Can you hear that?"

"No," I say.

"Listen carefully," he urges. "Can you hear that?"

I strain my ears, searching for the sound that has him on alert. I'm just about to say no again when he says, "There. That. The little tinny whining of…"

"A drill," I say. "They're here, aren't they?"

He just breathes for a few seconds. Then, "Yeah. A drill. You're right. They're drilling the iris gate. Probably from the center point where it spirals closed. That's the weakest point."

A faint *pop* sound makes both of us hiss in a breath.

"What was that?" I whisper into the darkness.

Sullivan is silent for a few moments. *Pop, pop, pop*, three more times.

"Explosives," he whispers back. "They're trying to break the seal first with small explosions. But once they have a foothold, they will use bigger charges to make an actual opening."

"Do you think it's them?" I ask. "Prodigy?"

I feel him nod next to me.

"It could be your friends," I say. "I got a message last night—or..." I pause. Because I have no idea what time of day it is, and this bothers me. "Before I fell asleep. Maybe it was just a dream, but they said they were friends. They were coming to get me."

"I don't have any friends," Sullivan says. "So no, I don't think they're friends."

"But Thomas's friends. I think it's Thomas's friends."

He's silent for a few seconds. Holding still as several more faint explosions sound off on the other side of the gate. "We should try at least."

"Try what?"

"To run, I guess. Can you stand?"

He gets to his feet just fine, all healed up from the massive crash, then bends down to grab my upper arm and pulls. I struggle, trying to get my bad leg to move, but he ends up doing all the work. I lean against the wall, huffing air and trying not to notice that my legs are definitely not ready for running.

"I'm not healed," I say.

"I'll help you," he says, putting my arm across his broad back so I can hold on to him.

He takes a step, but I stumble. "I can't do it," I say. "I won't be able to walk yet."

"I'll carry you," he says, leaning down into my neck. "We can't just let them get us. We have to try something."

"You go," I say, wincing as I put pressure on my leg. "You go and I'll stay here."

"No, fuck that. I'm not leaving you behind. That's bullshit. I'll carry you." He bends down and sweeps me up into his arms. I wrap my arms around his neck, so tired. Way too tired to escape anything right now.

We start walking, but it's very clear within only a few steps that his leg isn't completely healed either. He limps along, tripping over debris from the crash. We don't go down, but it's pretty evident that this escape will never happen. We will never get away. There is nothing around us but black. We have no eyes in this place.

He blindly kicks debris away with his foot, takes a few more steps, then stumbles again.

"Sullivan," I say. "It's over. We're going to hurt ourselves even more if we keep going."

"I'll just use the wall as a guide," he says, kicking his foot forward until he hits the hard stone. "I'm not gonna let them have you."

"I'll be OK," I say. But it's touching that someone I barely know… even… cares. I don't know what my life was like before this week, but I doubt it was good.

"No, Sadie. You won't. I'll be OK. Because Thomas will just take over again. They'll pump us with drugs and I'll disappear. I'll be nothing but chained anarchy in his head again. But you will not be OK and I won't let them have you."

I have nothing to say to that. I just lean my head into his shoulder and close my eyes. I have no idea how far away from the crash we make it before the little popping noises become bigger popping noises, but my best guess is not more than twenty or thirty feet.

We won't escape.

Sullivan stops walking. Leans his back against the wall and sighs. "I'm sorry," he says, putting me down.

I hold on to him, even when both my feet are back on the ground. He's all I have. "It's not your fault. None of this is your fault."

"No. It's not, but—"

An explosion cuts his words off. Then there's light coming through up ahead. Sparks are flying, illuminating the green gas, which has started to pour into the tunnel.

"They're cutting now," Sullivan says. "They've got a blow torch and they're cutting a door. They'll be here soon."

I start coughing, the gas entering my lungs. One breath is all it takes. One inhalation of the poison and I'm down. Choking and wheezing. Unable to get enough air into my lungs.

"I'm sorry, Sadie," Sullivan says. "I'm so fucking sorry."

The world goes black, then lights up again. But only in my head.

Sadie, Sadie, Sadie.

They're here.

They've come for us. Come to take us back and lock us up in their prison of darkness.

CHAPTER SEVENTEEN

Sadie slumps to the ground and I go with her. Her whole body is limp. The thick green gas is all around us. I breathe in, feeling the heaviness of it entering my body. For a few seconds, I wonder if we really are immune. If Thomas, and Lincoln, and Case and that weird computer, Sheila, got it right after all.

But we are. I exhale just fine. I am fine. Thomas wouldn't make a mistake like that.

I hold Sadie in my arms, staring at the small hole in the gate as the sparks from the blowtorch light it up. We're so close to it, it's sad, really. We aren't more than thirty feet away. My escape plans were pathetic.

There is no hope for escape.

"Thomas," I say out loud. I want him, I realize. I want him to take over and deal with this. He's the one who always took care of things. I'd never admit it to Sadie, but Thomas is the strong one. Thomas is the one with the plans that always work. Thomas is the one she needs right now, not me. "Come back," I whisper.

But he's not there. I look for him in my mind. I search for him as I watch the future unfolding before my eyes. He's just gone.

I don't hear voices, but I do hear clanging. They are pounding the metal with tools. Prying the small opening into a larger one.

After a few minutes of that, I see a face. A gas mask, actually. They are wearing something akin to a biohazard suit.

They knew about the gas. Or maybe they watched a few people die when they broke into the tunnel and reassessed. Reorganized. Got the right equipment to take us down.

I have powers. I am not helpless. I am a level ten mentalist, for fuck's sake.

Well, not really. Thomas is the one who knows how to use it. Thomas is the one with all the power. I can do a few things. I'm the one who had it first, after all. But I'm not the one who perfected it.

Still, one has to try.

So I wait. Patiently. I let them make their doorway. I let them come through, one and then the next. They have flashlights. Very powerful flashlights that illuminate the entire tunnel.

The full carnage of wreckage stands before them. The ruined train car, torn into so many bits of twisted metal. All of it glowing slightly in the shadow of the green gas. The beams pan back and forth over it. They are talking, I realize. On some kind of internal communication system. There are two of them, about the same size. Huge men from the size of their biohazard suits.

They split up, sweeping their light over everything— only halfway penetrating the green cloud and making the entire scene appear unearthly. I watch from the floor of the tunnel as one gets closer and closer.

His beam of light finds me. Shines right in my face, rendering me blind.

I don't blink. Just wait, absolutely still, as he makes his way towards us.

He stops a few feet away, still shining that fucking light into my face.

"You have something of mine," a tinny voice says from a speaker in his gas mask.

"Is that right," I say, my voice different as it makes its way through the thick cloud of green gas. It winds up his legs and around his body like a snake.

"Don't make this difficult, freak. You can't win," he says.

"Maybe not," I say. "But I can go down fighting."

The mind blast doesn't exactly burst forth. Not the way Thomas does it. But it still has power and it sends him reeling backwards with his arms flailing and his back bent. He crashes into a piece of sharp wreckage, and even though I can't hear his scream, I know he screams.

I smile at that and get to my feet, taking my attention to the other guy, who has his flashlight out in front of him as he does his best to run towards us.

I blast him too, but he braces himself. It rocks his whole body, but when the wave is over, he's still standing.

A tinny laugh from his gas mask. "That was weak, Thomas. I expected more from a guy like you."

He comes at me again, and again, I blast him. This time the force is even less powerful than the first. It doesn't even stop him, just makes him lean his body forward, like he's walking into a strong wind and nothing more.

"Weak," he says again. And then he raises his arms and unleashes his superpower.

His mind blast pins me to the concrete wall behind me. It's so powerful. More powerful than anything I've seen Thomas do, including that day at the hospital. The shockwave hits my mind, making me struggle to stay conscious.

Then it's gone. Like he flipped a switch. He's very in tune with his power.

Prodigy. Only Prodigy has powers like this.

"I'm gonna make you pay, asshole," the masked man says. "I'm gonna make you pay for what you did to my brother, Thomas."

I have no idea who his brother is, or what Thomas might've done to him, but it no longer matters. He aims a weapon at me and a dart bursts out of the barrel, hitting me square in the chest.

I look down, see the dart sticking out of my heart, and immediately know what he's done.

It's a drug dart.

The effects start before that thought is even through forming. I feel the chemicals inside me. They burn their way through the chambers of my heart, then empty into my bloodstream. Seconds later it's been delivered to my entire body.

I fall to my knees, laughing. "You fucked up, asshole," I say, crumpling to the ground, unable to control my body. I'm gonna turn back into Thomas and he's gonna power up his own mental ability and put up a good fight.

A great fight.

"You fucked up. You just wait."

My threats are ignored, but I have no time to wonder why.

The darkness is back.

I go into it relieved.

It really sucks being wrong. And I know I'm wrong the whole time I try to wake up. Because I'm not Thomas, I'm still me.

Asshole, I try to say. But it comes out as a groan. The one fucking time I need the guy to take over and he's not here. *Asshole.*

"Not time to wakey-wakey yet, you freak," a deep voice says off to my left. A sharp jab to my heart tells me all I need to know.

The chemicals flood my body and…

CHAPTER EIGHTEEN

His face is handsome, even with the scar. It's his eyes, I think. They are brown, but not just any brown. They are the light brown of autumn leaves, with golden flecks of brilliance shining through the darkness.

Sadie, he says. But it's in my mind.

I think I love him right now.

Sadie, come back to me.

I'm here.

Sadie, Sadie, Sadie…

I open my eyes and he becomes real. "Iziah," I say, my lips trembling and my voice shaking.

"Shhhh," he says, sitting down on the bed next to me. "Shhh. I got you, chick. I got you. Don't think about anything right now. Don't worry about anything right now."

"Where am I?"

"What did I just say?" He laughs, sweeping a strand of sweat-soaked hair out of my eyes. "Just relax. You're all good."

I close my eyes, mostly because they are too heavy to keep open. It's just too much effort. "I've missed you," I mutter, almost asleep again.

He leans down, making the bed move, and kisses my forehead. "We've missed you too. But forget it for now. Just sleep a little longer, Sade. You're safe here."

The next time I open my eyes, I see him again, but not him. "Uzi," I whimper.

The reaction is much the same. "Shhh, Sade. You're OK. I'm just changing your drugs. Your stupid fucking friend messed you up good with that gas. But we got a hold on it now. Don't worry. Just sleep."

"Cyan," I whimper back. "Where's Cyan?"

"She's been in and out the past week. She's sleeping now, like you should be. I'll tell her you're almost ready. She'll be so happy." Uzi caresses my cheek with his hand and then leans down and kisses my forehead, just like Iziah did the last time I woke up. "Just sleep."

CHAPTER NINETEEN

My body is cannibalizing itself from the inside out. I have no idea how long they've had me locked in this room, but it's more than a few days. Maybe more than a week. This is a prison cell. I've measured it by pacing more times than I care to count. About six feet wide by six feet deep. Gray cinderblock walls. Gray concrete floor. No windows. The ceilings are tall, at least. So I was able to stand up and move around. There is a toilet in the corner. No mirror. And a concrete bed. No blankets.

No one has come. No one has fed me. No water. No demands. Nothing.

I stopped pounding on the door days ago. I don't think anyone's out there. I think they locked me up in this room and left.

I'm hoping for unconsciousness soon. The pain in my stomach from not eating is constant. My mouth is so dry it feels like it's stuffed with cotton. The floor is cold and there's nothing to cover myself, so I shiver uncontrollably.

Thomas is gone too. I have no idea what happened to Thomas. He might be dead. Which is just fucking great. I tried to use my powers but nothing's there. I'm not talking about a weak wind, either. I'm talking about nothing.

I have been completely disabled.

I have no idea where Sadie is. If she's alive or dead. Where this place is. Whether or not anyone will come back, or even who these people are.

But I can take a good guess.

Prodigy.

Everything about this place has Prodigy written all over it.

This cell is one I'm intimately familiar with. It's just like the one they used to lock me in as a child. That's what broke me, I realize. That cell back when I was little. Back when I was whole. Back before Thomas, and mentalist abilities. Back before I knew anything, they put me in a cell like this and they broke me.

Split me right in two.

They created Thomas from parts of me.

They starved me back then too. It's a trigger. Something in me breaks free when I have no food or water. So they've already started the experiments again.

I can't pace anymore. I can't even crawl. So I just sit here, my back against the cold, hard, concrete wall, and wait. Shivering as I wait for the darkness to come.

I reach for Sadie's mind. We're linked. We know we're linked. I was in there. I can call for her.

Sadie, I message. *I'm still here. Help me.*

Nothing.

This is my past, my present, and my future.

There's nothing else I can do but wait.

CHAPTER TWENTY

"Sadie."

This time the voice is different. Soft. Feminine. Mine.

I open my eyes and see my sister. "Cyan," I whisper. I reach for her hand and squeeze. She squeezes back harder.

"How are you feeling?"

"Like shit. What the hell happened?"

"We're still trying to figure some of it out. But you're OK now. We've got you back and that's all that matters. Just rest."

"No," I say, pushing myself up on my elbows. "I'm done resting. I feel like I've been in this bed for weeks."

"You have," she says. There's fear in her voice. "That gas—" She shakes her head. "Whatever it was really fucked you up. But I'm almost done analyzing it. I wish I could've gotten that done sooner. It would've shortened your recovery period."

"Where's Uzi?"

"He's in the other room sleeping. We've been taking shifts with you. Keeping things going until you were strong again." She squeezes my hand. "The worst is over now. You're gonna be fine. Your leg is healing and—"

But I lose track of her words because a memory hits me in the head. "There was a crash," I say, interrupting her.

"Yes." Cyan nods. "A very bad one. Your leg was…" She shudders and makes a face. "Gross. But don't worry. It's healing nicely. The nanites have almost knitted

169

everything back to good as new. Maybe a few more hours and you'll never even be able to tell it was broken."

I go looking for more memories, but my mind is blank. "Why can't I remember anything?"

"I think it's just a side effect. Of the gas. But it'll wear off."

"Where did you guys find me?"

My sister pauses for a moment, looking down at me with that thoughtful expression I've always loved. I wonder if I look at her that way? We have the same face. The same eyes, hair, fingers and toes. Identical, with one exception.

I'm an illusionist and she's a mentalist.

But together, we are more than twins. We are complements. Yin and yang. Wondertwins.

"You were kidnapped by one of the Alphas. That's who poisoned you."

"Good God." My insides twist with that revelation. "How long was I gone? How long did those sick fucks have me?"

She pats my hand sympathetically. "Don't think about it now, OK? Uzi wants to fill you in on all those details later. Do you want to take a bath? I have your favorite bubbles."

"God, yes." I laugh. "That would be heaven." But then I remember something. "Wait. I think I saw Iziah here. Was I dreaming? Is he here? Did you find him?"

"Yes," Cyan says. Her sisterly smile beams down on me like rays of sunshine. "We found him about a month ago." The smile fades. "It was so bittersweet though, you know? You go missing just when we thought we were all back together again."

"Is he... OK?"

"He's fine." But it's a lie and she knows I know it. "He will be fine. He was pretty fucked up when we got him out too. But not as bad as you. And then they found you in that tunnel with the Alpha. He sent Iziah reeling into a piece of wreckage with a mental blast, tore his biohazard suit open, and then the gas got him too. But he's OK. He was mostly protected by the suit, so his dose was much smaller. He'll come say hi when he gets some time. We're very busy. We've got Prodigy within reach now. We're going to take them out, Sadie. Just like we planned."

Another flash across my vision. *Sadie*, it says. *Help me.*

"Are you OK?" Cyan asks me. She puts a gentle hand on my shoulder. "What's wrong?"

"I just got a flash. Of the Alpha." I look up at my sister. "Thomas Brooks was the one who took me, wasn't he?"

She nods, but says nothing.

"God. It's even worse than I could've imagined. Of all the Alphas to be caught by, it had to be him? What did he do to me?"

"We don't know yet," she says in her stay-calm voice. "But whatever it was, we can fix it. Don't worry."

Sadie, the message reads again. *It's me. I'm still here. Help me.*

"Don't listen to them," Cyan cautions me. "They'll twist your head. You know this. You know the kind of power they wield. You've been training your whole life to deal with their tricks. Don't let him have your mind, Sadie. Turn him off *right now.*"

She drops her carefully planned optimism as the last few words come out. They are harsh and stern. An order.

"You were tricked with his stupid mentalist powers. That's how he got you. Don't let him do it again. I can't lose you again, do you understand?"

I nod. "I won't. I promise."

"Good," she says. Her smile is back and she stands up from the bed. "Now let me help you to the tub. Uzi will come in when you're done and you two can have some alone time."

She winks at me, then smiles.

Uzi. We have been partners for as long as I can remember. Which, at this point, isn't long because my memory is so fucked up. But I know him. I know what he is to me. I know what we are together.

He's my other half. He's the one I belong to.

Things I know.

I'm in a house. A pretty big one, too. We're in the mountains because I have the most picturesque view imaginable as I soak in the tub. The bubbles smell like heaven. The hot water feels so delicious, I might drink it. And I have no clue what was wrong with my leg, because there's no sign of injury at all from what I can tell.

But every few minutes, that message flashes across my vision overlay.

Help me.

Why in the ever-loving fuck would I help that asshole?

I grew up terrified of them. All of them. I'd never met one personally, since the Alpha program was officially over before I was even old enough to understand what they were. But I've seen pictures. I've heard the horror story of how they killed all those other kids.

And Thomas Brooks was the ringleader. He was the one who did it. The others are just bad, but he's the worst of the worst. If evil is a real thing, that man is it, personified.

Cyan, Uzi, and I escaped Prodigy two years ago. Iziah was caught the same night. He was covering for us so we could all get away, and he was caught. I was caught a few days later.

That much I remember.

I have been with Prodigy for a long time.

The rest... well. It's a little bit fuzzy because that stupid fucking Alpha kidnapped me, put me into some kind of train car under the ground, and then we crashed, which released that green gas.

This is as much as I've figured out.

I remember the crash, the car, and the tunnel. Cyan told me about the kidnapping and the gas.

And I remember him too.

He's kinda hot.

Good God, I hope Cyan isn't trying to read my mind right now. She will flip out. Alphas are not hot, they are dangerous.

Sadie...

God, why is he doing this to me? *Go away!*

But just as I say that in my head, I have a flash of light. A feeling floods through my body. Fear, I think. Fear of... him?

No. Not him.

Them.

Which I can only assume is Prodigy. It makes me shudder even though the tub water is so hot, steam is still wafting up in hazy tendrils.

Don't let them take me.

I'll do my best.

He's holding me. Carrying me. His arm around me protectively.

And then it's gone.

I sink down into the water and wet my hair again. I stay like that, holding my breath, wanting that last part to come back, but I don't dare wish for it.

Too many people can see inside me. I've always hated that part about being an illusionist. There's no privacy when you have mentalists around. Cyan and Uzi are both mentalists.

I force myself to think of Uzi instead of Thomas. He's always been a part of our lives. Iziah too. They aren't twins like me and Cyan, just brothers. But they look enough alike that people assume.

We are a team. Been a team our whole lives. Iziah and I are illusionists. Uzi and Cyan are mentalists. We are perfectly matched. We are all linked, which means Cyan and Uzi can see inside Iziah and me.

But I wonder something as I sit in the tub and soak the ache from my muscles. I wonder how much Thomas saw of me. Because I feel his link. I feel his connection.

Sadie… Help me.

I feel… his pain.

"Cyan!" I yell, standing up in the tub. "Cyan!" I step out, grab a towel from the vanity, and wrap myself up.

The door flies open. Uzi is there. "What?" he asks, coming towards me. "What's wrong?" His huge arm wraps around my body, pulling me close.

Sadie… Help me.

Cyan appears in the doorway. "What's going on? Why are you screaming my name?"

"Where is he?" I ask, pushing Uzi away and slipping past Cyan. "He's here. Somewhere. Where are you guys keeping him?"

"Who?" Cyan asks, grabbing my arm. "Where are you going?"

"The Alpha," I say. "Thomas Brooks. He's here. Where is he?"

"Why?" Uzi asks.

"Because he's in pain, Uzi. He's dying."

Uzi laughs. "You know as well as I do, he can't die."

"You're torturing him, aren't you?"

"Sadie, just calm down." Cyan still has a hold of my arm, but I yank it away.

"I want to see him. Right now. I want to make sure he's OK." I turn around just quick enough to catch Uzi and Cyan sharing a knowing glance. "Take me to him."

"No," Cyan says. "I'm not letting him get near you. He linked himself to you, didn't he?"

I can't deny it, so I don't.

"Are you fucking kidding me right now?" Uzi asks. "Why the hell would you let that spawn of hell into your head?"

"It's not her fault," Cyan says, moving close to me. She takes my side and I appreciate that.

"It's not," I say. "I didn't let him do anything. But the link is there and I know you're torturing him. I can *feel* it!"

I feel Uzi inside me. It makes me sick. I don't know why. I've always loved it before. But Cyan kicks him out. She's there now. She has a special place inside me. She fills me up and makes me complete. She begins probing and poking. Looking for things she feels entitled to.

But there's a trick us illusionists learn early. We did it in the classrooms at Prodigy all the time. If there's someone in your head without permission, you can kick them out using another, stronger mentalist to take their place.

And normally I have no one I can use. Uzi and Cyan have been coming and going inside my head for so long— it's been just us for so long—I'd forgotten what it was like to replace them.

But now I have a third option. And he's much, much stronger than the two of them put together.

Now I have Thomas.

I call for him. He's weak, but he's still a level ten. The only level ten I've ever heard of. You don't have to be strong to take a mind. You just have to know the tricks.

I call again and this time I feel his attention on me.

"Stop it!" Cyan says.

"Get out of my head."

"Don't let him in there, Sadie. What the fuck do you think you're doing?"

I call again. "Get out of my head!" I say. This time it's loud. "Or I will let him in."

Cyan retreats. Uzi doesn't try to take her place. They both stare at me—open-mouthed—like I have lost my mind.

"What the fuck is wrong with you, Sade?" Uzi yells.

"Just calm down," Cyan says, grabbing Uzi's arm to hold him back.

I clutch the towel around my body and turn away. They follow me, still demanding answers.

I realize I don't have any clothes. I was wearing a nightgown when I woke up. "I need clothes," I say. "And then I want to see him."

"No," Cyan says. "That's absolutely not going to happen."

"Yes," I say back. Forcefully. "It absolutely is. You're torturing him. And as long as he's in my head, I won't stand for it."

Then I do something I don't think I've ever done before. I trip them. I trip them both. I make them see me as Thomas. The way he looks right now.

I don't know what he looks like right now, but that's the beauty of my power. I make people see what they know to be true. I don't have to know what people look like to turn myself into an illusion of them, I just need a face.

So they see Thomas.

"Stop it!" Cyan yells, yanking my arm. "Why are you doing that? What the hell is wrong with you? Did he brainwash you?"

"You're sick, Sadie," Uzi says. "You were with them too long."

And that stops me for a moment. The word… *them*. My illusion snaps and I'm Sadie again. "With… *them*? Who is them?"

"He means the Alphas. They did something to you. That green gas. Iziah has been complaining for days now too. He's—"

"Where is Iziah?" I ask, forgetting Thomas and the way they're torturing him.

"He's resting," Cyan says. "He's not feeling well today so he's resting. He told me to wake him for dinner. And that's what we're gonna do now, OK?"

She starts out speaking harshly to me. But her tone is that same soft voice of love and compassion by the time she's done.

Help me, Sadie. Please.

I close my eyes. His plea is so hard to resist. "First you take me to Thomas."

"No," Uzi says. "He's just gonna hijack you again. Take control."

"I'm a lot stronger than him right now. I can kick him out. Watch." I do. I shut off his plea and immediately, Cyan is back.

Her body is next to me, but her mind is inside me. Her shoulder relaxes with relief.

"I can control him right now. And I want to see what you've done to him. So get me some clothes and take me there right now. Or I'll kick you out again, Cyan. I can do it, you know I can."

I kick her out of me and let Thomas back in.

It takes every ounce of self-control I have not to smile about that.

For as long as I can remember, Cyan has been stronger than me. I have kicked her out before, but it takes a lot of effort.

Using Thomas didn't take any effort. It was instantaneous.

"He's done something to you," she says, letting go of my arm. "He's done something to you, Sadie, and whatever it is… it's not good."

"Clothes," I say.

Uzi shakes his head and walks out, slamming the bedroom door behind him.

Cyan walks over to a dresser, pulls out some clothes, and tosses them on the bed. "I guess I have no choice. But I'd just like to go on record that this is a very bad idea. He is what he is, Sadie. So whatever sweet-talk he used on you while he kept you prisoner"—she snarls that word—"it's not good. And you better think long and hard before you fall for it. Because if you take his side…"

"If I take his side what?" I ask. "You'll hurt me?"

She makes a face. "I'd never hurt you. You know that."

I do know that. But I don't feel like taking it back. So I get dressed instead. These are obviously her clothes because they fit me perfectly. And when I'm ready, dressed in jeans, t-shirt, and the red sneakers she's partial to, she opens the door and says, "Come with me."

CHAPTER TWENTY-ONE

Help me. I say it over and over, hoping she'll hear me.

But it's been weeks. Weeks since they locked me in this prison cell. I am unable to do anything but waste away on the floor, wishing for my final end that will never come.

Thomas is gone for good. I can feel it. He's never coming back. I'll be left here to rot. No one is even here in this place with me. No sound at all. Nothing. I'm deep underground. No one will find me. I will—

Footsteps outside the door.

Help. Help me.

The grinding sound of a bolt being slid. Then the creak of a heavy door.

"Thomas?"

Thank God, it's her. *Sadie.* I'm too weak to talk, so I do my best to project this to her. *Sullivan.* I concentrate on my name, trying to let her know I'm still here. That Thomas is gone and it's still me. The one she likes. I'm the one she likes. Me.

Lights flick on. It blinds me—even though my eyes are shut, it's too bright.

"What did you do to him?" Sadie asks.

"We needed to disarm him," a man says.

"We cannot afford to have sympathy for this animal," a woman snarls. "He is everything we've been fighting against."

"Feed him," Sadie snaps. "Now. And bring him water."

JA HUSS

"He won't be able to eat," the man says. "He's too weak."

"Then I'll feed him, Uzi."

Silence after that little declaration. For several seconds. Then, "I hope you know what you're doing," from the woman.

Footsteps. Two sets.

Sadie kneels down next to me. "Thomas?" she asks in a soft whisper. We're connected. Linked. That's what she called it back in the tunnel. So I can feel her even when she's not here. But it's so much better when she's near.

"They're bringing you food. I'm sorry. I was unconscious. I don't know how long you've been like this but…" Her words fall away.

I have no more fight left in me. She's here. It feels like a victory. It feels like the right time to fade away and let someone else take over.

But Thomas is still gone.

Where did you go?

The only response I get is darkness.

"Thomas?" It's Sadie again. I feel a lot different. A lot better. And I'm not filthy, cold, or lying on a concrete floor. "Can you open your eyes?" I'm on a bed. A very soft bed.

God. When was the last time I had the pleasure of experiencing a bed? I don't even remember. It was always Thomas who got to enjoy beds. Women. Drinking. Eating. I had none of that while I was locked up inside my own head.

I'm glad he's gone. Fucking ecstatic.

Something pushes against my lips. Plastic. A straw.

"I know you're waking up, Thomas. Drink from the straw. You need more water."

I try to open my eyes, but only a thin sliver of reality peeks through before I give up and close them again.

"It's OK," Sadie says. "You can rest. But can you hear me?"

Yes, I send her mentally. *I can hear you.*

"I know you've done bad things. And I know I should not think of you as a... friend."

Friend, huh?

She squeezes my hand. "We're not at Prodigy. We're with my sister. I have a sister!" She is excited about this. "I'm not..." She pauses. "I'm not what I feared. I just have a twin."

Twin. Well, that makes sense, I guess.

"Our friends, Uzi and Iziah, they're here too. We all escaped together a couple years ago. Well," she says, sighing. "Uzi and my sister Cyan did. Iziah and I were caught. Uzi and Iziah got us out of the tunnel. They came to save me. And I'm sorry for how they treated you. You don't deserve that. But you're getting better now. I've only fed you a few times and believe me, you look a hundred times better." She squeezes my arm and I realize I have no shirt on. "Your muscles are even back. I don't understand how we heal like we do. Cyan says she has the mesh and nanites too. So do Uzi and Iziah. I guess we were in the same test group. My memory is coming back."

"All of it?" I croak out. It's barely a whisper.

She squeezes my hand, then whispers, "Sullivan. I know that's you."

I manage a smile.

"I'd know you anywhere." Her whisper is so soft, I barely hear it. Which means she's worried about the others overhearing. She wants this to be a secret between us.

"There's still a lot I don't remember. Like… why was I with you?"

"Are you fucking kidding me?" I croak again.

She chuckles under her breath, trying to be quiet. "I know you're someone good. At least to me. But I was gassed or something. It took some more of my memory away."

"Fuck," I say. "I forgot, sorry."

"I got the earlier stuff back. I remember my sister. And Iziah and Uzi. But I have a big gap. The years Prodigy had me since the escape. I don't remember anything."

"Just give it some time," I manage to spit out. But shit, it feels like a very long string of words right now.

"Can you open your eyes?" she asks. "I need to see them. I need to see those eyes so I know you're going to be OK."

I try again, this time managing to bring them to half-mast. "Hey," I manage.

"Hey, yourself." She smiles. Then she inhales deeply and lets it out. Relief. "I was so worried. When I finally woke up and realized they didn't feed you…"

I try to shrug, but I'm not sure I pull it off. "No biggie," I say. My voice is hoarse but at least my mouth no longer feels like it's stuffed with cotton. "You can make it up to me later." I wink. Or… what I think passes as a wink right now. It's more of a two-eyed blink.

But it gets results. Because she smiles and maybe… yes, I think I see a blush.

"Do you know," I say, thinking I must be delirious for even going here, "I haven't flirted with a girl since I was twelve."

"Twelve?" She laughs. Then she looks over her shoulder, afraid someone might be watching her reaction. "Kind of a late bloomer, huh?"

I laugh this time. Or cough. She helps me sit up so I can do it properly, patting me on the back. "Sorry if I got you in trouble with your people."

"I'm not in trouble. They don't control me. We're equal partners."

"Thanks," I say.

"For what?"

"For using your... street cred, I guess. For getting me out of that fucking prison cell."

"I'm not done with you yet, Sullivan Brooks. Not even close. Whatever's going on, we're just getting started. So I've got your back if you've got mine."

This makes me look at her for several silent seconds. "Do you need me at your back?"

She shrugs, still very nervous about being overheard. "I don't know yet. But I'd like someone who didn't grow up with me on the team, if you know what I mean? An objective opinion, if you will. But I have to warn you, Sullivan. They see you as evil incarnate. The Alphas are the most feared project to ever come out of Prodigy school. I'm second-guessing myself a little too. But whatever you are, whoever you are... it's not what they think. So I'm gonna give us a chance."

Us. I like the way she just phrased that.

"We could be a great team, remember? Oh, that was Thomas. But it still applies to you and me, right?"

I nod, looking at her face. She's not pale anymore. Her skin is a soft light brown. Like she comes from a part of the world that has a blue-green ocean and a white-sand beach. I can practically picture her on that beach. Yellow bikini. Her hair all streaked with gold and red from the sun. Laughing. I have no idea what she looks like completely happy. I'd like to see her happy.

"But don't fuck me over. Please. If you're here to fuck me over, put me out of my misery first. Do it without me knowing."

I take her hand, ball it up into a fist, and bump it to mine. "Wondertwins?"

She laughs. "Yeah, sure. But that's a stupid name. We'll have to come up with something way cooler."

I appreciate her for a few moments. Enjoy her. Then whisper, "I'd really like to kiss you right now. And not just because you showed up when it mattered."

She holds her breath, then glances over her shoulder.

"But I'll wait," I say softly. "Just don't make me wait too long."

She blushes. Which almost makes up for the predicament I find myself in. "I need to get downstairs," she says. "Cyan is not happy with me for insisting they get you out of that cell. None of them are. You can rest. Or take a shower. I put clothes in your bathroom. Or come downstairs for dinner, if you feel like it."

"Sure," I say, letting go of her hand. "I'm up for all of that."

I watch her walk away filled with… longing.

A strange feeling, I realize. I've never had that before. Not even when I was desperate to be the one in control instead of Thomas. This is something new.

I like it.

"I'd know you anywhere."
Her whisper is so soft, I barely hear it.

Which means she's worried about the others overhearing.

She wants this to be a secret between us.

.

CHAPTER TWENTY-TWO

When I get downstairs Cyan is banging pots and pans around as she goes through the motions of dinner with Iziah. "Where's Uzi?" I ask.

"Out," Cyan snaps. "I hope you and your new lover enjoy the dark side." She slams a pan down on the stove burner, making the grates jump. "Because we won't be joining you there."

"Don't be dramatic, Cyan," Iziah says. He smiles at me when I look at him, his eyes warm and happy. "She's been through a lot and she went through it with this asshole. So…" He shrugs. "Cut her a break."

"Cut her a break?" Cyan says, sending him a sidelong glance that would make most people tremble. She might not be a level ten mentalist like Thomas, but she's got her talents. And she knows how to use them. Always has. Even when we were children Cyan was the one coming up with plots and plans. Cyan was the one who kept us safe. Cyan was the one with the idea to break out of Prodigy. "I don't cut breaks for Alphas."

"Would you just give him a chance?" I say.

"No," Cyan snaps back. "I won't. He's the one who killed them, Sadie. How the fuck do you just forget that?"

"I didn't forget that," I say, defensive. Well, I did. But that memory is back now. Not so for most of the memories with Thomas and Sullivan. There are still a lot of gaps

187

there. It's so strange. It's like I traded one set of memories for another. "I'm very aware of who and what he is."

"And you want to coddle him. Take care of him like a stupid nursemaid? I don't even know you right now."

"Well, I don't know you either," I mutter under my breath. But she's too busy banging shit around in the kitchen to hear me. I glance at Iziah, who didn't miss it. And he just sends me a sympathetic shake of his head and mouths, *It's OK*. Which is code for, *Drop it*.

Iziah turns away and starts grabbing some food out of the fridge.

"Thomas is coming down for dinner," I say. "So make enough."

Cyan slams a large metal spoon down on the counter. "Are you fucking kidding me?" She turns to Iziah. "You're OK with this?"

"Cyan," he says. Iziah has always been the calmest of all four of us.

"Don't Cyan me." She points her spoon at me from across the room. "Are you dating him now? Is Uzi aware that Alpha Thomas is taking his place?"

"What place?" I ask. "Uzi and I are just friends."

"Friends?" She looks over at Iziah, shooting him a do-you-believe-her-bullshit look.

"Cyan," Iziah says again. "Knock it off. She's been gone for two years. She doesn't even know him."

"Apparently, she doesn't know me either."

Well, I guess she heard my muttered response to her saying the *exact same thing*.

"Two years didn't stop us from getting back together," Cyan shoots back. And the look on Iziah's face is the only thing she needs to see. "What?" she asks. "What's that look for? You're having second thoughts about starting over?"

Iziah is just about at the end of his rope now. I don't know what happened to him when he got left behind at Prodigy. Just like I don't know what happened to me. I'm just going to assume it's bad.

"I never said that. I'm just saying... leave her the fuck alone."

Cyan looks hurt. She opens her mouth, then closes it and turns her back to him, busy with dinner again.

When Iziah looks over at me, I mouth, *Thank you.*

He doesn't respond.

I don't know why he took my side against Cyan. They've been a thing for as long as I can remember. Even as kids, they were always a team. Same with me and Uzi, but I never let him get any farther than that. Cyan always wanted more from Iziah. I always figured he was in love with her. But this... this is not the Iziah I remember.

And the tension in the air is almost thick enough to see.

"Hey," Uzi says, walking in the front door, slamming it behind him. He takes off his jacket, throws it on a chair as he passes by, then comes right up to me and slips an arm around my waist.

I smile. But... he sends chills up my spine. Just not the way he's supposed to.

I remember Uzi. I have lots of memories of Uzi. But there's something about him I can't seem to shake these days.

"What's wrong?" he says, feeling my apprehension. Probably reading my mind.

"Cyan's pissed off," Iziah says from across the room. He's looking straight at me when I glance over at him. Like he said that to cover up the fact his brother makes me uncomfortable.

Something's wrong here. Something is off. Ever since I felt well enough to come downstairs and join them, I've felt it. Uzi and Cyan have been on the outside for two years without us. Things have changed. And I know Iziah feels it too.

I wish I could talk to him in private, but we never seem to find ourselves alone together. If Cyan isn't with us, then Uzi is. In fact, now that I think about it, I haven't had one real conversation with Iziah since I woke up.

"When isn't she?" Uzi laughs. He looks down at me. "Right?" His smile is the same. His eyes, still the same. His face is just as handsome as I remember.

But he's not the same.

Maybe it's you, Sadie. Ever think of that?

Yes, I have thought of that. I've thought about nothing but that since I woke up.

I have changed.

"Right." I laugh, trying to lighten the mood. "And look, Cyan, I get it. We all know who Thomas is." Well, they don't, not really. They have no idea about Sullivan. And I'm not going to tell them. I decided this immediately, as soon as Cyan started asking me questions about him. "But he's not the same guy as he was when all that shit went down. And none of us were there. You should just let him tell his side."

"What side?"

All four of us turn our heads to the stairs to see Thomas—Sullivan—staring at us from the bottom step.

Cyan turns back to slamming things. Uzi's body stiffens next to mine. Iziah says, "Your side," with a long sigh that says he's tired of this fight and he's ready to move on.

"OK," Sullivan says, walking into the living area. He eyes Cyan with caution, then Uzi, and finally decides that Iziah is the only one worth talking to.

I have to agree with his assessment right now. Even though I feel like a traitor for doing so.

"But you're gonna have to help me out here," Sullivan says. "I came in on the middle of the conversation."

"How about an explanation for why the fuck you felt the need to kill all those kids at school fifteen years ago?" This is from Uzi.

"Not to mention the teachers," Cyan says. My mouth drops in shock. *Teachers?*

Sullivan laughs while I'm doing that. "Teachers?" And I might love him in this moment for being on the same wavelength as me. For making me feel—not crazy.

Then he lets out a guffaw. "Are you serious? I have no clue what your school was like," he says, again, deciding to focus on Iziah. "But mine wasn't filled with teachers. They were all certifiable mad scientists who used my body like a lab rat. They used my brother like a lab rat. And my baby sister. They used my friends. So if you think I'm going to apologize for what I did, think again."

"That doesn't give you right to blow people up. Kids," Uzi replies. He tugs me closer to him and I suck in a breath. This is not turning out right. I don't want him touching me. And it's not because Sullivan just made some kind of offer upstairs. It's just... *I don't want him touching me.*

"You Alphas think you're in charge. You think you're so powerful. Well," he says, gripping the skin of my waist so hard I let out a gasp, "you have no idea what Sadie and I can do together. Or Cyan and Iziah. And if you think you're going to put us down like rabid dogs, just like you did those other kids, you're in for a big surprise."

I don't think Sullivan even heard him. Because his eyes are trained on Uzi's grip on my waist. He drags his blazing eyes to mine. Squints.

I don't know him very well but I think that squint is... something bad.

I push Uzi off me to deescalate the situation and walk over to the kitchen. "Can we just have dinner and talk this out like grown-ups?"

"Pffff," Uzi says. "You barely count as a grown-up, Sadie."

"Fuck you," I say. "And just in case you don't remember, Cyan and I are twins. We're the same fucking age."

"Yeah, but you've been at Prodigy for two years. She knows what's up. You?" he says. "You have no clue what's happening. And you're the one who invited this monster into our house."

I open my mouth to yell at him, but Iziah says, "OK. That's enough."

But I'm not done. Not even close. "Whose fault was it that I was left behind?"

I'm talking to Uzi, but I can feel Cyan looking at me.

"We did our best," Uzi growls. "And I cannot believe you're taking this asshole's side over us. It makes me sick thinking of what they did to you while you were there. Just like it makes me sick thinking about what they did to Iziah."

I don't know what to say after that. I just want to leave. But I can't. I'm stuck here. And it sucks that I feel this way about my sister and my friends, but I do.

Something is wrong. Something has happened to the two of them while Iziah and I were still at school. Something very, very bad.

"Hey," Sullivan says. "I'm willing to tell you almost anything you want to know. About the past, anyway," he clarifies. His tone is calm now. Like he's interested in smoothing things over. But we're linked. I can feel that link right now. It's a buzz. A feeling of being... occupied. And

I like it. And just when I think that, he sends me a message. *Just stay calm and let me handle this.*

I look at Uzi, since he's the one who's supposed to be in my head, not Sullivan. But I haven't felt a link with him since I kicked him out when I made them take me to Thomas. Sullivan. God, that's confusing.

There's been no humming, at least. No electricity. No feeling of occupation or completeness.

He's not in me, I realize. He's not in me and this is probably why Cyan is pissed off. They think I'm compromised.

"But let's eat first," Sullivan continues. "I feel like I've been starved for weeks."

I smile. Almost laugh. But Iziah sends me a warning look to hold that shit back.

"No hard feelings though, right?"

Iziah squints his eyes at Sullivan. "You sure about that?"

Cyan huffs as she cooks.

"Look," Sullivan says, walking over to the living area and taking a seat in a chair. "I really appreciate the fact that you got us out of that tunnel." He looks at Uzi, then Iziah. "And I know I hurt one of you with a mind blast, but I'm not sure which, so I'll apologize to you both. I'm sorry. I thought you were from Prodigy School. Sadie was out from the gas and couldn't tell me otherwise."

"And I didn't remember, anyway. I was sick, you guys. Sul—" *Shit.* "Thomas saved me, OK? That's why I trust him. He saved me. I already told you that Prodigy sent me to kill him. Then my memory got fucked up, or reset, or something, when he did this massive mind blast in the hospital. Whoever that girl was who walked into the hospital with orders to kill wasn't me. This is me, you guys. I'm back. I'm safe. And all of you helped me get here. All of you," I repeat, looking at Cyan. "Including Thomas."

We all just stare at each other for a few seconds.

"So we need to forget the past and focus on the future."

Cyan and Uzi share a knowing look. This, I decide, is the issue I'm having. They're up to something. And Iziah and I aren't in on it.

"Before we go any further," Uzi says, walking over to a chair across from Sullivan, "I'd just like to know what your intentions are."

"With?" Sullivan asks, glancing at me.

"Not her, you asshole. With Prodigy."

Sullivan shrugs. "Kill the fuckers. What else? So they can't do this again, and again, and again. So they can't hurt any more kids."

Uzi thinks this over. The rest of us wait in silence.

"Now let's hear your intentions," Sullivan says. And even though Uzi wasn't asking about me when he asked first, Sullivan is. And all of us pick up on it.

"Sadie and I are a team," he says, staring Sullivan down. "Just like Iziah and Cyan are a team. So I'm just not sure you fit into our intentions."

"Fair enough," Sullivan says. "But you've got a problem."

"Yeah?" Uzi says. "What's that?"

Sullivan smiles. "You're not linked to her anymore, my friend. I am."

I watch Uzi's reaction very carefully. He doesn't blink or flinch. He doesn't scowl or get angry. So he knew.

Of course, he knew. He can feel the emptiness just as much as I could.

"I'd like you to think long and hard before you try to take what's mine, Alpha."

My mouth drops. I want to scream at him for that remark. But Sullivan sends me a calming message. *Let me handle this.*

"I didn't take anything. It just… happened. I don't think I'm in charge of Sadie's link any more than you are. It's out of my control. But…" Sullivan adds, sending Iziah a sidelong glance. "I've got friends who might be able to sort it out. Get your link back, Uzi. But we'd need to go there and figure it out."

"Who?" Cyan asks.

I look over at her. She's stopped her cooking and her attention is completely focused on Sullivan now.

"The other Alphas, of course. Lincoln Wade has an asset I think could be helpful."

All three of them laugh. Even Iziah. Apparently, an invitation to meet more Alphas is his line in the sand.

"No way," Cyan says.

"Pass," Iziah says.

But Uzi—who is clearly in the leadership position—remains silent.

"Well?" Sullivan asks. "Do you want her back or not?"

We all hold our breath, waiting for Uzi to make up his mind. I feel a little sick over this deal, but Sullivan keeps sending me messages. *Trust me. Trust me. Trust me.*

So I do.

And when Uzi finally says, "OK," I have it all under control.

Sullivan has a plan and it begins now. Because he says, "Good. Then let's skip dinner and get this show on the road."

SULLIVAN

MENTAL MAN 2

CHAPTER TWENTY-THREE

Iziah drives, I sit in front, and Uzi, Cyan, and Sadie squeeze together in the back. It's a predictable arrangement. Uzi wants me to know Sadie is his and he wants to sit behind me.

Needless to say, I'm not worried about either of those things.

"Get off at the next exit," I tell Iziah.

We drove through Wolf Valley about an hour ago, and it took us an hour just to get there, so it's a good thing I didn't just walk out of that house and try to find my own way home. We literally were in the middle of nowhere.

No one's really been talking, and it got dark hours ago, so the beautiful scenery can't make up for the fact that this drive is just boring.

"Thomas?" Sadie asks from the back.

"Hmmm?" I say, trying to act uninterested to keep Uzi's possessive gene from surfacing. I need him compliant and the best way to do that is to let him think Sadie is not what I'm after right now. But she is.

"What are your friends like? Will they... hurt us?"

"Sadie," I say, huffing down a laugh. "I wouldn't bring you here if they were going to hurt you."

"Sure you would," Uzi says. "But the answer is no, Sadie. They won't hurt us. They won't be able to."

I let that remark go and finish answering her question. "Case is a good guy. I don't know if he'll be there or not, but you'll like him. Everyone likes Case."

"And Lincoln?"

"Well…" I smile. "He's a little bit… antisocial. But still, not a bad guy. And Molly will be there. And Sheila. So no, he's not going to start anything. As long as your boyfriend there doesn't start shit."

"If I do," Uzi says, "I'll be sure to finish it."

Sure you will, I think silently.

"How is it possible that the three of you got away so clean?" Cyan asks. She has not said a word since the cabin.

"Define… got away," I say.

"Well, they never came back for you," she says. "Didn't you find that strange?"

"We thought we killed them, Cyan. So no. We didn't expect ghosts to come looking for us."

"It was kinda naive on your part, right?"

"What was?" I say, wishing they'd just go back to shutting up.

"Letting yourself believe you got them all."

"As I said, Cyan, we didn't know there were two schools."

"There's more than two," she snarls.

"I've already gotten that impression. Take a left," I tell Iziah.

Now he is the only one of the three who intrigues me. He's been silent too. Only speaking when he's asking for directions. And I can't figure out if he's just subordinate to Uzi—I've since learned through conversation that Uzi is the older of the two brothers—or if Iziah is just biding his time.

He slows down as he gets off the freeway, stops at the sign, then turns left towards Lincoln's house. This is all

Linc's land out here. He's got hundreds of acres. But the house is hidden down a five-mile private road, which is a little farther up this particular mountain.

"What are we going to do once I'm… reconnected?" Sadie's asking Uzi this, not me. So I just listen.

"Go home," Uzi replies. I can't see him. He's sitting directly behind me. But I can tell he's not interested in answering that question.

"Well, you're welcome to stay the night," I offer. "It's late. You won't want to be driving home tonight."

I get an incredulous laugh from Cyan. But Uzi says, "We'd love to." Which means yeah, this guy definitely has an agenda.

I expect an outburst from Cyan over that little bit of news. But she shuts up.

"OK, it's right up here on the left," I say.

"Where?" Iziah asks.

"That reflector right there," I say. That's the only marking to Lincoln's private road. Iziah turns left and enters the long driveway. The pine trees lining the road are old and tall. It feels a little claustrophobic on the best of sunny days. So driving up here at night, with just the moon shining through the expansive branches over our heads— well, it's more than that now. It's eerie.

Everyone stays silent for the rest of the drive, and when Lincoln's mansion comes into view, lit up in all its glorious detail with outside lamps, I feel, rather than see, every neck craning to get a better view.

"Does he know we're coming?" Sadie asks.

"Nope. He doesn't even know I'm alive. I've been missing for, what? A good month, at least."

"I don't like this," Cyan says. "It feels like a set-up."

"A set up for what?" I ask, just as Iziah comes to a stop in front of the house. But she never has a chance to answer, because spotlights flick on and we're bathed in light so bright, we all have to shade our eyes.

Iziah's door opens and Lincoln is there, his weaponized arm gun positioned at his head. "Who the fuck are you and why the fuck are you here in my—Thomas?" Linc says. "Dude, is that you?"

Never in my life have I been so fucking happy to see Lincoln Wade.

"Where the fuck have you been, asshole? What the fuck, Thomas? I should kill your ass. I should lock you up in the goddamned lab and never let you out. I should—"

He's got a whole litany of things he'd like to do to me, and he never stops talking as he walks around to my side of the truck. When I get out he pulls me into a hug. "I thought you were fucking dead, man. I thought you were dead."

"Not dead," I say, prying his arms off me. It's kinda touching that he missed me, but this isn't the time or place for a reunion. We have business to finish. "Where's Case?"

"Home," Linc says. "But I'll call him. Sheila?"

"I've already alerted him and he's on his way," Sheila says from some device on Linc's person.

I look over at the house and see Molly standing in the doorway, arms crossed like she's cold. "Molly," I say. "Nice to see you again."

She shakes her head at me, like she cannot believe I just showed up out of nowhere after all this time. "I'm fine, thanks," I call.

"Jerk," she calls back. But her reaction isn't as mean as it could be. So I take that as affection. We are siblings after all. She can't really hate me. Just like Thomas can't really hate her. I've never had a problem with Molly. It wasn't me who wanted her dead. That was all Thomas.

"Who the fuck are these people?" Linc says, finally taking notice of who's in my little party.

I cringe, waiting for Uzi to say something back. He and Iziah have already gotten out of the truck. Iziah is walking around the front of the vehicle to join us, but Uzi is only a few feet away. Thankfully, he stays silent.

I don't think he's afraid—though he should be. I think he's a little in awe. It's hard not to feel awe when you meet Lincoln. Thomas and me? We're just regular-looking dudes. So is Case. On the outside, anyway. But Lincoln's uniqueness is on full display. His arm is a weapon. A very powerful weapon that shoots—shit, I don't know all the details, but from what I saw when they blew up Blue Corp… a whole litany of projectiles can be launched from that arm.

I introduce Sadie first, since she's the only one of them I care about. "This is Sadie Scott."

"Nice to meet you." Her voice is sweet and makes Lincoln smile. Cyan scoffs. "This is my sister, Cyan. And my friends, Uzi and Iziah." She points them out, so Lincoln won't be confused about who is who.

"They're Prodigy," I say. Because that's all Lincoln really needs to know.

He squints at them, eyeing each one as he takes them in. Then he lets out a long breath of air. "We should probably go inside."

I smile at Sadie when she relaxes. Even Cyan relaxes. Iziah was never tense, so he does nothing but follow Lincoln when he walks towards Molly. And Uzi only gets more wound up. His muscles are on high alert. I'd like to reach into his stupid head and see just what the fuck he's thinking.

But I don't want him to know I can do that yet. And besides, now that they're here… I have plenty of time for that later.

Dumb fucks have no idea what they've just walked into.

CHAPTER TWENTY-FOUR

Lincoln Wade's mansion is... opulent. That's the only word I have to describe it. It's as big as the Prodigy School, but that's where the similarities end. It's one of those homes with wings. East wing. West wing. Hell, the front of the house looks like they might call it the north wing. There's probably a south wing too. It's made out of stone, which should be enough to conjure up an image of filthy rich. But it's also got a bazillion windows. All symmetrically lining the entire length of the house on each floor.

Three floors, plus... a fourth? That might be an attic?

It looks like a hotel. Like it sleeps five hundred.

"I don't like this," Cyan whispers as we follow the men up the front walk. And even though Sullivan told me to trust him—and I said I would—I am having the same thoughts. "Something's going on here, Sadie."

"Yeah," I say. "Maybe. But just give him a chance."

"I am. For your sake. That's the only reason I'm going along with this."

"What do you mean?" I whisper as they reach the door ahead of us.

"I want you linked with Uzi. He's been upset since we got you back and he realized you're not connected. And he expected you to say something. So when you didn't... well. He took it badly, Sadie. He's hurt. You need to make it up to him."

I narrow my eyes at her. But she either ignores me, or pretends not to see. And then we're at the door and nothing else can be said. So I drop it.

There's a foyer, if that word is even strong enough to describe the three-story room we find ourselves in. I look up at the chandelier. It's got so many crystals hanging from it, the entire space shimmers with dew-drops of shimmering light.

When I look down at the floor I find it just as impressive. Wood—several types, actually. Because there's an inlay of intricate diamond shapes.

"This way," Lincoln says, motioning to the great room beyond. The focal point is a massive stone fireplace that reaches all the way up to the ceiling. I almost get lost as I look up.

"Stop gawking," Cyan whispers. "You look ridiculous." She walks off, following the men into the big room, leaving me behind.

But I ignore her. This place is just way too beautiful not to gawk.

Molly, Lincoln Wade's wife—girlfriend—whatever she is—is next to me. We're both looking at the fireplace. "Do you like it?" she asks.

"I love it." I smile.

"We got that stone from a cathedral ruin here on Lincoln's property."

"Really?" I ask, forcing my eyes down from the stones so I can find her face. She's pretty. Not beautiful or gorgeous. But very pretty. A cute sort of pretty that makes you want to trust her. She reminds me of Sullivan, actually. Then I remember they're siblings. It shows. "Well, it's certainly grabbed my attention."

"Ugghh," she says. "We've been building this house for almost a year. It's finally living up to its potential."

"Ladies?"

I startle at the voice behind us. There's a... woman. But she's...

"I'm Sheila," she says. "Nice to meet you, Sadie Scott."

"Don't mind her," Molly says. "She's creepy at first but she grows on you."

The woman is made out of light.

"I'm a hologram. Well," the Sheila. "I'm a computer, really. But I use the light to make a body. It makes people more comfortable to talk to a face."

"Mmmm," I say. No. Still creepy.

"We should join them, I guess," Molly says. "It seems we have a lot to talk about."

"Yeah," I say, and follow her into the great room. Lincoln is pouring drinks, Iziah is looking at the art on the walls, Cyan is glaring at me, Uzi is glaring at Sullivan, and Sullivan is smiling at me.

I smile back.

Uzi does not miss this little interaction. Neither does Cyan.

But I ignore them both. I don't feel the same way about them since they got me back. I don't know why. I can't explain it. But things are just different.

I feel more connected to Molly and Sullivan right now than I do to Cyan and Uzi. The rational part of me understands that it's because of the mind blast Thomas threw at me back at the asylum. God, that feels like lifetimes ago. It flipped something off. Or maybe it flipped something on. It doesn't really matter. I know this is the reason I'm having a hard time connecting to my sister and friends.

But there's another part of me that thinks it's because they're wrong about things. These Alphas, mostly. Thomas wasn't a bad guy. Not to me. He helped me a lot. And that sex in the shower. Good God.

And I actually like Sullivan a lot. It's weird to think that, considering I first met him when he had me naked and tied to a table. But damn, it was kinda hot. I almost wish he'd do it again.

Sullivan chuckles across the room. Oops. I think he just read my mind.

"Drink?" Lincoln calls out. He's still got his back to us as he finishes pouring. I can see the cannon he's got attached to his arm and I absently wonder how much that thing weighs. His arms are definitely big enough to carry it. He's bigger than Uzi, and Uzi is built like a tank.

I let out a breath, feeling a little relieved at that thought. It occurs to me that I'm... afraid of Uzi. Just a little. But that's more than enough. He's powerful. And intimidating. I don't like it. Iziah is built like Uzi, but he has none of the attitude. Iziah is calm and rational. Uzi is hot-tempered and angry.

Sullivan is built. His body is well-muscled and perfect. But he's not a tank. He's more like a sophisticated rifle, if I want to keep the weapon comparison.

All the men take drinks and stand there sipping for a few moments. Sizing each other up.

Cyan walks over to me and Molly. She takes my hand. "Come sit with me, Sade."

I dutifully follow her over to a couch and we sit. Molly wanders over to Lincoln and he slips his non-weaponized arm around her waist.

They know each other, I realize. That move was well choreographed. She knew which side of him to stand on. He knew she wanted him to claim her with that display of affection.

It makes my heart hurt a little. Every time Uzi has tried to show me affection since I woke up, it was unwanted. But he didn't care. He did it anyway.

Lincoln knows how to read Molly.

Uzi has no idea how to read me.

"So," Lincoln says, looking at Sullivan. "Who's the new crew, Thomas?"

Can't he see he's not Thomas? Because I can see so clearly. Sullivan and Thomas are almost nothing alike inside.

"They saved our asses down in the tunnel," Sullivan replies. "We were on the train car, heading towards the west tower so we could make our way up here and sort some shit out. But then…"

Then I fucked things up with that little… whatever it was.

"Then someone took over the grid or something. We lost power and the gates—"

"Shit," Lincoln says, obviously seeing where this is going.

"Yeah, we almost got split in half. Sadie and I were pretty fucked up after the crash. And we were on the wrong side of the gate. But then the cavalry came in the form of these two." Sullivan motions to Uzi and Iziah with his drink. "And they…" He stops and I wonder what he'll say about the fact that they starved him for weeks. "They saved us." Skips right over that little nugget of unfortunate truth.

"Well," Lincoln says. "We owe you then."

"That's how I see it too," Uzi says. He and Iziah are standing shoulder to shoulder across from Lincoln, Molly and Sullivan.

"So what can I help you with?" Lincoln asks.

Uzi nods his head to Sullivan. "Tell him," he says.

"Well," Sullivan says, looking at Uzi. "It's a long story. You see, my friends don't even know half of what you know about me."

Uzi narrows his eyes at Sullivan. "Do not play games with me, asshole."

"I'm not," Sullivan says, putting his hands up like he's innocent. "They have no clue I'm a mentalist."

"A what?" Molly asks.

"See," Sullivan says. "My superpower, Molly. I'm what they call a mentalist. Just like Uzi here. And Cyan," he adds, looking over at us. "Right, Cyan? You're one too?"

She says nothing.

"But the really interesting part," Sullivan says, looking directly at Lincoln now, "is that we mentalists all have an opposite. Kinda like you and Molly. Alpha and Omega. Only our Omegas are called illusionists. That would be Sadie here. And Iziah, if I'm guessing ·correctly. We're linked to them. Kinda like your genetic bond, but mentally."

"And your friend here," Uzi says, nodding his head at Sullivan, but looking at Lincoln, "has stolen mine away. I want her back."

"Purely," Sullivan says, opening his arms in an innocent gesture, "by accident."

"Ahh," Lincoln says. "Gotcha. Sheila," he says to the air.

The light woman manifests off to his left. "Yes, Lincoln."

"Can you look into this… procedure? I think our new friend Uzi would like his link back."

"It'll take some time for me to pull up the Prodigy records and understand it. But I'm confident I can be ready to help in the morning."

"No," Cyan says. Her whole body is stiff with resistance. "No. Absolutely not. We're not staying the night here. Out of the question. I'm sure if we take Sadie home, away from this stupid Alpha, your link will come back, Uzi. Let's just go."

"Doesn't work that way," I say, surprised that I'm speaking up. "You all know it doesn't work that way. Hell, even I know it doesn't work that way and I'm the most clueless person here. We need to sever it first. Then rebuild it. And the way it was severed in the first place was from Thomas's mind blast back at the hospital. I'm not saying I want him to blast me. I'm not on board with that at all. But we need to do more than just create *distance*."

I look over at Uzi, trying to figure out what he'll do. But he nods at me. I smile, trying to make him feel at ease.

But all I want is a fucking night alone with Sullivan. And I realize now that *this* is why we're here.

Yes, the message scrolling across my vision overlay says. *Yes.*

He wants to be alone with me and that was never going to be possible back at the other house. But here? In this monster of a mansion… here we can do whatever we want.

"So tomorrow?" the Sheila asks. "Say, nine AM? You should probably not eat," she says, looking first at Uzi, then at me. "Just in case the procedure requires general anesthesia."

"I'm not going under," Uzi says. "Fuck you if you think I trust you to put me under."

"It probably won't come to that," Lincoln says. "Sheila's just being cautious. Hell, she's done hundreds of modifications on me and I almost never went under. So unless you're a pussy"—he looks right at Uzi—"it shouldn't come to that."

Uzi glares at him, but then takes his attention to Cyan. "What do ya say?"

Cyan is still stiff with resistance, but she nods her head. Agreeing with him.

No one even bothers asking Iziah. And he offers up no opinion on the matter.

"Great," Molly says. "And you're in luck. If you had shown up last month there'd be no guest rooms. But the upstairs was just finished so we have plenty of space now. I'll show everyone to their rooms."

I'm the first to follow Molly. When I look over my shoulder Uzi is right behind me. Cyan has to be pulled to her feet by Iziah, but by the time we make it to the grand staircase and begin to climb, we're all lined up like ducks in a row.

I have to give it to these Alphas. They're great manipulators. I bet Uzi never thought in a million years he'd be going along with an Alpha plan, let alone spending the night in one of their houses.

We get to the top and begin walking down a long hallway, passing door after door. They are all closed.

"OK," Molly says, stopping at a door about three quarters of the way down the hall. "Who's rooming with whom?"

"Cyan and I can take this one," Iziah says.

"Perfect. Uzi and Sadie, you can follow me."

Oh great. I have to share a room with Uzi? How am I supposed to orchestrate dirty sex with Sullivan when I'm rooming with Uzi?

I smile internally at my audacity.

"I have a great one down at the end here. It's got an amazing bathtub," Molly says, winking at me over her shoulder.

I shoot her a weak smile just as Uzi grabs my hand. Why can't he take a hint?

"Here you go. Everything you need is in there. But if I forgot anything, just—"

"Excuse me, Molly?" The Sheila thing pops into existence.

"Yes, Sheila?"

"I'm going to need Sadie to come down to the lab. I looked up the protocol and just realized I have a lot of prep work to do. Tests," she says, looking at me. "But mostly painless."

"What the fuck is this about?" Uzi growls. "She's not going anywhere with that thing."

"OK," Sheila says, nodding her head. "We can do it in the morning. But you'll probably have to stay another night. The procedure appears to be long. Quite complicated. And we want to do it right the first time. You don't screw with people's minds without some forethought."

Uzi is ready to explode. I might not be linked to him anymore, but he's squeezing my hand so tight, it makes me wince. "Uzi," I say. "Let's just get it done. I want this to be over, don't you?"

He stares at Sheila a moment longer. Then Molly. Then his gaze lands on me.

I rub his arm to help him calm down. "I'll be fine."

"I'm going with you then."

"Well," Sheila says, sheepish smile on her face. Jesus. I don't know who programmed her emotions, but she's got this shit down. "She's going to need some privacy, Uzi. I'll have her completely naked for most of it."

"So?"

I laugh. "What do you mean so? I'm not going to let you hover over my naked body while I have tests done. It's invasive, Uzi."

"You want this, don't you?"

I know what he's implying. That I'm eager to get away from him. And I am. But I can turn that around. Manipulating what people see when they look at me also involves manipulating what they think. "I thought you wanted this too! Don't you want us to be linked again?"

"That's not what I meant," he says.

"Then what do you mean?" I ask. "Do you think I'm excited about this?" I raise my voice a little. Put an edge on my words. "This was your idea. None of this is my fault, Uzi. I'm here because you wanted to come here. I'm doing this because you said we should. And now you're going to accuse me of what? Ditching you?"

He shrinks back. Just a little. But just enough. "No. I'm not trying to be an asshole. I'm just…"

"Insecure?" Sheila offers.

He glares at her. "No."

"Good," she says, taking control. "Then she comes with me. We'll do all the prep work and tomorrow afternoon you can be on your way. I, for one, cannot wait for you to leave."

"Sheila," Molly says, chastising. "Stop it. They're guests. I tell you what," Molly says to Uzi. "I'll bring you status reports every hour. And you don't have to stay in these rooms. Just come downstairs whenever you want. Lincoln and I will be up for a while. And Case and Lulu will be here soon. We'll have dinner."

"He can't eat," Sheila reminds him.

"Ignore her," Molly says to Uzi. "I ignore her too. But her and Linc are a package deal. So we endure." Molly rubs Uzi's other arm. And holy shit. These people are way out of my league in the manipulation department. She's playing him like an instrument.

Uzi finally huffs out some air, giving in. "Fine."

"Great. Come with me, Sadie. I'll show you down to the lab."

I turn to follow the walking woman made of light. But Uzi's not done. "I want hourly updates," he says. "With video. Or I'll just find my own way to that lab."

"Good luck with that," Sheila mutters as we walk back towards the stairs. "Don't worry, Sadie. He'll never find it."

I'm not sure that's a good thing, even though she makes it out to be one.

When we get to the stairs, we don't go down them. Just keep walking. And when I look over my shoulder I expect to see Uzi watching this little change up, but he's got his back to me. He and Molly are having a heated conversation that involves lots of waving arms.

"Open this door here, Sadie," Sheila says.

I do, still checking to see if Uzi is watching. But no. Still arguing with Molly.

So I slip inside and he never sees a thing.

Yes. These people are all very coordinated and clever.

I close the door and find myself in a room. A nice one, for sure. But nothing special.

"I have no body in this room," Sheila says through some hidden microphone. "Molly won't let me into any of the bedrooms after that nursery incident. So I'll just talk you through it. Go over to the fireplace, find the seventh brick on the far left, and push."

"I don't think this night could get any weirder," I whisper. But I do as I'm told and yes, it's a secret door built into a fireplace. I stare into the darkness as it opens up, wondering just what the fuck I've gotten myself into.

"You haven't seen anything yet, sweetie. Now go down the steps like a good girl and meet me in the dungeon."

SULLIVAN
MENTAL MAN 2

CHAPTER TWENTY-FIVE

As soon as the new crew is out of sight, Sheila says, "Case just landed in the helicopter. He'll be here in a few minutes. I'll take care of Sadie." Then she disappears.

I take my attention back to Lincoln. He squints his eyes at me, then whispers, "Sullivan?" I nod, which makes him exhale in relief. "Follow me."

He heads towards the east wing of the mansion and goes into his office. I follow and close the door behind me.

"Are we on track or what?" Linc asks.

"Well"—I laugh—"it's not *exactly* going as planned."

"No shit. What the fuck are you doing? We had an agreement."

"I know," I say, sighing as I drop into a deep leather chair. Linc doesn't sit. Just leans on his desk and folds his cannon arms across his chest. "But Thomas, man. I don't know what's happening to us. The dude is in denial or something. I can't get him back now."

"I hate it when you talk like that. You know I hate it. You're the *same* guy."

I sigh. "How many times do I have to explain this to you?"

"Apparently once more. Because no matter what you say, you're still Thomas. He's still you."

The door opens and Case walks in. "Hey," he says, closing the door behind him.

"What the fuck are you wearing?" Lincoln asks Case.

"You like 'em?" Case replies, sliding the SpyGlasses down his nose. "I just got this model in today. They're going into distribution tomorrow. My end of this little catastrophe is done."

"Already?" I ask. "Damn. I really missed a lot."

"Hey, Thomas," Case says. "And yeah, we didn't appreciate your little disappearing act. Where the fuck have you been for the past month?"

"I was just getting to that," Linc says. "But this here isn't Thomas."

"What?" Case is not so much surprised as he is annoyed. "We had a deal, asshole."

"I *know*," I say again. These fuckers are giving me a headache. "But that stupid doctor pushed some drugs into him—unbalanced everything—and then he blasted the whole floor with his goddamned mind. It wiped Sadie Scott's memory. She came to get me, by the way. And take me back to Prodigy. Which is still very much alive."

Case almost snorts out his laugh. "Well, that was lucky. Did he mean to do that?"

"I don't think so. I didn't know she was in the building, so I highly doubt he did. Yasmine gave him some drug—which, from what I can tell, split us up again. He was in and out, and then we were on the train car heading towards the west tower and either he knocked out the power or Sadie did, but either way it resulted in a fuck-up of epic proportions. And ever since then he's been… missing."

"He's not missing, you dumbass." Case walks up to me and raps his knuckles on my head. "He's right in there where he's always been."

"Are you two going to complain? Or should we try to move forward? Because I'm not in the fucking mood."

"So the plan is shot?" Linc asks.

216

"The plan is only shot if the two of you fucked up your end."

"Hey," Case says. "I got the SpyEye software on every handheld device in Cathedral City. I did my part. Distribution is done."

"Good," I say, looking at Lincoln. "And the program? You got that ready?"

He nods. "It's ready. But it hasn't been tested yet because you and Thomas decided to go off the goddamned deep end. Why now? Why, after all these years?"

"I have no clue why he does this shit. He just... overreacted, I guess."

"You pissed him off," Case replies. "And he wasn't ready for it."

"It's not my fault you fucked up his protocol. I'm not the one who shot him with some interference cocktail while I was under the influence of a supercomputer."

"OK," Linc says, walking around his desk to take a seat behind it. "We don't have time for the blame game. Case fucked up. We get it."

"I didn't fuck up! Molly poisoned me with that goddamned lariat thing the Blue Boar gave her."

"It wasn't Molly's fault," Linc growls. "So shut up about that."

"Who cares whose fault it is," I say. Thomas was always the leader of this little operation. The rest of us were on board, but he's the one holding it all together. And right now, his absence is painfully apparent. Because he's got a way of handling things that I haven't quite mastered.

I need to up my game.

"It doesn't matter how we got here," I say. "We're here and we need to deal. So if we're ready, let's just press play, right? Get this show on the road."

"And just how the fuck do you propose we do that without Thomas?" Lincoln says. "He's got all the initiation codes."

"I have access to that too," I say. "We're good, I swear."

I look at Linc. His eyes are trained on mine. Narrowed down into little evil slits. I glance over at Case. He hasn't quite perfected that look, but it's close enough. They don't believe me.

"We only have one chance," Case says. "One chance to flip this fucking town upside down and set things right. We cannot risk doing it without Thomas."

I smile and look at Lincoln. "Well, according to Linc here, I *am* Thomas. So what's the difference?"

"The difference is," Case continues, "that Thomas has his shit together and you don't. That's why he's been in charge and you haven't. You're a loose fucking cannon, Sullivan. And what's this I hear about bringing that new crew here? They are not on our side."

"I didn't send Sadie to fuck things up," I say, staying calm. That cocktail of drugs Thomas was on really did keep him on track. And me. And as reluctant as I am to admit it, it was working pretty well. But now? Nothing seems to be working right. "And Thomas needed her to escape the asylum after the blast."

"So why bring them *here?*" Lincoln asks. "You really want to unlink yourself from Sadie? Because I have to tell you, it was pretty clear that she wants nothing to do with that Uzi guy."

"Wait," Case says. "I missed this part. Bring me up to speed."

I do, letting him in on all the parts that seem relevant, leaving out those that are not. Like… how much I want to fuck that girl right now. And that's pretty much the only reason we're here tonight. I end it with, "So they're staying the night and we're going to do the procedure tomorrow."

"It is a real thing?" Case asks. "This unlinking bullshit?"

"How the fuck should I know?"

"It's not," Lincoln says. "I'd know about it. And for sure Sheila is not setting up anything of the sort down in the lab right now. She's just stringing them along to buy us some time."

"What we need to figure out," I say, "is how to get Thomas out of whatever mental cell he's locked in right now. Because even though being in charge is kinda fun, we can't be sure we're on track until things are back to normal. You can doubt me all you want, you guys. But I'm just as interested in revenge as the rest of you. I'm not about to throw away fifteen years of planning over this little hiccup in the chain of command."

"You're definitely not in charge anymore," Linc says.

I laugh. "Like hell. I'm the one with all the initiation codes."

"We need to get rid of these extra people and I have a feeling that Uzi guy isn't going to go quietly. We can't have this kind of distraction if we enact the plan. So how do you propose we get rid of them without a fight since your whole idea is based on bullshit?"

"I propose…" I cannot stop the smile. "That we just drug the fuck out of Uzi, Iziah, and Cyan, drop them off somewhere to sleep it all off, and bring Sadie in on the deal. She and I are a great team, man. I'm telling you, her illusionist skills are phenomenal. She's highly trained."

"She was sent to kill you, dumbass. So you know, you should probably sort that out before you bring her in on the most fucked-up plan this world has ever seen!" Lincoln yells that last part. There might be veins sticking out from his neck.

"OK," I say. "I can see I haven't explained things well." So I start over, letting them in on my theory. "Prodigy still exists. Sadie and those other three came from another school. They escaped a couple years ago, but Iziah and Sadie got left behind or some shit. So whoever sent Sadie to kill me—can we just assume that was the Red Robber? I mean, it only makes sense that Prodigy was behind that computer takeover of Cathedral City last spring."

"Why not?" Case says. "Does it matter what we call them? Red Robber, Prodigy, they're just the enemy and that's all that matters."

"Right," I say, pointing at him. "So the enemy sent Sadie to kill me, Thomas went apeshit crazy with his little mind blast and fucked up all their plans, because while it didn't kill Sadie, it did wipe her programming. Meanwhile, Cyan and Uzi see this as the best opportunity to break Iziah out, then they go after Sadie to get her back too. They're just a bunch of dumb kids trying to break free, just like we were fifteen years ago. But either way, their part in this is fortuitous, but coincidental. So who cares about the new crew. We should just drug them tomorrow. Take them out of the equation."

"Even Sadie?" Lincoln asks, calmer now.

"I want her," I say, just to be clear. "And I'm pretty sure Thomas wants her too. But yeah, even Sadie. She and I are only at the very beginning stages of our soon-to-be lifetime partnership. She stays here with them. Then we go to town, initialize the program, blow everyone's minds, and watch them all fall down."

"Sounds like a plan," Case says.

We both look over at Lincoln. He's still thinking about it.

"What?" I ask. "It's perfect. Kills all the birds with one stone."

"I feel like we're missing something," he says. "Something important."

"We have the program," I say, holding up a finger to tick off boxes. "We have the delivery device," I hold up another finger. "We have the distribution." Three fingers now. "And we have the initiation all set up. All we gotta do is tell it to start."

"People are gonna be pissed off." Case laughs.

"Very," I say, laughing with him.

But Lincoln isn't laughing. "We're missing something."

"We've thought of everything," I say. "Thomas has been planning this for fifteen years. We've thought of everything."

He hesitates, still thinking it through. "I can't find a hole in the plan, even though I know there is one. Can't you try to bring Thomas back?" he asks. It's almost a plea. "I'd feel a lot better if it was Thomas in charge here and not..."

"Not me?" I say, finishing for him.

He shrugs. "It's not personal, Sullivan. But we all know you're the fuck-up in the family. Which was why you volunteered to be the secondary personality."

"Hey, I'm the first to admit that Thomas is the evil genius on this team. But I'm all you've got. So we move forward with me taking the lead or we wait it out for Thomas to find his way back. But this is our time, you guys. We've set it up, it's all ready to go, and if we let our moment pass by it might never come around again. So let's make up our minds right now and just move forward."

"I'm in," Case says, looking at Lincoln. "Sullivan's never been a traitor. He's not going to start now. And yeah, he's no Thomas, but he's as close as it gets. I say we move forward tomorrow. Let's do it."

Lincoln stares at us. First Case, then me. And finally, he nods his head. "OK. I'm in. Let's do it."

A collective sigh of relief fills the room.

This is it. After more than fifteen years of planning we're about to get our revenge. And when it's all said and done, Cathedral City will never be the same.

"Perfect," I say. "Someone got a phone I can borrow?"

Lincoln hands his SkyEye sat phone over and I take it and call the number Thomas set up. This will initiate the satellites and put them into the position to seamlessly interact with the towers. "Done," I say, once the codes have been entered. "They'll be ready in twelve hours. Now, let's take the new crew out without drama, OK? Divide and conquer. That's the plan right now. I need cover so I can take care of Sadie tonight."

Sheila blips into the room. "I've got them in their rooms. Uzi is alone, Cyan is with Iziah, and I'm taking Sadie down to the lab for her tests." She does air quotes when she says the word 'tests.' "Molly told them we're having dinner. So she's just gonna slip the drugs into their food, then they'll sleep it off."

"How long will it last?" I ask.

"We can re-dose them after they're out," Sheila says. "No worries on that."

"You can't babysit them, Sheila," Lincoln says. "That would require you to split in two and we need you *whole* for tomorrow. Sullivan just initiated the satellites. We're on a timer now and we need you one hundred percent present for when the shit goes down."

"We'll get the dosage right, don't worry about a thing."

Everyone, including Sheila, lets out a long breath of air. This is it.

We're really taking over the City and there's nothing anyone can do to stop us.

CHAPTER TWENTY-SIX

"Come on," the Sheila calls. "It lights up as you walk so you won't trip. I had some complaints from the last girl."

"Last girl?" I say, still dubiously staring down into the stairwell.

"Lulu. She has a lot of ideas," Sheila says, tapping her… head. Which makes her light pattern shudder. A chill runs up my spine because everything about her is… wrong. "She said someone could trip and fall when we lead them up and down those dungeon stairs. So, being the accommodating entity that I am, I had the bots install motion sensor lights. Now when you step, the next step lights up so you can see where you're going."

"Where am I going? It's not really a dungeon, right? You're messing with me, right?"

Her eyes twinkle. And I realize she's made of lights so most of her is twinkling, but… "Just walk down the stairs. But don't worry, Sullivan is coming as soon as your boyfriend calms down."

"He's not my boyfriend," I say. I don't even think he's my friend at this point. But I tuck that little detail down. I'm not sure these people are my friends either.

I have only two options though. Go with the computer woman or go back to Uzi. The thought of being stuck with Uzi all night instead of Sullivan is just… no. I don't trust him. Something is off with Cyan too. And Iziah. Why is he so quiet? Uzi wasn't so in charge before. Not that I remember. Am I remembering it wrong? No, I decide. Something is off with Iziah.

But something is off with you too, Sadie.

Yes. Something is definitely off with me.

So I step through the secret doorway, which immediately closes behind me, and the steps begin to light up under my feet as I spiral my way down.

"Almost there," Sheila calls out from the bottom. "Only a few more turns and you're done."

There's a shimmering pattern on the wall. Like there's a pool down here. It's creepy and soothing at the same time. But when I step out into the room I realize it's a giant aquarium filled with rainbow-colored luminescent jellyfish.

"Wow, that's some tank you have there."

"Lincoln loves them. We originally got them for experiments, but now they're just pets. Come this way. I have a room ready for you."

The rest of the... laboratory is filled with a mixture of science equipment and tools. There's a huge screen on one wall with lots of complicated-looking controls. But there's also a black muscle car up on a lift.

"Is he a mechanic or a mad scientist?" I mutter under my breath as I pick my way through a maze of toolboxes and try to avoid stepping on all the little scurrying robots.

"Which do you prefer?" Sheila asks. "Pick one. That's what he is."

"Great." I finally make it to the... operating room— what the hell am I doing here?—and wait for Sheila to tell me what to do.

"Lie down," she says. "I'm just going to do a quick brain scan and—"

"Wait," I say, grabbing her arm because I forgot she's not real. Touching her is a weird mixture of heat and vibration. I pull my hand away instinctively, which makes her chuckle. "I don't want to be unlinked from... Thomas."

"Cut the Thomas crap, Sadie. We know he's Sullivan. And don't worry, no such procedure even exists. I'm not sure how this whole linking thing works because Thomas was never one to let me poke and prod him much. But I do know there's no protocol for unlinking in our records."

"So why am I here?"

"Well, I am going to run some tests on you just to get a handle on this whole illusionist-mentalist dichotomy. I've never had that opportunity before. But mostly, Sadie, you're here so Sullivan can have his way with you tonight."

"Oh." I smile. "OK, then. On the... what is that? A chair? An operating table?"

"Both, really. Do you like it?" Sheila asks. "I designed it myself. It's been customized for Lincoln, since he's usually the one on there. But it worked fine for Case too. It's to give my robot minions proper access. Since, you know, I don't have arms."

And that's when a small army of robots roll into the room. Some of them are walking on metal legs, like spiders. One tries to climb up my pant leg, but I kick it off and it goes flying into the wall.

"Don't be rude, Sadie. That's just me in another body." Her words make me shiver. All this is so weird. "Now climb onto the table like a good girl and let me get my readings."

I hesitate. Everything in me is screaming, *Run!* But to where? I'm in the goddamned dungeon.

"Trust me," Sheila says. "I'm not going to hurt you. It would make Sullivan mad. And I like Sullivan. Not as much as Thomas, but he's the default lead while Thomas is... vacationing."

I laugh at her description of the missing Thomas personality. "I like Thomas too. I like them both equally, in fact. Where do you think he went?"

"I don't know," Sheila says. "But it concerns me. Believe me, as soon as we get rid of your friends up there, I'll have Sullivan in this chair too. They've had an agreement for decades. Thomas is the outward personality and Sullivan is the inner one. Why it's all screwed up now, I have no idea."

"So you guys all knew he was… split? By Prodigy?"

"I helped them do it," Sheila says. "But that's before Lincoln stole me from the school and reprogrammed me into what I am now. I'm not that machine anymore. He made me self-aware. It was my choice to work with the Alphas. I'm not a threat to you, Sadie. These three men are my whole life. I'd do anything to help them. And that help extends to Molly, and Lulu, and now you. Sullivan brought you here because he knows you'll be safe. I'll help you any way I can. Trust me and get on the table."

A memory hits me like a brick to the chest. I lean over and let it flow. My missing time from before the crash.

Thomas did say the name Sheila back at the tower. God, that seems like so long ago. Did he really take me shopping for clothes? It makes me smile, even though looking back, it was an absurd thing to do.

It was, I realize, a little gesture of friendship. Something to make me happy. Something to make me forget the shitty situation we were in.

It was… nice.

So I walk over to the chair, but just as I'm about to hop up, she says, "Take off your clothes, please. You need to be naked for this."

"I thought you were joking about that. To keep Uzi away."

"No," she says, her light mouth flickering into a smile. "I need you completely bare. There's a gown over in that closet. So strip and climb up on the table. The sooner we get the tests done, the sooner you can be back upstairs with Sullivan for the night. And don't worry about modesty. I'm a professional."

Her form disappears before I can argue further. I do not want to do this. Something inside me is screaming that none of this is good for me. That things are about to go very wrong and it all starts with this little room right here.

But I'm all about sucking it up and dealing. She's right. The sooner I let her get the tests done, the sooner I can get the hell out of this... laboratory and be alone with Sullivan. I have so much to say to him. So many questions.

I take all my clothes off and wrap the gown around my body as best I can, then hop onto the table. The little robots, which didn't leave with the Sheila light form, start scrambling around the room. Several climb onto the table with me, and just as I'm about to swat them away, Sheila appears again. "OK, Lincoln filled me in on the details. I'm going to do some scans to see if we can't find your missing memories."

"I got my memories back," I say. "Even those few days back at the tower with Thomas."

She smiles at me. It's one of those, you're-so-cute-but-naive-is-a-better-word-for-it, smiles. "Sorry, sweetie. But even I know you're missing more than that. Why else would you be with those people?"

These people. She means Uzi, Iziah, and Cyan.

And even though I am supposed to think of them as friends—no, more than friends, as family—I don't. I really, really don't. I know they're bad. I just feel it.

227

A bot pricks my finger, then another is attaching an IV. In seconds, I'm hooked up to a bag of drugs, and seconds after that, I'm starting to feel dizzy and tired.

"Don't worry, Sadie," the Sheila says as she leans over my body. "I know how to pry them out of you. I'll find out what really happened before Thomas blasted you with his mind."

She said she wouldn't hurt me… but she lied.

Then I'm nowhere. I'm in blackness. I'm floating in non-reality.

"Sadie."

I am swimming in darkness.

"Sadie. Wake up now."

The black water feels thick, but now there's a light above me.

"Come on."

I move towards it, slowly. So slowly.

"Sadie."

I reach the top and burst into the light.

My eyes open and Sullivan is standing over me. "Hey," I say. "What happened?" I reach for him. *Try* to reach for him. But I can't.

I'm tied down again.

CHAPTER TWENTY-SEVEN

Her expression is calm. Serene almost. Until she realizes I've got her tied to a bed.

"What are you doing?" she asks, lifting her head up to try to see what's going on.

"Shhh," I say, petting her hair. "Just enjoy it."

I get a chuckle for that answer. "Sullivan…"

"No, really," I say. "You liked it last time." She opens her mouth to protest, but I put up a hand. "Don't bother denying it. You've got some kink in you, Sadie Scott. I knew that the first time I tied you up. But…" I almost growl, that's how turned on it makes me. "The way you got off."

Sadie lets out a small, whimpering moan.

My dick grows in my jeans. The thick, hard shaft presses up against the fabric, begging me to set it free. It wants to be in her mouth. It wants to be in her pussy.

"Just enjoy it, Sadie. Relish it. I have a feeling you haven't had many enjoyable moments lately. Let me give you this one night, at least."

She stares at me for a few seconds. Wiggles her body. Tugs on the soft silk bindings on her wrists and ankles holding her captive on the bed, like she wants to reach for me.

"Sullivan… I haven't…"

"Shhh," I say. I'm not sure what she's about to tell me. Hasn't had sex in forever, maybe. But I don't care. "I know just what to do."

She holds my gaze just a little longer. Her eyes searching mine for encouragement. It scares her a little. To be tied up like this. To be out of control. To be powerless.

She's not powerless. One word would make me stop and she has to know that. She could say no. And if she did I'd be disappointed, for sure. But I'd stop. I'd untie her. I'd fuck her whatever way she wants or not at all. It's up to her.

I say all that with my eyes and she gets it. We're linked. She knows me. I know her. We're already a team, whether she knows it or not. Partners.

Her whole body relaxes. Her breathing softens, her heart rate slows.

"Good girl," I say, enjoying her young, nubile body as I take her in. Her skin is so soft I just want to stroke it.

So I do.

One fingertip touches her lips. Her eyes are locked on mine as she opens her mouth. She sucks on my finger and it takes every ounce of willpower not to close my eyes and moan. Her mouth sucks on me and my dick grows to its full length inside my jeans.

Not yet though. Not yet. Not until she's ready to beg me.

And she *will* beg.

I give her two fingers in her mouth as I massage her nipple with my other hand. Her eyes close—briefly—but fly open again, like she's been commanded to look at me.

I smile. She continues to suck. Her mouth is so wet it coats my fingers and begins to drip down her chin.

Good God. I have to take a deep breath. My cock wants to be inside that wet mouth. Wants to push its way down her throat. Wants to come inside her and feel her tremble with pleasure.

I pinch her nipple to break her building ecstasy. She whimpers, "Sullivan," around my insistent fingers.

I grip her breast firmly, making her back arch up a little off the bed. But my mouth is there on her nipple, sucking on her the way she's sucking on me. It's just a little teaser for what's to come next.

My grip relaxes and I let my fingertips wander down to her rib cage. My touch is soft, gentle, light. Her skin prickles from her shiver. She wants more.

I continue to learn the curves of her body with my hand. Across each rib. Down to her hip where I trace small circles on the soft flesh with my thumb. Her back arches again. She wants me between her legs. And I'll get there eventually. But not yet. I'm not done exploring her.

I take my kiss to her stomach, licking the skin around her belly button. Kissing her, then nipping until she has to draw in a deep breath. It comes out in a gasp when I continue, my mouth making its way towards her pussy. But I go slow. Agonizingly slow. I want my fingers in her first. I want to know she's wet for me. And when they find her entrance and push inside—she gushes. She coats me with her want.

Goddamn. I might die.

Her scent fills the air as I stretch her pussy to accommodate two fingers. She sucks harder on my fingertips still in her mouth, lapping her tongue against them, letting me push them towards the back of her throat.

And just as she's about to gag I sweep my tongue over her clit.

"Ohhhh," she moans, her whole body squirming. She strains against her bindings again. She wants to grab my head and push my face even further between her legs. She wants to wrap her legs around my neck and keep me here forever.

Indeed. This is heaven.

I flick my tongue against her clit. Her pussy tightens around my fingers. They are swimming in her desire as it pours out of her.

I want to taste that desire so bad.

When I pull my fingers out of her mouth and her pussy, she moans, "Nooooo."

I reach down for the hem of my t-shirt and drag it over my head. But I leave the pants on. I want her on her knees in front of me. I want her head back, eyes up—the only thing on her mind is my face—when I tell her to unbutton my jeans and take out my cock.

A moan comes out of my mouth now. God, I can't wait to fuck her.

But not yet.

I sit between her open legs. She's watching me when I look at her. I smile. She says, "Stop teasing me." But it comes out so throaty and low, it only makes me want to tease her more.

"No chance," I reply, lowering my head to her pussy. I place my hands on her inner thighs, pushing her legs open, making the binding around her ankles stretch tight.

But I hover. Just over the top of her sweet spot.

"Sullivan," Sadie whimpers. "Come on. This is torture. This is cruel and unusual—"

I blow softly. She sucks in a breath with a hiss and her legs prickle with goosebumps as the light current of air passes over her clit.

She squirms again. Desperately trying to make her pussy touch my hovering mouth.

I smile as I lower my lips to hers. She's so wet, her sweetness coats them.

And then I lick her.

"Oh, shit. Oh, shit. Oh… yes. Lick me!"

She arches for me with her hands, but the silk bindings keep her contained. She pulls on them so hard, it rattles the headboard.

She starts gasping for air as I sweep my tongue back and forth across her opening, lapping up her desire. She tastes so sweet and delicious, I lean in and bury my whole face in her pussy.

She's panting now. Like there's not enough air in this room to sustain her.

"Fuck me," she whimpers.

I ignore her and take my tongue to her clit.

"Fuck me," she says again.

I flick it back and forth a few times, then grab it with my lips and suck it into my mouth.

"Ahhh, shit!" she moans. And it's loud.

"Shhh." I laugh, my head still buried between her legs. "I'll gag you if you scream."

"You're driving me crazy," she says, a little more in control.

"I thought that was the point?"

"Fuck me, you ass!"

I laugh again, but this makes a little vibration against her already over-stimulated nub and only serves to drive her wilder.

When I look up from between her legs and find her face, she's got her eyes tightly shut. Her lips are pressed together.

"Do you want to come, Sadie?" I ask her between licks.

"Mmmm-hmmm," she hums. "So bad," she whispers.

"Should I let you?"

"You better." She chuckles. "I'm going to die right now if you—" I flick my tongue back and forth across her clit as she says this, so the last word falls away.

She twists her hips like she wants to fuck my face. And good God, I picture her hovering over my face as I continue to lick. I picture her soft thighs pressed up against my scratchy jaw. I picture her rubbing her pussy over my chin as my tongue tickles her clit.

"Then come," I say. "Come right now and let me lick it off you."

She's panting hard. Her hips are moving in little circles as she seeks out more friction. My hands grip her thighs, pinning her legs to the bed as I spread her open and bury my face in her pussy.

Her body stiffens. She's so close. But I pull back, just to keep my supervillain street cred in good standing, and deny her at the last minute.

"Sullivan!" She laughs. "Stop it right now."

"I did stop." I chuckle.

"No, keep going! You know what I mean! You fucking tease!"

I take a moment to watch her struggle. She opens her eyes. She begs me silently. I see it inside her. I can feel her.

"We're partners," I whisper.

She's holding her breath because when she stops, it rushes out in a huff. "Yes," she says, like this was a question.

"You can't change your mind, Sadie. I don't want you to change your mind."

"I won't," she insists. "Just please… keep going. Let me come, Sullivan. Let me come. I will be yours forever if you do. I promise. I swear. I will. I will. I will—"

I spread her pussy open with my fingers and dive back down.

This time she's ready. She won't let me deny her again. She strains on her silk bindings. The headboard rattles against the tension.

And then... she has her release.

Her pussy begins to contract. I stick my fingers inside her so I can feel it happen. She squeezes them, her muscles clamping down as a pool of heat and desire coats my skin. Her back arches and she moans. Loud, at first. But then she presses her lips together and takes it like the Supergirl she is.

I watch all this looking up between her legs, my tongue still going crazy as she tries to deal with the overstimulation.

But I don't pull away until her pussy stops gripping my fingers and she lets out a long sigh.

I sit up, reach over and untie one leg, then the other.

She just lies there. Eyes closed. Body relaxed. I crawl up her body and kiss her mouth, make her taste the sweetness of her climax with her own tongue. "The deal is done now, Trip Chick. It's official. You're mine."

But then... out of nowhere, I say, "And mine too." Only it's not my voice. It's not me.

It's Thomas.

CHAPTER TWENTY-EIGHT

"What?" I say, confused. What the hell was that? Sullivan's voice is deeper. The jokes and fun are gone.

"Shit," he says.

"What just—"

"Thomas," he says.

Then his face changes. Not a lot. It doesn't contort or turn into something I don't recognize. But we've been through a lot together, so I recognize what's happening.

"That's right," Thomas says, but to Sullivan, not me. "It's me. What the fuck is going on? Why was I locked out? Why was I—"

"Dude," Sullivan says. Holy shit, this is weird. "I didn't lock you out. You're the one who over-reacted when I surfaced again."

"You," Thomas growls back at... himself, "were supposed to stay buried. We made a deal, asshole."

"A deal? That's what you call it? You forced me down with drugs, dickhead."

"What the—" Thomas looks down at our bodies. He's on top of me, his bare chest pressing against my bare breasts. My wrists are still tied to the headboard with silk. But then he smirks. "Did I interrupt something?"

"Umm…" I have no idea what to say.

He flops over, but one hand rests on my breast. He squeezes it. "Were we done?" He laughs. "Or just getting started?"

"Umm…"

He smiles at me. Thomas. Wow. This is so strange. "It's just me, Sadie. We've already had sex. I mean, before. Back at the tower. Are we at Lincoln's?" He looks around, taking in the room. "I guess they finished the guest rooms. Never seen this one before. But this room has Molly written all over it."

"Yeah…" I say, unable to form any coherent words right now.

"It's weird?" he asks.

I nod.

"Too weird to deal with? Or just a little weird and you need a minute?"

I swallow hard as I try to get a grip on the situation. "Can you untie my hands?" I ask.

"We're done with that?"

I nod my head again. "Please."

He reaches up and releases one arm. Then leans over my body to release the other one. He smells like sex. Like me. My sex. All over his face.

He's the same man who just ate my pussy like it's delicious. Who stuck his fingers inside me and licked my clit. Who tied me up and drove me crazy.

And yet… he's not.

He relaxes back on the bed. "Something's wrong."

"Yeah… well." Shit. What the hell do you say in this kind of situation?

"Do you like him better than me? Is that it?"

"No," I blurt out. "No, that's not it."

"I'm a freak? But by the way, you're a freak too. So. You know. Wondertwins and all that good shit."

There's a tingling in my head and I realize he's in there. "Stop it."

"I'm just trying to figure things out, Sadie. I'm sorry. The last thing I remember was the crash. Something happened. And then... blackness. How the fuck did we get here?"

"It's a really long story." I sigh. And I don't want to relive it, actually. But I don't say that last part out loud.

"Totally understand," he says, reaching for me. He hugs me close and even though it should freak me out, it doesn't. He's inside me. For real. Not the same way Sullivan is. Sullivan's in control of... the *super* parts of me. Whatever's running the... *software* in there. Thomas has access to the emotional parts.

He soothes me. Just his touch soothes me. My climax is waning, and that should come with at least a little disappointment since Sullivan and I were just getting started. But it doesn't. Thomas is fulfilling a need I have, something I can't quite explain.

"Love," he says, reading my mind.

"I thought you couldn't read minds? Sullivan said you only grab memories when people die or something."

"Well"—he sighs—"things changed, I guess. I got an upgrade."

"Are you OK?" I ask. "And where does Sullivan go when you... take over?"

He hesitates for a few moments. Like he's thinking really hard about this question.

"Thomas?" I ask again.

"I don't know how I feel. Weird. But I can't decide if it's just because I'm not used to Sullivan being around, or if it's because something else is going on."

"What could be going on besides that?"

"You tell me. I'm sorta lost right now."

I shift my body so we're looking at each other. I study his face. Trying to finds signs of a stranger. But he's the same. They *are* the same person.

"And Sullivan's still here," he says, tapping his head. "There's... compartments in there, I guess. He's retreated for now. It's too confusing if we're both active at the same time."

"Has it always been this way?"

"No," he says, shaking his head. "No. When we were small we came up with this deal, you know? Our power—the Prodigy power—it's only useful to them when they can control both of us. So we make sure one of us is always submissive to the other. I came up with a drug to help us do that. It suppressed him for years. Decades, almost. But the... It started falling apart after Case—my friend, the other Alpha, you know?"

"I haven't met him yet. But I think he's here."

"Right. Things started going sideways after Case shot me with that drug when we were taking down the Red Robber a few months ago. And when Case took that control away..." He shakes his head again. "I don't know what happened. But things are very different now."

"He said you tried to kill yourself. That's why you were locked up in that hospital."

"I wasn't really gonna do it. I was just pissed off that day because he came out of his little dark hole. But it happened at work and everyone saw me. They called the police, put me on a seventy-two-hour hold at the hospital, and then... shit just got worse and worse. People kept dying in that goddamned place. I kept collecting those memories. It drove me insane, I think. It wasn't Sullivan's fault. Where's he gonna go? I mean, really. He's me. If the drug won't work, where's he gonna go? I should've realized that, but things were so... weird."

"Do you feel more in control now?"

He offers up a small smile. "I'm in bed with you. And you're naked."

I smile with satisfaction. I can't help it.

"So I'm gonna have to go with much better now." He averts his eyes, studying something on the other side of the room. "But what do you think? About all this? You're probably ready to run, right? It's too weird."

"I'm not running," I say. "I'm still here. And I'm still naked."

He chuckles this time. And I get a real grin out of him. "I feel so lost right now. God. What's been happening?"

I try to sit up, but he holds me tighter. "Don't leave."

"I was just going to get one of your friends. Or the Sheila thing."

"They can wait. Sheila will want to run tests and shit. I'm not up for that right now. I just want to be here with you for a little longer."

He hikes his leg over mine, a little possessive gesture that makes me relax. "Back to your original question," I say. "We weren't finished. We were just getting started."

He closes his eyes as he smiles. "I figured, since I still have pants on."

We laugh together this time and he squeezes me. His cock is still hard. It's pressing against my thigh. Making my pussy tingle with excitement.

Thomas raises his eyebrows at me. Reading my mind.

I shrug. "I could go for another round. I'm not even sure an oral orgasm counts."

"Oh," he says, leaning in to kiss me. "It counts. But it's only a part of the satisfaction I'm capable of."

"Is that right?"

"Mmmm," he says, his tongue slipping inside my mouth as he grinds his hips against mine. One hand plays with my breast. He pinches my nipple, just the way Sullivan did when he was in charge. He traces the bumps of my ribs, then slips right between my legs and plays with the evidence of what Sullivan did to me a few minutes ago. "He must've been good, huh? He's got your release all pooled up for me to play with."

Oh, shit. I'm so turned on right now, I think I gush.

"You can tell me no," he says, pulling back from the kiss.

"Are you kidding?"

"It's not weird?"

"You're the same person. It's not weird, Thomas. I like you both. Equally," I add, so he knows. Whatever's happening to him, he doesn't need me to make it worse. I want him. Flaws and all. I want them both. One at a time or all at once. I don't care.

He kisses me again, probably reading my mind. Then his hand takes mine and places it over the hardness under his jeans. "Take me out," he whispers in my mouth.

My fingers fumble with the buttons for a few seconds. But I get it together and pull the fly open. His cock is hard, and hot, and thick when I wrap my hand around it and pull him free.

"Yes," he says, taking his whispers to my ear. "Hold it in your hand. Squeeze it, Sadie. Squeeze it hard."

God. I forgot. This one's a talker. So fucking sexy.

"Do it," he says, biting my earlobe.

I squeal, but I also obey.

"Now pump it up and down. Yes," he says. "Just like that. It feels good. I can't wait to put it in your mouth."

Oh, shit.

"Your pussy just gushed all over my fingers, Sadie. Does that mean you like it?"

"Yes," I moan.

"Yes, what? Tell me what you like."

"I like your cock in my hand. I like the way you talk to me. I like picturing how it will feel when you push it inside me. When you fuck me."

"Do you want me to fuck you hard, Sadie? Like last time? Or should I go easy on you this time?"

"Do whatever you want."

He laughs. "That's my girl. Now scoot down. Scoot down and put your lips over my head. I need to feel your mouth on me."

Good God. I have won the lottery with this guy. These guys. Oh, who the fuck cares. I'm fine with all of it.

I reluctantly break away from him. But I keep my hand busy stroking his cock as I position myself at his waist. I lick his abs. They are hard. Muscular. Perfect.

"Mmmm," he says. "You're teasing me." There's a little hint of warning in his voice. "Keep moving. You're driving me wild."

I look up at him as I continue to lick and kiss my way down his groin. His eyes are open, but only halfway. Like this feels so good he's having trouble.

I lick my lips just as the head of his cock touches my lips. His crooked smile is all the encouragement I need. I take him in my mouth. He's so thick and hard, I worry that I won't be able to take much of his length.

"Go slow if you want. I'll let you get used to it. It might be too big for you. You might not be able to take it all the way down your throat. But don't worry, little Sadie," he says, petting my hair with one hand while he reaches down to squeeze my breast with the other. "I'll *make* it fit in your pussy."

I pull away to look up at him. "Keep talking."

He laughs, making his cock jump in my hand. "If you keep licking."

"Deal," I whisper. I stretch my mouth around his tip and suck. He fists my hair and groans. I like that he likes it. So I look up and watch him as I push his fat cock deeper into my mouth. It hits the back of my throat, making me gag, but he just fists my hair harder and pushes my face into his groin. I flatten my tongue against his shaft, let him slide in as deep as I can, then pull back, saliva spilling out of my mouth. I grab my spit in my hand and begin stroking him, twisting my hand up and down as I tease the tip of his head playfully with my tongue.

"You're gonna make me come if you keep doing that," he says.

"So come," I say, still looking up at him. "I'll swallow you down like it's candy."

He grins, yanking on my hair until I have to tip my head back. "No."

I don't take the denial personally. It's fun after all. Why rush it?

"I want you on the floor. On your knees. Kneel for me, Sadie."

I give his cock one last lick, then ease myself onto the floor and kneel. He swings his legs over and stands up, still holding on to my hair. He grabs it on both sides of my face and brings my mouth towards his cock. It looks huge from this angle.

"Look at me, Sadie." His command is soft but still stern. He expects me to obey him. Right now I'm in the mood to do just about anything he says. "Good girl," he says when my eyes meet his. "I want to see your pretty eyes when I sink my cock into your throat. So make sure you look at me."

"I'll do my very best," I say through my smile.

"And put your hands right here," he says, patting his muscular thigh. "Palms flat. Keep them there. You won't be needing your hands."

Oh, man. I feel heat between my legs from that prediction.

He pulls my hair, bringing my head towards him. "That's it," he says. "Open wide for me, Sadie."

I open my mouth and a thrill runs through my whole body. I want to touch myself. I want to play with my clit while I suck his cock. I want to come on my fingers when he comes down my throat.

"You're daydreaming, Sadie. Tell me what you're thinking about."

I look up at him. All smiles. So very handsome and perfect. He hasn't shaved in a few days and it's hot as fuck. "I want to play with myself."

"No," he says, still grinning. He's having fun with me.

I'm having fun with him too.

"I want to rub my pussy all over your face."

"Soon. What else?"

"I want you to come down my throat."

"No again." He kneels down to look me in the eyes. "I will come inside you, but not in your mouth. I want to feel your pussy squeeze me. I want to feel you clamp down on my dick so hard I have to suck in air. I want to be buried deep inside you, Sadie. That's the only way I'll be satisfied." He leans in. Kisses me softly on the lips. Whispers, "Do you want me to be satisfied?" right into my mouth.

"Yes," I whisper back. Our eyes are locked on each other. This is the most intimate moment I've ever had.

"Good," he says, kissing my lips one more time before standing back up. "I want you satisfied too. Now suck my cock and make us both happy."

I lean in and he meets me halfway. The soft, wet tip of his head bumps against my lips, so I open. I let him in. He lets me take control of how deep inside. I wrap my lips completely around his head and suck.

"Yes," he says, crooning the word down to me. I keep my eyes on him, just the way he asked. "That's very nice. Keep going."

I swallow around the fat cock in my mouth and he groans. His fists grip my head, pulling me forward. Urging me on. I open as wide as I can and let him enter my throat. For a moment, I know I'm going to choke.

But then he says, "You're OK," in such a soft, tender voice, I believe him. I am OK. "Just let me handle this. You concentrate on how good it's going to feel when I finally push my dick inside your pussy. You want that, right?"

I nod my head, tears forming in the corners of my eyes as I try to breathe through my nose.

I really want that.

"Me too," he says. "But I want this for a little bit first."

He begins to pump his hips. Slowly at first. His cock slides in and out of my mouth. So much saliva is pooled in my mouth, it drips down my chin and falls onto my nipple.

I almost die with want.

"Now a little faster. You're OK." He starts fucking me. Not hard. He's still gentle. Still reassuring. Not trying to force me.

And I have never been so turned on in my whole life.

He thrusts in, but then he stops. Almost none of his cock is outside my mouth now. I have tears in my eyes. And him in my head. Telling me to trust him.

I relax and he smiles. A tear drops down my face when he places one hand on my throat and one hand on the back of my head and he... goes deeper. Pushing himself inside me.

My palms are still pressed flat against his muscular thighs. And I push, trying to make him back off.

"Not yet, Sadie," he moans. "I can feel my cock in your throat."

Oh. *Yes.* I can feel his hand there.

He presses forward again, until my nose is buried into his groin.

I have to close my eyes.

Not to get through it. But because I am so turned on I might come without anyone touching me. I might come just from the thought. Just from the image I'm holding in my mind.

I gag, and he pulls out. Long strands of saliva drip down my body.

He kneels down and kisses me on the lips. "Now I want to fuck you."

"Yes," I whisper into his mouth. His tongue is there, twisting with mine. His fingers are between my legs. I'm so wet, he slips inside with almost no friction. I need his fat cock. I need to feel him. "Then fuck me, Thomas. Now."

He pulls away from my mouth, breaking our kiss. "Come on. You can be on top."

He sits on the bed and lies back. I climb on, straddling his hips, lifting up just enough to place the tip of his dick under my entrance.

And then I sink down on him.

We both moan. There's no way in hell I can keep my eyes open now. I just want to drift away into bliss. I sit down even more, letting him fill me up.

His hands grip my breasts, squeezing them hard. The gentle fucking is over. I want to ride him.

"Fuck me," he says.

But his voice has changed. I open my eyes and see Sullivan.

"Fuck me," he says. But now he's Thomas.

"Fuck me, Sadie." It's both of them.

I do fuck them. Both of them. I lean down, letting my hair fall over my shoulders and drag over their shoulders. They grab my ass, urging me to move quicker. Everything is suddenly urgent. They wrap their arms around my back, pinning me to their chest. They thrust their hips upwards while I try to sink down.

"This is fucking," they growl into my ear.

I can feel my climax surfacing. It's swimming up from some dark depth and there's no way I can stop it from breaking free.

"Squeeze our cock, Sadie." And that simple switch, that one word—*our*—it unravels me. I come apart as they fuck me so hard from below, their balls fly up to smack me on the ass.

Then I gush. Their hot semen spills into me and I coat their dick with my climax. They hold me close, kissing me like we've been separated after a long absence.

I brought them together.

So they are mine.

CHAPTER TWENTY-NINE

We hold her for a little bit, our eyes closing, ready for this day to be done.

"I'm glad you're back," Sadie says. "I mean that."

I open one eye so I can look at her. She's pretty fucking adorable. I mean, really... she's completely adorable. Her face is so sweet. And I don't know what she was like before we met at the hospital—I can take a good guess, knowing Prodigy—but I really love this version of her. "You mean you're not gonna play favorites?"

She opens one eye too. Smiles at me. "There's no way in hell I could choose, Thomas. I like both of you. Besides, you really are the same person."

At least she knows it's me and not Sullivan right now. I'm not even sure Case and Lincoln could be that sure about it. They know about Sullivan. Have known for a long time. But they don't know as much as Sadie does.

I filled them in some when you started going crazy after Case shot you, Sullivan says inside my head.

I figured.

I saw you struggling and, yeah, I was all about taking over again. It was a good opportunity for me. Couldn't pass it up. But... I need you, Thomas. I think we're better as a team than we are alone.

I have to agree. I never thought I'd feel that way, but he's right. *We're better as one. Maybe one day we'll even merge? Who knows. But this is OK with me.*

He relaxes inside my head, content to let me lead for now.

"I'm so tired," Sadie says.

I stroke her hair and close my eyes again. "Me too."

"Well, snap out of it." Sheila's voice comes from the pile of clothes on the floor. My phone in my jeans. "Uzi is pissed off right now and I need you downstairs to help mitigate things immediately."

"Fuck him," I say back.

"No," Sheila says. "I'm telling you, this is going to be a huge problem in a matter of minutes if you don't show up down there. I've been feeding him video of Sadie from when she was under in the lab. But I'm out of footage. Someone needs to talk him down and he wants nothing to do with Lincoln or Case. So that someone is you. Get up."

"Did you find out anything from the tests you ran?" Sadie asks Sheila.

Sheila is silent for a few seconds.

"Sheila?" I ask. "Did you?"

"We need to talk about that."

"Well, talk." More hesitation from Sheila. "What the hell is going on?"

"We need to take care of Uzi first—"

"No," Sadie says. "This is my private business. If you know something you need to tell me. Like *right now*."

"Come on, Sheila. Tell us what's going on."

She sighs. God, sometimes she's so damn real with her voice inflection. "In the interest of getting Thomas to take his ass downstairs and help his Alpha brothers, I will. But you're not going to like it. How much do you remember about the last two years, Sadie?"

"Nothing," she says. "It's like... I have a memory of escaping with Cyan and Uzi. I have a memory of Iziah getting caught. Then me. But after that it's... me standing in the asylum looking straight at Thomas. That's it. Just a huge black hole of emptiness."

"Well, the human mind is a very interesting specimen. It's like a recorder. You never really forget things. Your brain just files your memories away. That's how they erase people. They find the right file, tuck it somewhere unexpected, and presto, you forget things."

"Who does that?" I ask. "I mean, there's some crazy fucked-up people in this world, but for real. Who has that kind of power over a brain?"

"Well…" Sheila says. "You do, Thomas. This whole mentalist thing? I don't understand it. But that's something you can do. If you knew how, that is. I found memories inside Sadie. Memories of her being… altered in this way."

"By who?" Sadie asks. "When?"

"Those two years you thought you were with Prodigy?"

Oh, shit. Here it comes.

"You weren't, Sadie. You were with Cyan and Uzi the whole time."

"What?" she gasps, sitting up in bed. "What are you talking about?"

"I don't know," Sheila says.

"What do you mean you don't know?" I snap. "You're a goddamned know-it-all."

"I don't see a school in her memories, Thomas. I see underground bunkers or something."

"Wait," Sadie whispers. "I remember that now. I was in a room. But I wasn't with Cyan and Uzi." She stops to massage her head, like it's painful to think about these things. "I was with Iziah."

"They had both of you, Sadie. They were using you. Training you to be a weapon."

"Good God," she says. "I *knew* there was something between them. I *knew* it. They were acting all funny."

"Well, they're acting funny again right now. And I don't think we fully understand just how dangerous these two are. They're like you and Sadie, Thomas. Mentalist and illusionist. Except they know what the fuck they're doing."

"Shit. Get Case and Linc right now."

"Well, I could do that," Sheila says. "But… I'm telling you, Uzi is raging downstairs right now. He can't be left alone. There's no telling what kind of damage those two could do. I don't know if Case or Lincoln could fight an attack like that. They've never been exposed to that kind of thing."

"So what do we do?" Sadie asks. I'm only half surprised that she's ready to jump ship so easily. Sheila is right. Somewhere deep inside her, she knows everything Sheila said is true. Those memories they stole are still in there, filed away for secret-keeping. But they're still there. "I don't want them to get a hold of me again, Thomas. Ever. I want to stay with you."

I pull her close to me and hug her. "I have no intention of letting them get you, don't worry. Uzi needs to sever that link to have any control over you, Sadie. I'm your link and I won't let him cut it. I promise."

"OK," Sheila says. "Now that all that stupid emotional stuff is over… can we please come up with a plan to get these freaks out of Lincoln's house? All we need is for them to find the lab and things will get really ugly, really fast."

"We need to tell Lincoln, Sheila. Send him a message now."

"I can't. Uzi and Cyan are right there. I can't even ask him to leave the room. You don't understand the level of tension down there right now."

"You know what I want to know?" I say.

"What?" Sheila replies.

"Why the fuck can't you talk to Lincoln in his head? You really need to work on that."

Sheila huffs. "I'll take your upgrade suggestion into consideration, Mr. Brooks. Now stop being so... not-Thomas. I need that cold motherfucker back, pronto. Get dressed and get your ass down there. Now!"

"I don't want them to get a hold of me again, Thomas. Ever. I want to stay with you."

I pull her close to me and hug her. "I have no intention of letting them get you, don't worry. I'm your link and I won't let him cut it. I promise."

CHAPTER THIRTY

"Shit," I say. "I'm so sorry, Thomas."

"What for?" he asks. But he's already out of bed, pulling his clothes back on.

"This is all my fault. I think they set us up." I get out of bed and look around the room for my clothes too. They're in a neatly folded pile on the chair.

"What do you mean?"

"Listen," I say, tugging my jeans on. "I think they sent me to the hospital for you."

"Yeah, I got that part," Thomas says. He's got his shirt on now and he's looking for shoes.

I get my shirt on too, then turn to look at him. "I think they sent me there, not to kill you, Thomas. We know that's not possible. They sent me to bring you back. And I did, didn't I?"

He's got his shoes on and he's waiting for me to finish with mine. "They couldn't have planned this."

"No?" I say. "Think about it, Thomas. We're here. At Lincoln Wade's *house*. With all three Alphas, and their greatest weaknesses. Lulu and Molly and... me. Oh, fuck, Thomas. They *wanted* you to bring them here. They're here on purpose. They're here to get all of us. And who knows if they're working alone or with Prodigy—" God, that makes my stomach sick when I think about it. "It doesn't matter. They sent me to bring you back to them. They want us together, Thomas. They want us as their ultimate weapon. But now—this is turning out even better than they planned. Because they have you, me, Lincoln, Case, Molly, Lulu, and Sheila. They have every weapon in your arsenal, Thomas."

We're ready now, so Thomas is at the door, pulling it open as I join him. We enter the hallway, and already I can hear the arguing going on downstairs.

"Look," Thomas says. "That might be true. In fact, it's highly probable you're right. But we still have the element of surprise. They don't know we know about their little plan. OK?" He's shaking me a little to make sure his words sink in. "They have no idea what Lincoln is. They have no idea what Case is, either. I don't even know what Case is, but he's a smart, formidable motherfucker. Plus we have Sheila. We can take them down, OK? Just let us lead the way. You stay hidden while I try to diffuse the situation." He grabs my shoulders, making me focus on him and not Uzi's and Cyan's voices down below. "Do you understand me, Sadie?"

CHAPTER THIRTY-ONE

Sadie stares up at me. I shake her shoulders again, a little harder this time. "Tell me you understand."

She nods her head, but then begins to shake her head no. "I don't think you understand, Thomas. I don't think you know how powerful we are."

"We?" I ask. Is she with me? Or them?

"Not that way," she says, struggling to clarify. "We, like who Cyan, Iziah, Uzi, and me are together. We're not just your average Prodigy project. We're not Alphas," she says. "We might be worse."

"Yeah," I say, giving her a small smile to try to make her feel better. "I'm getting that impression. But we're not your average Prodigy project either. We're so much better than they could ever have imagined as a team. And your friends fucked up by thinking they could take us on in our own domain. We have everything going in our favor, Sadie. Trust me. I know what I'm doing."

"They are very powerful in teams, Thomas. You can't even begin to understand what Iziah and Cyan can do. And Uzi and me…" She lets her words drop off. "Well, we're perfect killers together."

"OK," I say, trying to keep her calm. "But you're not linked with him. You're linked to me. So he can't combine his power with yours. He's only half the monster he thinks he is right now."

She just stares at me.

"Understand?" I say, still gripping her shoulders.

She sighs, looks down the hallway towards the stairs where the voices are getting louder. Doesn't look the least bit convinced. But she finally nods. "OK. I'll follow your lead."

I grab her hand and half-walk, half-jog down the hallway. When we get to the stairs I stop and look at her again. "Stay here. If things get out of hand, go back to that room Sheila took you in." I point down the hallway, past the stairs. "And go into the lab. It's safe in there. They can't get in, I promise. Molly and Lulu will join you and we'll come get you when it's over. Got it?"

She's still not convinced, but she swallows down her doubt and nods her head. "OK."

I place my hands on her cheeks as I look down into her eyes. "Trust me," I say. I lean in and kiss her. "I want you, Sadie Scott. We are the perfect team." She kisses me back, her hands clutching my shoulders like she never wants to let go.

I don't want to pull away, but I do. She grabs my hand as I try to walk over to the stairs. I let her keep it for two steps, desperate for me to change my mind. But there's no way I'm going to change my mind. We have Prodigy right here and there's no way I'm not gonna take this chance to end them. We might all be almost indestructible, but there are worse things than death. I know that better than anyone.

We make our way to the stairs and Sadie holds on to me for as long as she can. But one more step… she squeezes my fingertips as they slide through her hand… and then she lets me go.

CHAPTER THIRTY-TWO

"What's all the fucking yelling about?" Thomas yells as he descends the stairs.

"Oh, there he is," Uzi snarls. "Did you have fun fucking my little Sadie?"

Thomas laughs, but I have this deep, sinking feeling in the pit of my stomach. This is wrong. Everything about this is wrong. Thomas has no idea what Uzi can do. He has no idea—

"I thought we had a deal, Uzi?" Thomas says.

"Yeah, your friends here," Lincoln says, nodding at Thomas as he walks up to them. His friend Case positions himself on the other side. They are a team. And they are powerful. But I'm so fucking scared for them. "They've overstayed their welcome. I'm gonna have to ask you to leave."

"Get Sadie," Cyan says. "And we'll be on our way."

"No," Thomas says. "Sadie stays. But the three of you, you're leaving. Right now."

"Not without her," Cyan says. "I'm not leaving my sister in the hands of you freaks. Who knows what you'll do to her."

"That's funny coming from you, Cyan. Do you really think we don't know who you are? What you did to her?" He nods at Iziah, who has not said a word. And, come to think of it, he hasn't said a word since we got here. "And him?"

Cyan and Uzi both look at each other.

And then a message flashes across my field of vision. It's fast. Barely a blink and it's gone. I don't even get a look at the letters. Was that from Thomas? Sullivan? Is he trying to warn me about something?

Pain shoots through my head. Pressure, so severe I feel like I might explode. I fall to my knees, holding my head like this is the only way I can keep my brain intact.

Downstairs everything is pushed. Case and Lincoln go flying backwards. Lulu and Molly are slammed against the fireplace and slump to the floor.

But Thomas is still standing. He sends one back towards Uzi and Cyan and gives them a little taste of their own medicine.

Iziah is the only one of them who takes the hit. He crashes into a window and disappears from sight. God. Thomas threw him like a rag doll. Iziah didn't even try to defend himself.

Why didn't he react? Uzi and Cyan must have some kind of control over him.

Uzi and Cyan raise their arms, like they are magicians, wielding power. How? How are they doing this without me and Iziah? Two mentalists? Linked? Not possible. It can't be—

But it is. Because they push the next mind blast towards Thomas and send him flying.

Then—little robots appear. From every corner of the room. From every doorway. They emerge from their secret hiding places like a swarm. Some have pincer claws, some are flying around Uzi and Cyan's heads. They crawl all over them, making Cyan scream, her hands desperate to try to swat them off her clothes.

Sheila, I realize.

But that's when I notice Uzi. He's not fighting—he's laughing. They are crawling all over him like ants. "That's all you got, Alphas? Really? Robots?"

Case and Lincoln are getting to their feet. "No," Lincoln says. "That's not all we've got." He raises his cannon arm, aims at Cyan, and shoots her.

I gasp, my hand over my heart. My sister! That's all I can think as her body explodes into millions of shards. She shatters. Like glass.

What the fuck is happening?

I feel her for a moment. Inside my head. Memories go flashing by. Her whole life runs out like a movie in super-fast-forward. She's reaching... looking for...

Shit.

Oh, shit.

Thomas stands up, a smirky grin on his face. "Finally," he says. "Finally." Only this time he cackles with laughter. It's the most diabolical sound I've ever heard.

And it's not Thomas.

It's not Sullivan either.

It's Cyan.

She's not in my head, she's in *his*.

I take my attention back to Uzi, that evil laugh filling the room until it echoes. "You did it!" he yells. But who he's yelling to, I'm not sure.

Not me.

Not Thomas.

And not even Cyan.

He's talking to Lincoln Wade. Who aims his cannon arm at Uzi now. But Uzi pushes him back with another mind blast. Lincoln smashes into a wall and sinks down, momentarily stunned.

The little robots are all over Uzi, but he ignores them as he walks up to Lincoln. "That's all I wanted, Bike Boy.

How do you kill someone who can't be killed?" Uzi laughs as he grabs Lincoln's collar and pulls him up to his feet. "You get an Alpha." Suddenly every squirming robot on Uzi's body goes still. Then they drop off, like someone… *turned them off.*

Good God. He was the one who stopped the train back in the tunnel! He can control mechanical things with his mind.

"We need you, Linc," Uzi says, right into Lincoln's face. "So Cyan could die and slip right into Thomas's mind to take over. If you think two mentalists linked together are powerful, just wait till you see what we can do with three."

He throws Lincoln down on the floor with the most powerful mind blast I've ever seen. It makes a crater in the floor so deep Lincoln's body disappears into a dark hole.

And then Uzi looks right at me.

CHAPTER THIRTY-THREE

"No," I yell, clutching my head. She's in me. That bitch, *Cyan*. The second Lincoln shattered her, I collected her memories. *She's inside me.*

No. It's Sullivan. *Sorry, bitch. No room for you in here.* Sullivan, the master of the dark places in my head, has some kind of hold on her. Some kind of quarantine.

Take control, Thomas. But that's not Sullivan. It's Cyan. She's here. Inside me. She's got my thoughts. She's controlling me.

"Get out of my mind, you bitch!"

Fight her, Thomas. Sullivan is trying to hold on to me. Desperate to keep me with him. But there's a link... there's always been a link, I realize. Ever since I let Sadie in my head.

We come in twos, Cyan whispers. *When you let my sister in, you let Uzi in too, you fool!*

How many fucking people are inside me right now?

"Thomas!" Sadie's call for help makes me struggle to open my eyes. Uzi's got her by the hair and he's dragging her into the center of the room. Sheila's robots come over the side of the broken front window, dragging Iziah's body behind them.

"Thomas!" Sadie calls again.

I reach for her with my hand. But it's stupid. I'm all the way across the room. And Cyan is there anyway. Fighting with Sullivan.

He's strong, but she's... a force. *I have to help him.*

"Thomas!" Sadie is still calling me. And that's when I notice... none of my friends are still standing. No Lincoln, no Case, no Molly, no Lulu....

"Thomas!"

I need to help them.

Thomas.

I need to help Sullivan too.

Thomas.

But it's too late. Because that's Cyan. Inside my head. In control.

You're mine now, Thomas.

Sullivan is gone. Molly gone. Lulu, Case, and Lincoln, gone.

I need to help them. I need to help them all.

Silly Thomas, Cyan croons inside me.

"Help me!" Sadie calls.

I open my eyes, the pain from Cyan's takeover so severe, my blurry world spins. I squint, try to focus. And then I see it. I realize just how badly I've lost this fight.

Uzi has Sadie in the middle of the room. Iziah is lying down beside her. Already lifeless.

But she's next.

I can feel Uzi's build up in my mind. I am *linked* to that motherfucker, so I feel it.

He lets loose a mind blast right over top of Sadie and Iziah. It literally blows their minds. If Iziah wasn't dead, he surely must be now. Sadie's body goes limp. She crumples under his force.

Everything is silent.

"Silly Thomas," Cyan says, through *my* mouth. "You have far too many loyalties, my stupid little puppet. Didn't your Prodigy school ever teach you about divide and conquer? You have to pick and choose who you will be loyal to. And you can only have one. Lesson learned, huh?" She *tsks* my tongue. "But you learned it just a little too late."

"Come on," Uzi says, reaching for my hand. I take it. Only it's not me. It's her. Cyan. I am Cyan now. "He initiated the satellites, remember? We've only got about eight hours before the whole thing goes down."

"I can't wait," I say. Then there's a sick moment when I realize... I'm still me. But now Uzi's my partner.

Thomas...

But it's faint. She's gone. Sadie is gone. She doesn't matter anymore. Uzi and I are the only ones who matter now.

"We're gonna take over the world, Thomas."

"Yes," I hiss. "But don't call me Thomas again, you dick. I'm still Cyan."

Uzi laughs as we walk out the door. "You know I'm gonna come back for Sadie and wake her up. I'll need her to be my little fuck-doll again when this is all over."

"I wonder if I like girls now?" I ask Uzi. We laugh together.

"You can like whoever you want, Cyan."

We get in the car and slam our doors at the same time. And we laugh all the way down stupid Lincoln Wade's five-mile-long driveway.

"Isn't it great that these Alphas set up the whole thing for us?" I say.

"We are gonna fuck that city up good, Cyan."

"Yesssss," I hiss back at him. "We are."

It's still dark but it won't be for long. And by the time we get down the mountain it will be a brand-new day. We'll be the ones to take down Cathedral City, not these worthless Alphas. And when we're done... Prodigy will control everything and everyone.

Bye-bye, Alphas. Your delusions-of-grandeur schemes are ours now.

CHAPTER THIRTY-FOUR

"Sadie?"

Someone is shaking me. Who? Where am I? What's going on?

"Sadie, can you hear us?" A new voice. Female this time. But my mind is swimming with illusions and doubt.

Sadie…

They're talking to me. They're gonna wipe my mind again. They're gonna wipe my mind and make me powerless. I will have to obey.

Who?

I don't know, I just know that I can't let it happen again.

"What the ever-loving fuck?" a third voice says.

"She's tripping, you guys. Don't pay any attention to her illusions, it's fake. Uzi blasted her and she's out of control. We need to get her to the lab. Get her arms, Case."

I fight. I thrash in their grip. I won't be taken back there. I refuse to be someone's loyal puppet of death. I won't do it…

Sadie, he calls. *Sadie… help me…*

A sharp prick in my arm and I'm swimming again. This is it. This is the end for me. I'm done.

I am in a dark place. Four walls, no light except for a thin strip leaking in from under a door. The room smells like the earth. Damp dirt and stale air. There are lots of voices outside and I recognize all of them. Uzi, Cyan, and the others.

I wait in the dark until I hear the locks disengage. Fear jolts me to my feet as he enters the room. "Time for some fun, Sadie." Uzi walks towards me, one arm reaching. In my head, I fight him. I grab that outstretched arm and flip him over. Smash his face on the hard floor. Snap his neck and relish the sickening crack of bones breaking.

But in reality, I let him hold my hand. I let him lead me from my prison cell. I let him take me down the hall, feeling shame as everyone looks at me, grinning. Knowing what he's about to do. Knowing that I will let him.

"Here you go, Samuel," Uzi says, holding my hand out to the other man. "She's all yours."

"She doesn't look like Azure," the man called Samuel spits.

Uzi laughs. "Not yet. But she will. You just have to get used to it. Ask anyone. Right, Gordon?" Uzi nods his head towards another guy in the hallway with us, asking for his validation of my skills.

"She looks just like Jayleen when I fuck her." Gordon shrugs. "She flips in and out. Her trips are short. But she's pretty enough and you get used to it. Plus, Sadie here gives some first-rate blowjobs. And it's as close as you'll ever come to fucking your dead wife again, right?"

"Take it or leave it," Uzi says. "I have dozens of people lined up, Samuel."

"Just relax," Samuel says. "I just needed a little clarification. How do I make her look like Azure then?"

"That's the beauty." Uzi laughs. "She just does it. You show the picture and hold the image of Azure in your mind and she just… becomes her."

Samuel thinks about this for a few seconds. "How do you keep her so… docile? Will she wake up from this trance—or whatever you have her in—and try to kill me? She's one of you, right?" Samuel shakes his head with doubt. "And everyone knows what you four are."

"Hey," Uzi says, getting angry now. "I've been doing this for two years. No one's died yet. You've got five seconds to take your turn and then I'm moving on to the next client on the list."

"Fine," Samuel says, pulling out his wallet.

Uzi takes his money and places my hand in Samuel's. He leads me to an open door and we enter, closing it behind us.

I walk to the bed and start getting undressed. When I'm naked I turn to look at the man who wants me to be his dead wife. He's holding out a picture of a woman. Early twenties, blonde hair, green eyes, pretty face. I drag my eyes away from the picture and find it in his mind too.

He smiles at me. "Azure?"

I nod, but don't speak. He's got a few more seconds on this trip and I don't want to end it early with speech.

He doesn't care. He takes me over to the bed and I lie down. He slides in next to me, but doesn't remove his clothes.

I flicker in and out between Azure and Sadie. But Gordon adapts as we lie in bed looking at each other. He closes his eyes when I become Sadie. He learns to wait a few seconds before opening them again so he can see his wife. And each time he opens his eyes, he smiles at me.

At Azure.

He talks. That's it. He talks to Azure. He tells her all the things he's been holding inside since she died years ago.

It's a disjointed conversation with all the trips I have to throw to make it as believable as possible. But Gordon doesn't care.

"I'm sorry," he keeps saying. "I'm sorry I didn't save you. I'm sorry I wasn't enough to save you from them."

He's talking about Prodigy. Somewhere in my head I know this, but I'm not supposed to think about them. And Uzi always knows if I think too hard. He's always in my head, poking around to steal all my thoughts and keep them for himself. So I try not to think at all. I just concentrate on being Azure. On making Samuel happy. On giving him his money's worth.

Most of them want to fuck me, all the while pretending I'm someone else.

Uzi interrupts his quiet confessions of guilt, and unworthiness, and regret as a voice through a speaker. "Five-minute warning."

Samuel stops talking and this time when I flick back into Sadie to restart the trip, he keeps his eyes open. "Why do you let them use you like this?"

I'm confused for a second. But I don't respond.

"You're strong, Sadie. The best illusionist this place has ever seen." Samuel is whispering now, probably wondering if Uzi is watching. Or listening through some recording device. "You could get out," he says. "You could trip them all and—"

The door flies open and the next thing I know, Samuel is being dragged out of the room by a whole gang of men.

"Fucking asshole," Uzi says, watching as he disappears down the hall. He turns and tracks me with his eyes as I get up off the bed and start getting dressed. "I hope you don't get any funny ideas, Sadie. You're mine, honey. And I have big plans for you."

"Sadie?"

I sit up, breathing hard, sweat running down my face. I look around wildly, expecting Uzi to be here. Expecting to be dragged back into that prison cell they keep me in.

But I'm not there. I'm in Lincoln Wade's creepy dungeon, sitting on his supervillain operating table. I break out in tears from the relief. "I'm not there," I say, to no one in particular. Lincoln, Case, Lulu, Molly, and Sheila are all looking at me with shocked faces.

"Are you OK?" Molly asks.

I just stare at them, the memory of what Uzi was doing to me all these years still way too fresh in my memory. How he used me.

I look down at my trembling hands and shake my head. "No," I say. "I'm not OK." And then I remember everything that happened. I'm at the Alpha lair. I came here with... "Thomas? Where's Thomas?"

"Uzi has him," Lincoln says. "And I know whatever that nightmare was you were having, it's a pretty big deal. You were thrashing and screaming. But we need you now, Sadie. I cannot stress how badly we need your help right fucking now or everything we're doing is gonna go to shit."

"You tripped into hundreds of people," Lulu says, ignoring Lincoln's plea for help as she rubs my arm. "What was that?"

"It's her superpower," Case says. I don't know him, I just know of him. And everything they told me—everything they made me believe about these Alphas—was wrong. They're not the bad guys in this story. They're the only good guys I've ever met.

"Sadie?" I turn my head to see Iziah standing on the other side of the room.

"He's one of them," I blurt. "Don't let him near me! Please—"

"No, Sadie," Iziah says, walking forward into the room. "I was with you. These past few years, I was with you. I was down in that cell too. Remember?"

My head hurts when I think about my missing years. So I shake my head. "No," I say. "I don't want to remember."

"You don't have to," Lincoln says, grabbing my shoulder. "Not yet, anyway. But we need you, Sadie. But somehow Cyan... she took over his body."

"The memories," I whisper. "Sullivan told me that Thomas can collect memories from dead people. And Thomas is a mentalist, so he can form a link to Uzi. Shit," I say, rubbing my aching forehead. "When Cyan was shattered she jumped into his head and formed a link with

Uzi." I look up at them, so much fear coursing through my veins, I suddenly feel cold. "She took control of him. She's got them both now. Thomas and Sullivan. We'll never get them back!"

"We're not going to let that happen," Sheila says. "But Lincoln's right. We need your help, Sadie. We need you and Iziah. He's already told us what he knows."

"They had me too, Sade," Iziah says, forcing his way into the tight circle of people who surround me. "Cyan was controlling me too. But when Lincoln scattered her and she... died, I guess—I don't know, maybe she forgot she was controlling me. Or maybe they thought I was never going to recover. I took two hits, from two of the most powerful mentalists to ever come out of Prodigy."

But he's not dead.

No, he says in my head. *I'm not dead. Neither are you.*

He's in my mind.

"We're linked now, Sadie," Iziah says. "If they can link two mentalists, well..." He smiles. "We can link two illusionists. It took me years to figure this out. I wanted to help you. While we were still at Prodigy... but...."

Iziah trails off. I feel his sadness. His regret.

"We need you, Sadie," Lincoln says. "We can't pull this off without you. We need Thomas back and we need to get him before those fucking satellites align and rain a shitstorm of chaos down on Cathedral City."

"I don't know what they're planning to do with my SpyGlasses," Case says. "Or Thomas's satellite phones. But I can tell you this—it's not what we had in mind. And now that we've unleashed this plan and can't stop it, it's our duty to make sure it's carried out properly."

"Will you help us?" Lulu asks, still holding onto my arm. "Will you help us get Thomas back and take down this totally fucked-up city, once and for all?"

I look at each of them, one at a time. "Who *are* you people?"

All of them laugh, even Iziah.

"We're Alphas," Case says, smiling.

"And illusionists," Iziah adds.

"And a fucked-up Omega detective," Molly says.

"I'm just a lawyer." Lulu laughs. "But I got your back."

"And don't forget about me," Sheila says. "I have control of every computer in that city. Every phone, every tablet used in the schools, every bus-stop map, every jail cell. I'm inside all of it. Every device with Spy or Sky in front of the name is *me*."

"Cathedral City belongs to us, Sadie," Case says. "It's ours. And we want it back."

"We can do this," Lincoln says. "With your help, Sadie. So what you do ya say? Wanna join the team? Wanna be on Team Take Down the Assholes? Wanna get Thomas and Sullivan back? Wanna get your revenge and help us get ours at the same time?"

I picture it in my head. What would it be like to be in control again? What would the world look like with no Uzi controlling me?

Paradise, I decide. No matter what these supervillains have in mind, it's got to be better than this. And there's no fucking way in hell I'm gonna let Cyan have what's mine. She will not take Thomas from me like she's taken everything else.

"Yes," I finally say. "Yes, I'd very much like to be a part of this team."

"Good," Lincoln says with an evil, crooked smile. "Now listen carefully, here's the plan…"

CHAPTER THIRTY-FIVE

"Are you ready?" Uzi screams the words at the top of his lungs. We're in a large warehouse in the Merchant District. All around us are hundreds of people dressed in black holding up baseball bats and tire irons. They scream back, waving their clubs in the air, nothing but confirmation in their echoing replies. Yes, they're ready.

Sullivan and I have retreated to his safe place. The place he's been hiding for fifteen years. The place I put him.

I'm sorry, I say.

Don't worry about it, he says back. *If you hadn't put me here, we'd have nowhere to hide. We'd be dead in all ways but one. But we've still got a chance, Thomas. We're not out of this game yet.*

He's right. If he didn't have this little compartment we could retreat to, we'd be slaves. Stuck here in our own mind, watching Cyan and Uzi make us do... well... *What do you think they're gonna do?*

I think we're about to find out.

"In exactly thirty minutes," Uzi yells. The whole place goes quiet to hear his instructions. "Every Sky and Spy device in this city will start a protocol. Courtesy of Alpha Thomas and friends."

Shit, Sullivan says.

Fuck, I reply. *They're gonna use our own tech to get what they want.*

Can't Sheila stop it?

No, I say. *It's all automated until the program stops running.*

So it'll work like we planned?

But before I can explain the finer details of what Lincoln and Sheila have set up, Uzi explains his side of things.

"In thirty minutes, every device in Cathedral City will start flashing. And you, my friends, will be the first to experience what revolution really means."

Tell me you didn't use Lincoln's flashing lights to reprogram people.

We did. Well, he did. Asshole. I told Case to keep him under control and now look, all that shit he did last year is what's finally gonna bring us down.

"Now the Alphas," Uzi continues, "thought they'd use this little scheme to open eyes and make people see the truth. But we're not Alphas, are we?"

"No!" his minions scream.

"We're Prodigy!" he yells.

"Prodigy!" they scream.

How? Sullivan asks. *How the hell did all these people come out of Prodigy when you blew it up fifteen years ago?*

I never saw it coming, I realize. I remember the flyers all over the city. I remember the news articles. The parents, desperately seeking their missing children.

All those missing kids didn't go missing. They became part of the Prodigy program.

Sullivan is silent. What can he say? We missed it. We all missed it. Prodigy was never gone. It was here, right under our noses, this whole time.

"And we've got the Red Robber on our side!" Uzi continues.

Ecstatic, raving cheers at that little revelation. Hundreds of people are shouting and screaming as...

Fuck. Sullivan and I think it at the same time.

You have got to be kidding me, I say.

Randy Shits walks out and joins us at the front of the warehouse. Smirking at me like he's the most evil genius on the planet. He's dressed in black from head to toe, just like everyone else except Uzi and me. Motherfucker even has a goddamned logo splashed across his chest. A red anarchy symbol outlined in blue.

He stole our fucking anarchy sign! Sullivan says.

That asshole was setting Case up last spring. All that bullshit about the banks and the power plant. The water treatment center. The coffee shops. All of it is...

He's corrupted the Spyware, I suddenly realize. The flashing lights in the police station. The way all the monitors and lights started to blink out Lincoln's unauthorized program to make people violent. He did all of it and he used *us* the entire time.

"We have control of everything," Randy yells. "Every SkyEye phone. Every SpyGlass tablet. Everything in this city will be ours!"

He's going to make the whole city crazy with violence. Just like the riots he most certainly started last spring. I picture what this will mean. Total chaos—no. Total *anarchy*.

I still have the images of all those people in my head. How they turned on each other. How they tried to kill each other. How they walked around like zombies and...

"All thanks to the Alphas!" Randy continues. "Lincoln Wade made our little light show possible. Case Reider delivered it into the hands of every citizen of this city. And Thomas Brooks..." He cackles. "Well, he gave us the ability to do all this without any government interference. Welcome to the winning team, Mr. Brooks."

The crowd goes *insane* with cheers. "Prodigy, Prodigy, Prodigy," they scream, arms in the air, bats and tire irons pumping with the beat.

I think we just lost, Sullivan says.

I try to remain positive. I do. I try to talk myself up. I'm the mastermind here. I'm the brain. I'm the plotter of plots. *I'm* the most evil genius on this planet. And I'm teamed up with two more, with powers and intellect almost as equal.

But they have no idea. None. They have no clue this is what's happening. So even if they're coming for us, even if my friends have a plan… it won't work.

Sullivan's right. We just lost this game we've been playing. Fifteen years of planning can't prepare them for what's coming. Because you don't know what you don't know.

Lincoln, Case, and Sheila will show up. They'll come with false bravado that we, and we alone, are the most badass motherfuckers this town has ever seen… and they'll be wrong.

Because this was never our plan. This was never what we intended to do with all our carefully curated resources. With all our evil ideas.

This is some real *bad* supervillain shit right here.

I miss the rest of the speech, too busy imagining all the ways this day can end. All the ways we will lose. All the ways this city will go down.

I have nothing left. There is no brilliant mad scientist idea that can stop them now. I sent the codes last night and in just a few minutes, the program will start.

CHAPTER THIRTY-SIX

"I have him," Sheila says through the helicopter headsets. Case, Iziah, Lincoln and I are crammed into the small space. I'm practically sitting in Iziah's lap. Lulu and Molly had to stay at home. They only have one helicopter after some crash a few months ago. So no room. "He's in a warehouse in the Merchant District."

"Motherfuckers," Lincoln says. "That's my hood, goddammit."

"Well, it's theirs at the moment," Sheila replies. "There's hundreds of people in there with him, and I've got to tell you, just from my limited view from a security camera mounted inside, I think we might have a big problem."

"What are they saying?" Case asks.

"No sound," Sheila replies. "But Uzi and Thomas are addressing the crowd and... oh, shit."

"What?" Lincoln asks, banking the helicopter over the top of the last mountain we need to clear before Cathedral City comes into view.

"That DA, Randy Shultz, is there with them."

I shudder at the name. *Randy*.

"Shits, you mean," Case laughs into his headset.

"It's not funny, Case. He's dressed in black too. And..."

"And what?" Lincoln says.

"And he's wearing our logo. The anarchy symbol. It's like... he's a—"

"Fuck," Lincoln says.

"What?" Iziah asks, just before I can do it myself.

"He's one of us," Case finishes for Linc.

"He's Prodigy," I say.

"How do you know that?" Lincoln asks.

"I know that name," I say. "He came to the…" I almost say school, but that's not what it was. "He came to see me. Uzi made me…"

Iziah puts a hand on my arm. I don't know if he knows what Uzi was making me do while they were controlling us, but I appreciate the gesture.

"He made me turn into someone for him."

"Well, I, for one, have no clue what that means," Lincoln says. "But fuck that guy. Sheila, how long do we have?"

"Three minutes until initiation," she replies.

"In three minutes, we'll have control over the entire city," Lincoln says. "We didn't plan it this way, and it sucks that we have to do it, but we gotta use everything available to get Thomas back. Prodigy cannot have him again. Ever."

But they already do. They have him and Sullivan too.

The helicopter dips suddenly as Lincoln takes us south towards the Merchant district. My stomach flips, and not just because of the quick descent.

Something is very wrong here. I can feel it.

Then the letters start flashing across my vision.

Sadie, Sadie, Sadie. Come closer, Sadie. We're waiting for you.

But it's not Thomas and it's not Sullivan.

It's Cyan. *Thank you for bringing the boys along too. We'll bring you all back into the fold in just a few minutes. It's over. You belong to Prodigy. You always have and you always will.*

CHAPTER THIRTY-SEVEN

"Ten. Nine. Eight…" The minions are counting down to world domination when the roar of a helicopter fills the room.

Cyan looks over at Uzi. I feel her—me—*us*—smile.

"Seven. Six…" A garage door begins rolling up on the other side of the thug-filled space. Everyone turns to watch. "Five. Four…" A hard thud as the helicopter lands on the roof. The enormous warehouse doors are halfway up.

"Three. Two. One…"

The anarchists burst forward, trampling each other as they push their way out of the warehouse and spill out into the city.

"Get them," Uzi says to Cyan.

I feel my head nod. Then words come out of my mouth. My voice says, "Our purpose is chaos, but our prize will be the Alphas. All three of them will be back under Prodigy control. Just like we planned when we set Sadie loose."

Uzi takes my hand and we follow their minions out of the warehouse.

Riots fill the streets as the protocol begins. Bus stop screens are flashing. Lights in all the open businesses are flashing. Traffic lights, and street lights. Every SkyEye phone is ringing.

The blinking lights and ringing phones create a trance that no one can escape from. We made sure of it. We planned this down to the very last detail. I see the moment things change. It happens right before my eyes. Their faces go slack. They stand completely still as anarchy explodes around them, their eyes trained on the signal flashing across their faces. Red. White. Red. White.

Then they all look up. The haze of the trance evaporates. They scream. They *roar*, arms in the air, waving whatever they're holding in their hands. They strike each other. Some of them have nothing to hit back with, so they throw their phones. One phone hits a woman in the forehead and a burst of blood spurts from her split skin.

Cyan makes us look around, take it all in. Burns it into our memories. And then she spies the prize.

Lincoln, Case, Iziah and Sadie. The four of them are standing on the roof of the warehouse, staring down at us.

"There she is," Cyan says through my mouth. I feel her reaching for Sadie's mind. I try to stop it, but I can't. I can't. She's not under the control of another mentalist right now. That place inside her mind where we fit together like a lock in a key is empty and open.

So I slip inside and Cyan takes over.

I'm sorry, Sadie, I say in my head. *I'm sorry.*

CHAPTER THIRTY-EIGHT

No, no, no. She cannot come back in.

But it's too late. She's there.

While I was distracted by my intruder sister the helicopter has landed on the roof of the warehouse. Lincoln and Case jump out and Iziah is pushing me to go next so he can follow, but I double over and scream, "Iziah!" I grab his arm as a pain goes shooting through my head.

"What?" he yells back over the thumping helicopter rotors. "What's wrong?"

"Cyan!" I yell back. "She's inside me!"

"Fuck that," he says, pulling me out of the helicopter.

"Fight her off, Sadie," Lincoln says, grabbing my other arm to keep me upright. "Sheila's coming right now."

"What's all that noise?" Case asks, running over to the edge of the roof. "Shit! What the fuck is happening?"

Lincoln and Iziah drag me over to the roof with them and we look down onto a horror that takes my breath away.

An entire city block of rioting people. Some of them are wearing all black. They hold bats and clubs, and metal bars, swinging them at storefront windows.

"They did it," Lincoln yells over the roar of the crowd.

The helicopter has powered down, and I can feel Cyan even stronger now. Then I see her looking up at me. She bares her teeth in a diabolical smile. *I've got you*, she whispers in my brain.

The hell you do, Sheila whispers back.

Now I have them both inside me. Sheila, in the computer interface Prodigy implanted to control me. And Cyan, the one who thinks she owns that space.

I fall to my knees just as bullets begin spraying up at us. Case takes one in the chest and stumbles backwards. Lincoln has his arm cannon powered up and aimed down below.

"Don't hit Thomas!" But that makes no sense. Thomas is Cyan now. We might have to take him out. That was Lincoln's instruction before we left the mansion. *We won't let them get him, Sadie. Ever. So if it means we have to splatter him into pieces, so be it. We made a promise to each other when we started this plan. No one goes back. We'd all rather die.*

But he doesn't shoot. He can't shoot. He'll kill all those people down there and that was never their plan.

My head is nothing but pressure now. Cyan is winning this battle. I feel her powering me up. Getting ready to do something. What is she doing?

What do you think she's doing, Sadie? She's gonna use you to mind-blast us!

No. Thomas is the most dangerous mentalist ever known. But Thomas and Uzi combined...

That's when I realize, it's me. I'm the one in control of Thomas. I'm the link between them both.

That thought defeats me. I lose all control over my powers. I lose Sheila too. I double over, the pain in my head unbearable, and she's in. She's in control now.

When I stand up I am her. I am Cyan. I am Thomas. And Sullivan.

I look at Lincoln and Case and know what I have to do. Cyan trips my illusion, even as Case and Lincoln try to figure out what's going on. I become Molly. Then Lulu.

Back and forth. They are after all, their greatest weaknesses.

My objective is, and always has been, to take them alive. And that's just what I plan on doing.

CHAPTER THIRTY-NINE

Be ready.

The words flash through my head and confuse me for a second.

I was ready. Sadie came for me in the hospital and we got out.

No, Thomas. You're not thinking clearly. Quick! You don't have any more time to decide. Are you ready now? Because this is your last chance. I won't give you another one. Yes. Or no.

Who—

Time's running out, Thomas. Better make a decision.

Everything but what's happening all around me falls away into the nothingness I've been in since Cyan took over. Uzi's in control now. But that's not who's talking to me. Someone else is inside me too.

How many fucking people can fit inside my mind?

Doesn't matter, the unknown voice says. *Just be ready.*

Pressure builds in my head. Pressing against my skull until I feel like I will—

The mind blast explodes out of me. Uzi, I realize. He's aimed the concussion wave up at the roof where Case, Lincoln, Sadie, and Iziah are standing. Case, Linc, and Iziah are all distracted by something Sadie is doing. They don't even see it coming. The mind blast hits them head on and all four bodies tumble over the side, crashing into the ground below. Mobs of people attack as Uzi moves forward to take our prize.

No!

They will never get us back alive.

But you can't die, my friend. Are you ready? Because they will get you unless you let me help you.

Who are you?

Does it matter? Your friends are about to be made into good little minion slaves again. So does it really matter who I am?

No, I guess it doesn't. It's the only chance I have. Whoever this person is, they're the only way out of this fuck-up now.

There is more pressure, but this time it comes with mental screaming. I bend over, my hands cupping the sides of my head, like that can do anything.

Obey me! It's Cyan. She's… struggling.

Sadie is screaming in my head. Then Uzi is there along with Cyan and the newcomer.

My mind is filled with nothing but insane screaming.

Then… quietly… *Thomas.*

One word. From a voice I recognize. Mine.

Sullivan, I realize. Sullivan is back. But how? How is he so in control?

Who cares, he says. *Who fucking cares. Just get that bitch out of us!*

We come together, maybe for the first time ever, and fight our common enemy.

Fight, fight, fight… Sullivan is chanting in my head.

Then Iziah is there too. Cyan is one stupid bitch if she thinks we'll give up on fifteen years of planning. Fifteen years we spent dreaming about one thing and one thing only.

Revenge.

Because we are two Alphas teamed up with an illusionist.

And we are *pissed.*

CHAPTER FORTY

The anarchy isn't on the streets of Cathedral City. It's inside my head as I wrestle back a little bit of control.

But I'm not me anymore.

I am everyone.

I am no one.

I can feel all of them at once. Cyan, Iziah, Uzi, Thomas, and Sullivan. For a few seconds we are three bodies, but one common entity.

This is the definition of insanity. I have lost myself. I am gone. I have been wiped away and replaced with… a collective.

My body is twisted up on the ground in a defensive position as rioters come at us. They have clubs and bats, and flying fists. They want to end us.

But when they reach Iziah, they don't try to kill him. They pick him up and hold him steady as he wobbles back and forth. They do the same to Lincoln and Case.

That's when I realize. No. They're not here to kill us, they're here to take us back.

I lose a little more of myself as Cyan gains power. But Sullivan, Thomas, and Iziah are right there, fighting for me. Fighting for us.

A little bit more, Sadie.

Sheila! I want to cry with happiness. But I can't even manage a single moment of relief, because the arms and hands are on me now. Pulling me to my feet, restraining me. Taking me prisoner until…

Uzi walks up to me *tsking* his tongue. "I was worried you'd get away, little Sadie. But not anymore. You are mine, bitch. My little fuck toy. We have a business to run down in the underbelly, remember? We're such a great team, aren't we?"

"Fuck you," I spit, struggling in the arms of my captors. My mind is clear now. Everyone gone. Nothing left inside me but… me. "Fuck you, fuck you, fuck you!"

But I'm powerless. Because in the instant it takes for me to realize all the others are gone, Uzi is there, filling me up again.

I struggle against the hands holding me steady for Uzi. He walks up to me, sick smile plastered across his face.

Sadie, Sheila whispers. *Give me control. I know what to do.*

I do it without hesitation. I blank myself out to make room for her. I am not going down without a fight this time.

Sheila's awesome computing power sweeps through my whole body. Every nerve ending belongs to her now. Every thought, every motion, everything of me is hers to command.

I stand up straighter, the pain in my head gone. Cyan, gone. All of them gone. I am more myself with the creepy supercomputer inside me than I ever was with my sister or the psycho who thinks he owns me.

Uzi stops, some secret message from Cyan making him doubt his approach. He's not far away though. And dozens of hands are still holding me captive.

But Sheila is with me. Sheila and all her big ideas. Sheila and all her insane power.

She laughs through my mouth.

"What's so funny, little Sadie?" Uzi asks me. "You might've kicked Cyan out, but you're not going to win." He turns and sends a mind blast towards Iziah, Case, and Lincoln. They blow back from the force of his power.

And just as he's distracted, Sheila uses me to throw a trip into the crowd.

A concentric wave bursts out of my mind and hits every one of Uzi's little minions. They squint their eyes in confusion as they look at me.

I smile, and this time it's not Sheila controlling my face. It's me.

Because I know what she just did. Thanks to Prodigy, I have a hard drive in my brain.

Thanks to Lincoln and his software, I have data flowing through my brain.

Thanks to Case and his SpyGlass tablets, every face around me comes with a name. Facial recognition is a fact of life that no one even questions anymore.

And thanks to Sheila, I am myself, and I wield the trip with awesome power only I'm capable of.

I flicker in and out, my face changing every few seconds. I am him, and her, and him and her. I am that parent, that baby. That girl they wish didn't get away. I am their loved ones in these moments. I am the only person that matters in their life.

The hands holding me release as the crowd stumbles back in confusion.

I watch Uzi for the moment, that one glorious moment when he realizes what's happening. When he realizes who he's really dealing with.

They don't call them Alphas for nothing.

He turns, just a fraction of a second too late. And this time he's the target of a mind-blowing blast that catches him off guard, throws his body back against the brick wall of the warehouse, and knocks him unconscious.

He's not only dealing with one Alpha, he's dealing with two. Thomas and Sullivan work as a team and Iziah is there too, helping them. Making them stronger together than they ever could be alone. They pound Uzi against that wall with blast after blast. They pummel him like a force of fucking nature.

Fuck the wind, I think to myself.

Fuck the wind to hell and back. We are more than *one* force of nature.

We are all of them.

We are all Alpha now.

CHAPTER FORTY-ONE

It takes more strength to stop the beating than it ever did to start it. Sullivan and I pull back. Iziah eases his link to us and we stand there, panting hard with the effort as we take in the scene.

Uzi is… limp. I'd call him dead, but somehow, I don't think he's capable of dying. There will always be evil in this world.

The rioters are on the ground, weeping as they look up at Sadie. They encircle her like worshippers, only I know they're not worshipping her. They're being tripped.

She's not Sadie though. She's… everyone. Her face changes every few seconds. This person, that person. And the effect it has on the crowd is… sobering. *They're tripping,* I think, then laugh out loud. What a nice trick to have in one's arsenal.

"Thomas!" Case shouts. "Watch out!"

A force hits me in the back, making me stumble forward. I look down at my chest. At the gaping wound. Blood pours out of the bullet hole and it takes me a moment to realize I've just been shot.

"Fuck, no!" a voice shouts from behind.

I turn slowly, my head spinning from the massive chest wound and the blood loss. And I wonder, as I sway back and forth, if this is what Lincoln experienced when he took a bullet from the Blue Boar.

"Fuck, no! Fuck, no!" I force my head up and find Randy Shits coming at me, shotgun out in front of him. He pumps the barrel and pulls the trigger again. This time I go flying backwards, crashing against the ground so hard, my head bounces, cracks, and then blood spills out of there too.

"I did not," Randy Shits spits, "come this fuckin' far to have you Alphas rip victory away from me at the last second."

"Think again, asshole," Case says.

I turn my head towards his voice. He's walking straight at Randy, eyes blazing with hate. Lincoln is behind him, cannon arm raised. He shoots, but Randy dives behind a corner. I hear the telltale sound of pump action. Randy reloading.

He shoots, hits Case dead in the chest, just like me.

Only Case doesn't go down and blood doesn't spill. Because... well, he's fucking Alpha Case, that's why. His superpower is healing.

Randy Shits is dead and he knows it. He reloads, pumps, shoots again. But Lincoln is behind Case, using him like a shield as they walk forward. They shoot each other at the same time. Randy's shot hits Case in the leg, which only slows him down a little. But Lincoln's... I laugh. Lincoln blows that motherfucker's head off.

The whole city goes silent.

Every rioter, minion or otherwise, slumps to the ground. Every flashing light blinks its last blink as Cathedral City goes absolutely still.

Eternity passes in a moment of silence.

I take it in. The whole scene. Anarchy is everywhere. Everywhere but inside my head. Inside my head... everything is calm.

Lincoln walks over to me, claps me on the back. "You two OK?"

Case stumbles up, limping a little as he holds the two pieces of open flesh together. His nanites are doing their job efficiently, and right before my eyes, he heals.

"Damn," I say, still looking at Case's amazing power. "I might need a nanite upgrade. I'm not dead and I'm not out, but I'm definitely feeling the two bullets I took." They both manage a smile.

"Sadie?" I ask, whirling around. My eyes searching for her.

She's standing in the middle of the circle of slumped bodies, looking around like she can't believe this just happened.

I know the feeling. I've been here at the edge of insane battles too many times to count.

I walk over to her, take her in my arms, and hold her tightly to my chest. If she minds the blood on my shirt and the half-healed hole in my body, she doesn't show it. Because she holds me back just as tight. "Hey, Trip Chick?" I say, looking down at her head, which is pressed into my neck.

Her body shakes a little with her relived chuckle. "What, Mental Man?"

"That's a helluva trick you have, baby."

Her face turns up to mine and she smiles. Relief washes over her. I can feel her again. I don't want to invade or anything, but she feels like home. And I want nothing more than to be inside her right now. "OK," she says. "Maybe it's not so stupid. You can be the wind, I guess."

We both take a moment to appreciate the joke.

We made it. They threw everything they had at us, and we made it.

I turn both of us around and look at my friends. Case is healed already. Lincoln looks charged with adrenaline and satisfaction as he looks around the city.

"It's not exactly how we planned it, is it?"

"No," Case laughs. "Not exactly."

"There's still time," Sheila says. "The program is still running. I made the necessary adjustments. They didn't mess with it."

"You mean couldn't mess with it," Lincoln sneers. "I made that shit bulletproof."

"Where's Iziah?" Sadie asks.

"Over here," he calls. He's standing over Randy Shits' body, tugging on his shirt. He takes a knife out of his pocket and starts cutting it off, then holds it up for us all to see.

"Anarchy," I say.

"Anarchy," Case and Linc repeat.

"It belongs to us, motherfuckers."

"You ready then, asshole?" Lincoln asks me. "Finish what we started and all that good shit?"

I take one more look around the city. Remember it the way it was.

It was nice, once. The unknown voice inside my head is back.

Yeah. I think it probably was. But it's not now.

No, she agrees.

Thanks, Yasmine.

You knew?

No. But I figured out just now. I'd know you anywhere. But what I don't understand is… why you helped me break free. Especially after I killed you back at the hospital.

Because, dear Thomas, there's a saying that goes a little something like this: The enemy of my enemy is my friend.

Are we enemies? I ask.

Until death do us part.

She fades away after that. I don't know where they go when they leave me. The dead memories. And I don't know if that's all they are. Just memories. If she was just a memory she'd be no help at all. Maybe I'm just insane. Maybe I've been chained to the anarchy in my head for so long, I don't know the difference anymore. Or maybe I just need to get used to the fact that I'm whole again.

At any rate, Sadie and I follow Linc, Iziah, and Case over to the warehouse where Sheila and the little helicopter are waiting on the roof. We take the stairs up, slowly, since I'm definitely in need of a nanite upgrade, then pile in. Linc and Case are up front. Iziah and I are squished into the back, and Sadie sits on my lap.

All five of us look down on our city as we ascend into the sky to wait things out up in the mountains, wondering what will happen when our plan finally takes hold.

People start to wake up. Just like last time when the Red Robber had Case in his grips. At least that threat is over.

No more Blue Boar.

No more Red Robber.

But Prodigy... yeah, those motherfuckers are still out there. But in a few days, it will be impossible to hide from the justice we've unleashed on Cathedral City.

EPILOGUE

"Welcome to the show, Mr. Brooks. I'm sorry you couldn't be here in person, but we'll take a satellite feed if we must." The reporter smiles at me. "As long as we don't lose transmission."

Haha. Funny. Don't quit the day job, honey.

Be nice, Sullivan, I chastise him. "No chance of that, Miss Manchen," I growl out. "SkyEye is the most reliable service this city has ever seen."

I give her the creeps because she leans back in her chair at my dangerous tone. Creeping is my main superpower and I like it. So I'm keeping it.

She clears her throat and says, "The whole city's wondering just what it is you've unleashed on us. Can you explain it a little better? We've all watched the statement you gave earlier this week, but still..." She cocks her head. "It's so... weird."

"Is it weird?" I ask her back. "Is it really? I mean, in my mind, it's just the next logical technological step."

"But I think everyone was under the impression SkyEye and ToyBox were developing a... kind of virtual reality game. Something educational. Something that involves the history of the city."

"Well," I say, smiling. "I think if you look closely, you'll see that's exactly what we've done."

"You think this is a game?" she asks, her tone incredulous.

"Why not? It's got all the makings of a game."

She huffs out some air, ready to be a little more confrontational. I bet she's thankful for this satellite feed now. Makes her feel brave to have creepy me on the other side of the screen and not sitting four feet away. "It's an invasion of privacy."

"Is it?" I ask again. "Is it really? I mean, we didn't force people to buy the ToyBox console. Or the SpyGlass tablets. Or the glasses."

"But you did give the phones away for free." She raises an eyebrow at me. Like she's about to get the upper hand.

She's not. "We did. After the district attorney hacked into the banks, shut down the power, contaminated the power plant, and blew up all the city's cell towers. How could I not give them away, Miss Manchen? How? I'd be a heartless bastard if I didn't come to the rescue of Cathedral City. I love this place. Dearly. It's my home. The only home I've ever had. The only home I will ever have. I'm just trying to take care of it and the free sat phones were just the first step. I have many plans for this city. I've just begun to leave my mark."

Just the first step in our little coup d'état, *you mean?*

Shut up, Sullivan. But I like having him around. He's funny. And cool. And easy-going. Which means I'm all these things too. At least in private.

Miss Manchen scowls, undeterred. "So the fact that you had software running on those tablets and consoles, as well as the free phones, that maps every user's facial characteristics and puts it in a database... that doesn't bother you?"

"Why would it? Everyone signed a release. They gave us permission. We're just trying to do what's right."

"With your game?" she sneers.

"Well, technically, the game belongs to Case Reider and ToyBox."

"Your software then?" She's losing her cool now.

"The software belongs to Lincoln Wade and Wade Industries."

"So you take no responsibility for what's happening out there?"

"Oh, sweetie," Sullivan interjects, speaking out of my mouth. "We take all the credit."

Manchen recoils. "What?"

"We're proud of our product, Miss Manchen." I put my hand out—off camera—and Sadie places a set of SpyGlasses in my palm. I put them on my face and Manchen looks like she's ready to bolt. But we're live on air. I told them I'd only do the interview if we were live. And I'd only do it with Manchen.

Because I know her dirty little past. And everyone else knows it now too.

That's what SpyGlasses do. The facial recognition maps everyone who comes into your field of vision, tags them, then displays every piece of dirt Sheila could gather on them. Every newcomer who enters our little city nestled among the tall mountains is also tagged. By license plate as they pass through the tower's invisible magnetic field. Or through cameras in the bus stations. Or the airport security.

No one gets through unless they have a tag. If they don't have a tag… well, that just makes it easier to spot the criminals.

Manchen gathers herself. Straightens her chin. The dirty deeds she's done are displayed above her head in red letters. The towers take care of the broadcast. And if people are out of range of the towers and have a SkyEye phone or a SpyGlass tablet, those devices will tag them too.

Manchen's secrets are not as bad as some, but we did find a record of her working as a stripper in college. It's nothing to be embarrassed about. Manchen probably made a great stripper when she was young.

"Hundreds, maybe even thousands, of people in Cathedral City have been fired from their jobs over this little invasion of privacy."

"Maybe they deserved to lose their jobs? Ever think of that?"

"Mr. Brooks. If you're not socially conscious enough to realize this is indeed an invasion of privacy, then I'm afraid you might not belong here among the citizens of Cathedral City."

"Well," I say. "We'll have to agree to disagree. I'm not out to invade privacy. That wasn't our objective. Our objective was to open eyes. And we've done that."

"To the detriment of society."

"Says you," I reply.

She shakes her head at me, unable to believe what she's hearing. "Look," I say. "Information gives people power. They then use that information to make decisions. Decisions based on fact."

"Your facts," she snaps.

"My facts are accurate, Miss Manchen. If anyone has a dispute, we have a hotline. And we remove all mistakes from the database."

She sighs, clearly done with me. But I'm not done with her. Because she just doesn't get it.

"People always say they want the truth, right? Well, here it is. The truth is ugly, Miss Manchen. No one cares if you were a stripper in college." She gasps, unable to believe that I just went there. But why not? It's on fucking display everywhere she goes. She can't turn it off. The only way for people not to see her dirty deeds now is to take the glasses off.

But it's all too new. They won't take them off. Not yet. Not until they've had their fill. Not until they feel comfortable with their neighbors, and friends, and bosses again. But one day they might.

"Life is nothing but one long string of mistakes," I say. More to the camera than to the reporter. "Everyone makes mistakes."

"Yes," she agrees. "Everyone does. But they shouldn't have to be reminded of them."

"You can't see your tag unless you look in the mirror wearing the glasses. Don't wear them in the bathroom, Miss Manchen. No big deal. So you made some mistakes. There's five million people watching this program right now. If they're wearing glasses they're seeing all kinds of shitty things I've done. It allows them to form an opinion about me."

"My opinion of you is very low," she spits out. "And I'd bet most of the audience agrees with me."

I shrug. "So what? I can live with that. And my best advice for everyone watching is to learn to live with their mistakes too. One day, Miss Manchen… one day we'll all wake up and decide we're done with the glasses. We're done with the truth. And we'll put them away. We'll learn to trust each other again. And that's why I did this. There's no trust in this city right now because it's filled with liars, and criminals, and deadbeats who think they're cheating the system. But they're not now, are they? We know who the liars and cheats are. We get to decide who we'll forgive and who we won't."

"It's virtual vigilantism," she sneers.

"People are a force of nature. You can't control them, even when you think you can, you *don't* control them.

Because the collective is made up of individuals and everyone gets a say in the matter. SkyEye and ToyBox aren't about judging people, Miss Manchen. It's about forgiving people. Including yourself. And then moving on. Bad guys are real, yes. But the good guys are out there too. And isn't it great that now we can tell the difference?"

I take my SpyGlasses off and hand them to Sadie. Then I reach out to the camera and switch it off.

Sadie climbs into my lap and plants a kiss on my lips. "That was perfect."

I have a crooked smile for her. I don't give one rat's ass if people like what we did. But four hundred seventy-two people on the Cathedral City payroll were fired this week.

"It's a very good start," I say. "But enough of this bullshit. We're tired. We want to take you to bed."

She winks at me. Us. Because Sullivan is still here. And that side of me is one kinky motherfucker. I wouldn't get rid of him for anything now.

He might've started out as chaos. And yeah, I thought being chained to that anarchist bastard was a punishment. A sickness.

But I'm getting used to his chaos.

And I have discovered… I don't mind watching.

An evil laugh bursts out of our mouth as Sadie takes our hand and leads us towards the bedroom.

We're ready, I decide. We're ready for the revenge to be over. We're ready for things to sort themselves out down in Cathedral City. And we're ready for Sadie Scott to make us happy.

Because happy, ya know? Happy is the only thing that counts.

Yes, we're a bad guy. The SpyGlass tag above our head proves that to anyone who's interested.

But we're thinking about getting out of the supervillain business.

Anarchy might have to live on without us.

Because happy, ya know? Happy is the only thing that counts.

Yes, we're a bad guy. The SpyGlass tag above our head proves that to anyone who's interested.

But we're thinking about getting out of the supervillain business.

Anarchy might have to live on without us.

END OF BOOK SHIT

Welcome to the End of Book Shit. This is the part of the book where I get to say anything I want. Well, this trilogy is done. That's not to say that I'm done with this world because I'm not. Not at all. I feel like I'm just getting started. The third book in a trilogy is always awesome for me because I know the world, I know all the main characters, and usually I've set up something big and it's like putting the all the leftover pieces of a puzzle together so that the readers can see the "big picture". I think I did that with Chained and I'm very happy with how it turned out.

Since this is a superhero story and was written in the "spirit" of comic-book tradition, I've left a few things dangling. And I did that on purpose. So if you've got questions about parts of the story you can bet I'll be answering them in another book… eventually. Questions like – What about when Lulu pricked her finger on the SpyGlass window at the ToyBox office? Or, in this book – what's the deal with Yasmine?

So if you have a leftover question, don't worry. I've got a plan for it. ;) Three books is really just a sample when you're building a world like this. I don't have any idea how many books I'll write about supervillains falling in love, but six at least. That's a good starter guess. And I probably won't write more than one a year after this because I have to squeeze them in as personal projects and I have two personal projects in addition to the supers to write next year.

One thing I really did try and develop in Chained was the connection to Junco. There was that little nod to tunnels under the city. There was no green gas in any of the Junco books but what's that gas do anyway? Ha, another question. I'm pretty sure it's come up again at some point. Also, the reporter at the end – if you've read Junco you'll recognize her last name.

I think the coolest thing about writing a superhero world is all the crazy tech I was allowed to put in with no explanation. Lol Green gas, for one. And the super cool (or maybe super disgusting) way some of these characters can heal themselves. Or how about those "gates" in the tunnels? What the fuck is up with that? Overkill, anyone? Did you ever see that movie Galaxy Quest with Tim Allen and Sigourney Weaver? And they're deep inside their ship and have to run the gauntlet between these giant crushing, hammer thingys. And Sigourney Waver (Gwen) says:

"What is this thing? I mean, it serves no useful purpose for there to be a bunch of chompy, crushy things in the middle of a hallway. No, I mean we shouldn't have to do this, it makes no logical sense, why is it here?" -Gwen

"'Cause it's on the television show." -Jason

"Well forget it! I'm not doing it! This episode was badly written!" -Gwen

lol. I love that fucking movie. I might to go watch it right now. But the reason the gates are there is because it's a superhero book and things don't necessarily make sense if they have great visuals. The chompy, crushy things in Galaxy Quest just make life difficult. And so do the razor-sharp gates. I think that's probably the best thing about writing this genre. It's all about the visuals.

I took a little non-scientific poll in my ARC group after my ARC readers finished with Missing and asked them if they wanted Randy to be a good guy or a bad guy. They overwhelmingly said bad guy, so here he is. Well, there he was. I'm kinda glad to get rid of him. But we have so many people left to bring back into the story, we won't miss him. I'm pretty sure that Chief O'Neil will come back. He reminds of the Penguin so much, I can't not bring him back.

But anyway… I hope you had fun with this series and I hope you come back next year and check out the next one. I will have Atticus's story, as promised. And he will be sexy and fun. So thanks for taking a chance on this series and high-five if this was your favorite book of mine this year!

Oh, and if you want to hang out with me on Facebook you can join my fan group, Shrike Bikes. I'm in there every single day just shootin' the shit with readers. Just request to join and one of us will add you to the group as soon as we see it.

Thank you for reading, thank you for reviewing, and I'll see you in the next book! (His turn, bitches! His Turn is coming in just three weeks!!!!)

Julie
JA Huss

ABOUT THE AUTHOR
JAHUSS

JA Huss is the New York Times and USA Today bestselling author of more than twenty romances. She likes stories about family, loyalty, and extraordinary characters who struggle with basic human emotions while dealing with bigger than life problems. JA loves writing heroes who make you swoon, heroines who makes you jealous, and the perfect Happily Ever After ending.

You can chat with her on Facebook, Twitter, and her kick-ass romance blog, New Adult Addiction. If you're interested in getting your hands on an advanced release copy of her upcoming books, sneak peek teasers, or information on her upcoming personal appearances, you can join her newsletter list and get those details delivered right to your inbox.

JA Huss lives on a dirt road in Colorado thirty minutes from the nearest post office. So if she owes you a package from a giveaway, expect it to take forever. She has a small farm with two donkeys named Paris & Nicole, a ringneck parakeet named Bird, and a pack of dogs. She also has two grown children who have never read any of her books and do not plan on ever doing so. They do, however, plan on using her credit cards forever.

JA collects guns and likes to read science fiction and books that make her think. JA Huss used to write homeschool science textbooks under the name Simple Schooling and after publishing more than 200 of those, she ran out of shit to say. She started writing the I Am Just Junco science fiction series in 2012, but has since found the meaning of life writing erotic stories about antihero men that readers love to love.

JA has an undergraduate degree in equine science and fully planned on becoming a veterinarian until she heard what kind of hours they keep, so she decided to go to grad school and got a master's degree in Forensic Toxicology. Before she was a full-time writer she was smelling hog farms for the state of Colorado.

Even though JA is known to be testy and somewhat of a bitch, she loves her #fans dearly and if you want to talk to her, join her Facebook fan group where she posts daily bullshit about bullshit.

If you think she's kidding about this crazy autobiography, you don't know her very well.

You can find her books on Amazon, Barnes & Noble, iTunes, and KOBO.